Appearances

Joanne Greenberg

Also by Joanne Greenberg

Age of Consent

The Far Side of Victory

Founder's Praise

High Crimes and Misdemeanors (stories)

I Never Promised You a Rose Garden

In This Sign

The King's Persons

The Monday Voices

No Reck'ning Made

Of Such Small Differences

Rites of Passage (stories)

A Season of Delight

Simple Gifts

Summering (stories)

Where the Road Goes

With the Snow Queen (stories)

Appearances

Joanne Greenberg

Montemayor Press

Millburn, New Jersey

For information contact:
Montemayor Press,
P. O. Box 526, Millburn, NJ 07041
Web site: MontemayorPress.com

1 3 5 7 9 10 8 6 4 2

Library of Congress Cataloging-in-Publication Data

Greenberg, Joanne.
    Appearances / by Joanne Greenberg.
      p. cm.
    ISBN 1-932727-03-5 (pbk. : alk. paper)
       1.   Fathers and sons--Fiction. 2. Prisoners--Fiction.
       3. Secrecy--Fiction. I. Title.
    PS3557.R3784A86 2006
    813'.54--dc22
                              2005021003

To Edward Myers

One of the Mountain-Drawn

Appearances

Joanne Greenberg

Chapter One

The problem was that his father had died away somewhere, and his mother had covered the facts of it with vagueness and silence. Steven wasn't even sure when he had died. Was he seven or eight? There were no details of illness, hospital, or funeral, only "away from us." In the hollowness of loss, he had constructed fantasies. Don't people say "dead and gone"? Doesn't that show that some people die and aren't gone? In his dream time and fantasy life, Steven believed his father to be one of these, dead but not gone. Even now, out of habit, he sometimes looked hard into the faces of bikers beside him at traffic stops, peered at them in roadside coffee shops until his looks brought glares or threatening gestures in return.

A treasured memory: Lon Howe wore a studded leather jacket, the arms fringed like a bird's wing, because on the bike he would fly, and the fringes would stream behind his arms like feathers. Steven saw himself reaching out to touch those fringes, and the black leather gloves, fringed also, shining like an eagle's talons.

Connie said, "Were you dreaming about him again last night, or about Annina? You were moaning and thrashing."

"I'm sorry. I threw the blankets off. You must have been freezing."

"Oh, Steve, it was awful, losing your mother that way, so suddenly, and there, with everyone."

"It'll certainly change our Thanksgivings for years to come. It's funny, though, that I should dream about my dad and not about Annina. She was so shy and withdrawn, poor woman; she doesn't even get a dream out of me. Con, thanks for taking care of things."

"Did you expect to jump up and be normal? You're still in shock."

Connie was the one who had made the calls and managed and decided things. She closed Ring and Wreath for two days; she called Steven's secretary and had her cancel Steven's appointments and defer his depositions and court appearances. Ring and Wreath was a bridal service, but Connie, a wedding planner, slipped easily into organizing the funeral. It was she who decided the service, the burial, the casket, the cost. Steven wanted to do some of his work at home, but he had no concentration to give. His mind slipped the line to his subject and floated off, carried by the wind of loss into a fog of sorrow.

A few days before the funeral, Connie sat down with the children and asked them if they wanted to go to Annina's apartment for something to save—a keepsake. Steven said, "Before we do that, I'd like to go back to the projects where I grew up. Then I want to see Callan, where my dad's people lived. Do any of you want to come?"

To his surprise, the three kids said yes, and the next day, he drove them back to his old neighborhood. It was a district still in the news for drug arrests and violence. He'd never taken any of them there, or Connie. Blocks of the old area had been swallowed by the highway interchanges Denver had put up in the seventies and eighties, and on the north side, by remodeling and gentrification.

The talk in the car was subdued. Their grandmother Howe had died sitting at the table in the Scotts' big dining room. They had all thought she was dozing. She was the only Howe relative they had, Annina Masachetti Howe, the Italian war bride of Alonzo Carl Howe, PFC, also dead. She'd been proud of her grandchildren, stunned by their American success, and she was the only Italian on record, they'd joked, to cook spaghetti badly and make inedible lasagne. Steven realized with surprise that Jennifer, Jeremy, and Mike were being tactful for his sake, not kidding or playful as they brought up memories of her, going into an old event carefully, touching it delicately, and coming quickly away.

"When did you leave this part of town?" Jennifer asked. She was staring at the collection of struggling small businesses, the body and fender shops and boarded-up and decaying houses and stores. Other places sported signs for palm readers and psychics, and the handwritten notices of rooms for rent. Here and there, the struggle for beauty went on in tiny homes whose iron gratings against break-ins were hung with flower boxes, bare now in the winter, but some strung with early Christmas decorations.

"I left when I got work with my first law firm. Then I could take Annina with me."

The three were silent. Steven thought they must be trying to imagine him growing up in such a neighborhood, trying to see themselves coming and going on these streets. He rounded the corner and there it was, the complex, four stories high and four blocks wide, set off at each end by liquor stores. The abutting streets had been intended to open onto a garden, but the central patch had always been bare, littered with garbage and broken glass. The pink stucco walls of the building were pitted with bullet holes.

3

"Wait . . . stop," Jeremy called as Steven began to drive past. "Let's get out and look the place over."

"Yeah, Dad," Mike said, "which window was yours?"

Steven pulled to the curb and they all alighted with care.

Steven was a man, now, fit and well muscled, but he felt the old fear moving him and he looked around for Dill or Shiv or B.C., the bullies of a hundred encounters and a thousand clutches of stomach cramp and heaves of nausea. All the lower windows were barred and locked. The four visitors stood at the entrance to the screened-off yard in silence, imagining.

"Where does all this broken glass come from?" Mike asked.

"From broken liquor bottles. The kids find the bottles in the morning, sometimes with drunks still attached to them. They take the bottles, drink what's left, and throw the bottles against the side of the building. It used to be an official game—someone would spray paint a target and the kids would keep score."

"Where did you go to school?"

"It's four blocks over. We can stop by there, if you want to. The junior high was about ten blocks away."

"You fought . . ." Jeremy said.

"Oh, yes, within the races and between the races. People'll tell you racism is taught to kids by their elders, but I think the grown people here, white, black, and brown, all wanted to live in peace. It was the kids who kept the wars alive, particularly in junior high."

Mike, the youngest, was just out of high school and his memories of junior high were fresh enough for him to shiver for a moment.

"Did you have gangs?" Jennifer was turning, letting the scene unfold around her.

4

"The white gangs were into heavy commerce," Steven said, "selling stolen goods. The black kids were just discovering drug dealing, and the Chicanos—they weren't called that then—were making and selling weapons: zip guns and switchblades. Life was hardest on the kids who wanted to stay out of the gangs. To be honest, the kids like me, the ones who stayed out, weren't the brightest or the most gifted."

They stood and took that in. Steven still marveled at the differences among his three children: Jennifer, the dramatizer; Jeremy, the organizer; Mike, the thoughtful one.

Jennifer gestured toward the heavy battered door. "Could we go inside?"

Steven shook his head. "I don't want to leave the car."

"I'm getting cold," she said, "but I want to look around. Why don't we go two by two, case the joint."

"I'll stay by the car and the three of you can walk around together, but don't go inside."

"Can we drive to the school, too?"

"Sure, if you want." Steven was surprised at their interest. "Be careful," he said.

He meant that they should look out for the young residents, two or three of whom had drifted in and out of the building. The apartment dwellers eyed them with suspicion but not with hostility, or at least not yet. That could change with an electrical suddenness, he knew, and the three of them, his precious, carefully raised children, who were neither streetwise nor angry, didn't even know what their innocent looks or gestures might signal.

A chain-link fence separated the sides of the building from the street, probably for the protection of the small children. Each structure had four floors, each floor four apartments. Four buildings, all the same, made up the complex. Steven remembered how his

5

anxiety had always risen as he passed the other buildings, then eased as he turned into his own, rising again as he entered the foyer. In that unprotected place, he'd seen beatings, had had a few, and had witnessed, from the stairs, two rapes. Cries and screams had always been studiously ignored by the four tenant families on the ground floor.

The memory made him wonder why he had felt such an urgent need to come back here. He was watchful, leaning against the car in a too markedly casual way. If something went wrong, he wanted to be ready to act.

The three had disappeared from sight around the corner. Jeremy looked strong enough, and although Mike was smaller, lighter, he wasn't someone who seemed easy to intimidate. Steven marveled at how narrow his and Annina's days had been in this ugly place, how pinched life had become in the years after his father's death. He had been brought here from Callan, the mountains, the light and air, and his father. All around their barricaded rooms in this place, violence and noise had heaved in waves through the evenings and nights. Holidays intensified the clamor, and long before he began making the money that would free them, fear must have clamped Annina mute and shrunk her spirit.

Here they came around the corner, laughing and talking. He watched them cross the central area, now paved. The concrete there was buckled and upthrust, covered with gleaming scatters of broken glass. He saw Jennifer trip and go upward over the lip of the fault. Mike was reaching out to pull her from the air and Jeremy turned as she fell.

For a moment, Steven thought she might have been shot. He ran to where she lay, Mike still holding on to her down jacket. "Are you all right?"

"I tripped, that's all."

6

He was relieved and the relief erupted in annoyance. "Didn't you see the bad spot? That piece of concrete was sticking up like a shelf."

"I was talking," she said defensively. "I didn't notice it." She lay in the broken glass. "Wait, I'm all right. Let me catch my breath."

Some young girls had approached, gathering to see what had happened. Their presence made Steven try to urge Jennifer up.

"Has any of that glass cut you?"

"I don't think so. Just let me lie here for one more minute."

When she rose, he saw that she hadn't been cut, although her down jacket had small rips here and there, and from several of them, delicate feathers had begun to escape. The jacket, Steven realized, had saved her from the glass.

"I'm really all right," she objected, and noticing the increasing crowd, she began busily to dust herself off, waking a small swirl of tiny white down. "Let's see the school," she said.

At the school, they got out again, and Jennifer made a point of walking around it. Steven noticed that when she thought she was out of his sight, she limped slightly and held her left arm.

Chapter Two

How was your blast from the past?"

"Good—ugly. I forgot how cramped and poor it is—a buckled courtyard. Jen fell. Did she tell you?"

"Jen never outgrew all her adolescence. She's half graceful, half klutzy."

"But it was good for me to check in. Today we go to Callan. You're sure it's all right?"

"You and Annina," Connie said, "all but swamped by my big loud family. It's not such a mystery, your wanting to locate some kind of reality. After Grandma Scott died, I went through all her things, the closets, the drawers. I felt like a spy, but I needed to assure myself—of what, I still don't know. Go."

"I'm no help here."

"No, you aren't. Go."

So, the day before Annina's funeral, Steven drove Jennifer, Jeremy, and Mike up into the mountains, a full day's trip to the Ute Valley towns. He enjoyed being alone with them. He even enjoyed listening to their chatter as the car wound its way up through the foothills and into the high country. He often went that way and over Prospector Pass to Aureole and past the valley towns to the Gold Flume ski area. There had been little downhill skiing in the four valley towns when he was small and Aureole's Prospector ski mountains and a glittering upscale Gold Flume were years in the future. He hadn't been on skis himself

8

until friends from law school took him. Now, his law practice was principally with skiers. He had been taken instantly by the elegance and beauty of the sport and was drawn into it naturally as his personal injury practice became what was now called ski law.

Steven had lived in Callan and the other valley towns for the first years of his life, but he hadn't visited them since he and Annina had left them. For years, he had passed their exits on the highway as he drove to the sites of injury or death, to conferences or depositions at the county seats. Now, he listened to the sun and shadow of Mike's description of a teacher and Jeremy's defense of a change of major—yet again. Jennifer was telling them about her theatrical designing and how crowded the field was becoming.

"I've been thinking about going to Mexico," she said. "They have a big film industry there. I'll study Spanish this spring. My start may be there or South America."

How easily and casually she was planning the lines of her life, going here and there, specializing in that. The world was their employment office, heady stuff. Steven had never dreamed of leaving Denver.

Mike began to talk about a rock concert he'd been to. This led to an argument about their varying tastes in music. They threw the weird names of groups to one another as the car lifted them into the mountains, going away. Going away is what Americans do, Steven thought, and he tried not to be sad.

The trip he had taken from the valley into Denver when he was eight had seemed very long to him and held a special place in his memory. Who had driven them? He remembered their things piled in back of a dented, rattling, and rusted pickup truck, where he had ridden half sitting, half lying on a rolled-up mattress, the bedding in big bundles tied with rope. It had been exciting to be in the open, facing backward,

9

always going farther down until they were in Denver. By the time they had arrived, it was dark, and he was very cold and very hungry. He didn't remember where they had gone or who had fed them, but the next two days they were in a group place with other families of women and children. After he'd become familiar with that, they'd moved to the projects, with more people than he'd known could be in one place. Day and night, there was the shouting, the meaningless noise. He'd been forced to learn the menace of older boys, and in his fear and mental exhaustion he'd lost the face of the man who'd driven them that day and helped them to unload in the streetlight night of shadows and strange sounds. The driver must have been a Howe uncle or cousin, angry, perhaps, that the widow had chosen to leave the valley with her son, to end all contact with her husband's people.

They passed the Vail and Beaver Creek ski areas, with which he was very familiar as lawyer and skier. He and Connie had started the children skiing very young, and they were all good at it, but without the sense of miracle that he'd enjoyed by discovering it late and making it his own.

"Don't you ever listen, dorkhead?" Jeremy was remembering a friend's accident. "Things happen on the slopes. People run into you, and you run into them, or into trees. You go over on your ass. I don't go bong-bonging down like you do."

"How about you, Jen, are you going to do some time on the slopes?"

"I don't like being cold and wet."

"Learn to ski better and you won't fall down so much."

"Tell me," Steven asked, "do people at the smaller areas, Loveland, Beaver Creek—do they know who you are—I mean, that I'm your father?"

10

"I think so," Jeremy said. "I sign passes sometimes. Howe isn't a name like Smith or Jones. Once or twice, I've seen people's eyebrows go up."

"I'd hate that," Jennifer said.

"Hate what?"

"Their thinking they know me because of who my father is—special treatment because they're afraid of getting sued."

"That doesn't bother me," Jeremy was crowing. "I'm up for all the special treatment I can get." Everyone laughed.

Steven took a conscious satisfaction in their good health. He dealt with many young people as litigants and had seldom seen suffering ennoble them. His own hard childhood had done nothing at all to improve him spiritually or mentally. It had made him overcautious and over-serious. These laughing heirs of his would, on the best equipment, ski downhill past the vicissitudes of poverty: shame, helplessness, and loneliness.

"Jen, how are you feeling today? That was quite a fall. Are you black-and-blue?"

"Oh *Dad*."

"Jen doesn't like being reminded that she's a klutz and a three-footed butter-fingered calamity," Jeremy said.

"Tell me more, oh gallant one, who will never get a girlfriend because his mouth holds both feet."

"Did you see what she did this morning?"

"*You* put the egg there, where it could roll off the counter. I brushed it with my sleeve."

"You walk around in a dream, Jen. You're in outer space somewhere, designing clothes for the little green men."

"Yes, Jennifer, and on little green men, what's the part you have to cover up?"

And suddenly, they were arguing. It went from sun to storm with them whenever they were together. He endured it for five minutes and then said, "Any more and I will drown you out with *my* favorite music, *my* groups."

"Not Mozart—not now."

"Your mom got me hooked on it. We tried to introduce you numbskulls to it and look what happened. Reggae, rap, back to the projects, loud, louder." There was a temporary peace. He had never mentioned the projects before.

They stopped in Aureole before going over Victory Pass. Steven had tried cases there and knew the best places to eat. At the bottom of the pass, they turned off the highway onto the old back road now, potholed and barely traveled. The vehicles passing them on the broken two-lane were being driven by old people and the rural poor, rattling pickups and junkyard remakes. Past Granite Creek and Bluebank, Steven was amazed to see that a huge trailer park had been built, and there were new houses and condos pushing up into the mountains. Everything here looked cleaner and sprucer than he had remembered.

The town of Callan itself was little changed, but there was a library he didn't recognize. The school to which he had gone briefly had been turned into a museum. Steven drove up the main street, turned west, then south, not thinking, but feeling the turns, moving into the place where he had first learned to define location and direction.

The houses were still there, the ground around them still there. His heart began to beat with excitement. He had expected dwindling but this weathered house was truly tiny; its two rooms would barely have contained their beds, a stove, table and chairs. Others had lived here and replaced with stone the steps down from the porch and shored up the buckled end he

12

remembered. No one had occupied the place for years. There was a rusted lock on the door. He walked around to the back while the three waited for him. Two of the outbuildings were leaning over and one had collapsed on itself and was weed-grown. He had remembered the yard as sunny. He had played with stones there, stacking them, piling them. There was a boy named Teddy. He noticed the back window; he had forgotten that, how Annina would stand there and watch for his father to come home. How they waited for that excitement, his father's arrival, his easy stride as he sauntered toward them. Then his mother would put her arms up. Steven had forgotten that gesture of hers, the wordless welcome of it.

They all strolled past the house in the cutting cold and looked at the remains of the last snow, eroded and lying in gray piles like sorted laundry.

"So, you lived here until Grandpa died, and then you moved to Denver?" Jennifer asked.

"No, there were a few years when Dad moved us from here to other places, but after the first move, I stopped caring about where we lived. That house there"—he pointed down the road to a larger, sprucer place where people still seemed to be in residence— "was where the grandparents were. I guess they were nice people and tried to be helpful to us, but some-thing always seemed to be worrying them. Things were hard then, I think. My strongest memory of them was of their saying, 'Stay out of the garden, don't go into the toolshed. Stay away from the river.' On down the hill were some uncles and aunts, all gone now. I checked all the valley phone books for Howes and Kendricks."

"Did you check on-line?"

"No, I stopped looking years ago. They'd all left. I never followed up." He studied the three as they stood hunched in their jackets.

13

"I'm glad you came up with me. Doing this is more of a good-bye for me than the funeral will be. Dad died in a place I don't know, and I don't even know where he's buried, but the Howes lived here and I wanted to remember them when we were still a family."

They peered at the ruined house. Steven saw them imagining themselves living there, too, fitting themselves figuratively into the cramped form that had been his to inhabit. Then they walked back through the town, now seeing it as their world with the same frisson they had felt in the projects. Steven picked them up in the car. They were silent on the way back over the pass.

Chapter Three

Connie said, "I'll get over to the apartment and take care of Annina's things. The kids have gone over and taken whatever they wanted."

"Wait till Tuesday afternoon, and we can go together."

She looked surprised. "You don't want to go through her clothes, do you, throw out the stuff in her medicine cabinet, box up her romance novels? The kids took her afghans, the jewelry, and I gave Jen the Capodimonte. I never knew she had that. It's wonderful porcelain."

"Yes, four pieces. We picked them up at a Goodwill store, where they must have crept into the castoffs. She was very careful with them and used them only on birthdays and at Christmas. She must have some things from my dad, a watch or his ring—something she saved."

"We're not talking Graceland here," Connie said. "I'd be in the bedroom doing the clothes and the bathroom things and you could decide what else you want to take." She took a deep breath and let it out. "Duty done."

Steven realized that Annina's death would lighten Connie's life considerably. Left to herself, Annina would have subsisted on spaghetti and olive oil and worn her clothes to rags. She'd always needed urging. Connie had shopped for her and saw she got out now and then. He wondered if there'd been friendliness

15

between them. Connie never watched the soaps and had opinions on people who did. Was there anything they'd shared, were there happy or exciting moments in their time together?

On the day after the funeral, he sat on a rickety kitchen chair, listening to Connie packing clothes away in the bedroom. He was hearing Annina recount her voyage to America. "The ship stopped here and here and here, all the ports, to pick up the brides. Wherever there was the army—Egypt, Morocco, Italy, Sicily—there were the brides. Some were black and some had veils and eye paint, and some were hill girls, the farm, the city, and all of us sick together, and all thinking America, America." At another time: "All were told someone would meet them when they landed, and for some the men had run away and the women were standing, waiting. I waited, too. I didn't see him, your father. I began to cry, but then there he was, and he took me and kissed me and told me of the long train ride we would have to make to where his father was a landowner in Callan, Colorado." And another time: "His people had land, but they were poor. There were brothers and sisters, but they were not on the land, and I didn't understand. He said, 'Americans choose how they want to live.'"

She had never chosen. She'd been at the mercy of something more than poverty and her in-laws' dislike. What could it have been?

Connie came in with a battered leather suitcase. "This was under the bed."

"I'd forgotten," he said. "It's her valise from Italy."

"I've got the bathroom to do now." She smiled at him and left.

He lifted the valise onto the table and undid the old-fashioned leather straps. He had the guilty feeling of a voyeur but took a deep breath and opened it anyway. He remembered its presence down the years

16

before Denver, when they seemed always to be moving. Often it was the signal of their move, standing ready on the floor. He yearned for her to be there, to tell him where those moves had been, where they'd gone. Where was the place with the horses? Where was the place where the floor was cracked and the cockroaches came? Where was the place where the school was so small that all the grades were in one room? His childhood was gone from him now, breathed out in the last soft, invisible breath she'd taken.

These were her treasures, carried from move to move, ending in this small apartment. The handle had been broken and repaired with wire, clumsily, and the objection was out of his mouth before he could stop it. "Why didn't she let me take this to a leather shop. They would have—"

The contents: a plastic bag with a handful of loose pictures. Mother and Father in Naples, sisters, brothers, the funeral cards of Grandfather and possibly other relatives. The dates were 1943 and 1944. Her wedding picture. Those shoes must have been borrowed. The dress was denim or coarse cotton and it was a grayish color. The veil, white, had probably been rented, or borrowed. She looked like a little girl, a starveling. The groom, Alonzo Carl Howe, was a smiling GI, a little stiff in unaccustomed dress uniform. His sleeve in the second picture, where he stood in profile, showed PFC. There were four pictures of him, one with his company mates, standing at a gun emplacement, bare-chested and squinting in the Italian sun. One was standing with her family, legs apart, hair tousled, and his wide grin. He had his arms draped loosely on their shoulders. They were unsmiling, pinched, not allowing their bodies to take an inch of extra space. The other pictures were of Steven at various ages, school pictures. In two group

17

pictures at schools and among children he no longer remembered, he stood stoic, stolid, and lost.

Steven put the pictures back and saw another plastic bag, this one holding travel brochures. He lifted the bag out of the valise. They were tied with string, and Steven remembered how Annina hated rubber bands and wouldn't use them unless forced to. "Faithless," she said. All the brochures were for the Caribbean: Jamaica, Saint Kitts, Barbados. He was amazed. Were the pictures alone what she wanted, the pristine beaches and blue ocean, or had she a secret wish to go to those places, to open the doors of those luxurious rooms? Why hadn't she told them she wanted to go to the Caribbean? "I would have taken you," he insisted. "You never told us you wanted to go." Every reference she had made to a voyage had carried the memory of all those sick and morning-sick war brides, pregnant or parturient on the heaving sea. He tossed the brochures into the trash.

Another plastic bag held all the forms, inquiries, and letters pertaining to her status as immigrant, wife of a citizen, prospective citizen, and, finally, her citizenship certificate, "Granted, this 17th of June in the year 1952, in Lincoln, Nebraska." Steven would have been going on four then, but he didn't know they'd been in Nebraska. They must have come back later, then, to Colorado, to the house he'd first known as home.

In a third plastic bag was her marriage certificate, in Italian, elaborately worded and elaborately printed, uniting Anna Suzanna Massachetti to Alonzo Carl Howe, PFC, USA. There were his discharge paper and his birth certificate, Callan, Colorado, September 24, 1922.

Steven read these documents with the pleasure of one who hears a familiar story he has been told for years, in which he is the heir to a secret treasure. Here

18

was the meeting of his parents, the shy girl, her parents poor, suspicious, and vigilant. He could see the young couple meeting, street English and street Italian, the few words GIs mislearned. From somewhere in his memory, the marching cadence: "Signorina, veni qua'/"Come and get your chocolate bar." Her gravity would engage the conquering soldier. Soon he was supplying her starving family with food, clothing, and medicine.

Their courtship, as Annina had told it, consisted of walks all over Naples. Here was the marriage certificate the army had tried to keep him from being granted. Annina had told him of the roadblocks the army created at every turn. She had told him these stories while she was bathing him, in the intimate moments of nuzzling and playing Find the Belly Button. "Yes, I had a white veil and a crown of flowers." In the wedding picture, she held a prayer book, but he couldn't remember her ever going to church or saying beads as Catholics did. They'd never had religious pictures on the wall or the candles he had seen in other people's houses. He'd never known whether the Howes were Catholic or not and was surprised now that he'd never wondered.

Other papers: lease documents, receipted rent checks, Social Security and bank documents. He remembered helping her set up that account. She had kept all of his school reports, evaluations, inscribed with the names of teachers forgotten or partly remembered, even the smallest mentions in the school news; his name in *The Denver Post* when he graduated; college notices, law school; pictures of his wedding; pictures of the children.

Something began to nag at him, an echo out of all these saved and cherished things. His father had died in 1957 or 1958. Where was the death certificate? Alonzo Howe seemed to have slipped away some time

19

before his death, and why was there no mention of him after 1947? Perhaps papers had been lost in the awful changes contingent on his death, the confusion and dislocation of their move to Denver. Had the move been made in anger? He couldn't remember, but, of course, they hadn't been living in the Callan house by then. There'd been all those other moves, and maybe in one of those moves, pictures, bills with signatures, letters might have been lost.

"My father, who served in the army during and after World War Two, in Naples, as a PFC, died when I was eight." He was muttering to himself. "We were living in a cabin near the river then. There was a yard—and a shed. There was a clothesline like a tree. I broke it, riding on it, and Mama was angry. When Dad came home, he laughed about it. He used to hold his hand up to greet me. He had a motorcycle and a black leather jacket. He wore jeans and boots." Where was that jacket? What had happened to the motorcycle?

Connie had come from the bedroom and was standing at the entry. Well, that's done. We're moving along. I heard you say something—were you calling me?" She was wearing a kerchief, looking efficient and brisk.

"No, talking to myself. I'll take this suitcase to our attic. Con, my mother saved every scrap of paper that had my name, every picture and notice of my existence. Why didn't she save anything about Dad? He was good to us. If he hadn't been, I would have known it and remembered. There was nothing but his discharge paper, his signature on her citizenship application. Why wasn't there anything else?" He looked at her helplessly and began to weep. "I can't ask her. I can't ask her anything again."

Chapter Four

Christmas came with the usual Scott festivities. On the day before New Year's, Steven lunched with his law school friends, who had long ago christened themselves the Witty Committee. At first, these get-togethers had been strongly flavored with the slightly acetic tang of competition—a comparison of job offers, contacts, vistas; later of clothes, watches, and computers; later still of cars, houses, and memberships. The friends dropped names and preened and told stories of brilliant ploys and frightening risks, but gradually the measuring and comparing had given way to appreciation and companionship. They were easy with one another now. He looked forward to the meetings.

The group had once been eight; one had died of cancer, one of a sudden heart attack; two had moved away. The group weathered its waves of divorces and other attritions.

The four left of the Witty Committee were very different in personality and work. Of the four, Steven was closest to Terry. Terry did collections for the four Catholic hospitals in the state. In law school, Steven had been the grind, the only one working full-time and living with his mother, but after law school, his way up had been steadier than the others and his family life happier and more harmonious. The friends had gone through the coming out of Paul's gay son

21

and the constant, nagging fear of the boy's exposure to AIDS. Terry's daughter had died in an auto wreck, and then there was Jack's divorce and womanizing, pursuant to, as Terry said. They had all been at Annina's funeral. Paul asked, "How's it going, Steve?"

"I wanted to take her back to Italy for a look and to introduce the kids to her side of the family, what we could find of them. If we went now, it wouldn't be the same."

"Your dad died a long time ago, didn't he?"

"We seem to have lost all his family. I don't even know where they are."

"Have you ever thought of tracing them?" Jack asked. "I could do that, or Terry, here, the skip-tracer of deadbeats nationwide."

"No—but there's a strange kind of nothing about him, no fingerprint or footstep—he seems to have disappeared even before he died. There are no pictures, no papers. . . ."

"That's odd—some widows keep things longer than they need to," Terry said. "My mother walked around jingling with my father's relics; my aunt harangues everyone to death with long reminiscences of a man no one in the family could stand."

"Even his death certificate is missing."

"He died in Colorado, didn't he?" Terry was looking interested. He liked puzzles.

"I think so, but I may be wrong. I always assumed Annina got her citizenship in Colorado, but I saw the certificate was issued in Nebraska."

"You said your dad had something to do with ranching."

"Years ago, there'd been a ranch at Callan, but it was gone by the time he came back from the war. He seemed to get work at different places. We moved a lot."

"You have too little family," Paul said, "I've got too much. The Friedmans are into tracing their lineages. A family get-together has suddenly become a meeting of the genealogical society, complete with arguments over which software to use. We're saying, Steve, that if you wanted to find your dad's people, it would be easier than ever."

"Let's all go into probate law," Jack said, laughing. "There's no question we all chose the wrong branches. Steve here wastes hours talking people out of bad cases. Paul is too damn sweet for what he does."

Paul looked up from his vegetarian plate. "Maybe I did make a mistake. Shared custody can be one royal battleground."

Jack took a bite of his burger but kept talking. "Lady gets hit by a paint can falling off a scaffold. She isn't killed—amazing. She isn't hurt, either, because the can was turning and its point of impact was the strap of her shoulder bag, which deflected it. Result? A black-and-blue streak across her shoulder for a week and post-traumatic stress syndrome for what she swears will be the rest of her life. I take the case, do the job, but I can't help thinking she should be down on her knees thanking the saint of paint for not punching her ticket." He grinned at Steven. "You graze higher on the slopes of personal injury."

Steven nodded. "I think I do. Ski cases were all new law when I started. Every part of that was exciting, the daily caseload and the legal theory." He smiled at his friends. "And skiing is my chance to be what I'm not."

"Which is?" Terry was smiling back.

"Relaxed," Steven said.

"Generous," Jack said.

"Risk-taking," Terry said.

Paul laughed. "I'm not going to dump any more on this tight-assed friend. Why not? The free ski pass he got me last year."

Seven's friends were still somewhat artificially casual with him, self-conscious and careful, because of Annina's death. He hoped they would ease up soon. Their joking was familiar and dependable. He wanted to hear them at it again, even when he was the butt of it, discussing his conventional nature, his caution, Connie's work.

"A practice with its share of the very rich is not grazing in the Garden of Eden," Steven said. "Allow me to disabuse you of that notion. Juries don't like idle rich kids." He hoped they would pick up on his tone, their faces creased with false misery, that they would moan. Then he could laugh and tell them about seventy-year-old Bob Peterson (*Peterson v. Long*) being beaned by a flying ski.

On the way out of the restaurant, Terry said, "Steve, I wasn't fooling about finding out how your dad died and where, and even getting his death certificate. I've got a lot of skip-tracing software, and access to documents. Do you want me to run the query for you?"

Steven considered that for a minute. "Thanks, Terry, but don't bother with it. Maybe my mom lost the death certificate in the move from Callan. She might have been so distraught that she tore it up. He left her with nothing, after all—her in-laws in a dying town, being in a family she didn't understand and who didn't understand her. Anyway, the Howes are all gone. Thanks anyway."

Back at the office, Steven's secretary handed him the medical records for four of his current cases. The study of hundreds of these cases had given Steven an extensive knowledge of anatomy and the physics of trauma. He was now able to visualize a situation from an emergency room report, and as a result, he asked keener questions when he took depositions. Reports that had once taken him three hours apiece now took one. This increasing competence was gratifying. For the past few years, he had felt he was at the top of his game. Now, he buzzed and said, "Call my mom and tell her I'll be over before I go home." There was a long pause. He said, "Oh, sorry," and she said, "Me, too."

That night, just before sleep, he pictured his father giving him a ride on the motorcycle: the strong, able hands, the fringed black leather jacket, its special tang, the warmth of his father's wiry body. Once or twice, he had picked Steven up and put him on the backseat of the wonderful machine, and for years after, Steven had relived the glorious ride. Then he remembered the times he'd watched from the yard as his father disappeared down the long dirt road and away, followed by the sound that seemed to want nothing more than to surround him. There would be a lonely silence that left the world empty. When he had almost given up hope, the sound, tiny, almost insectlike at first, would announce the return, and there would be the great horse of iron, cinched in chrome, purring its music, reappearing whole, larger and larger. He remembered the joy of it, the awe, then the loss. These thoughts had become rarer over the years. He realized that his mother's death had stirred the memories like a wind.

Christmas and New Year's had gone by in a haze. Jennifer was back in Chicago and Jeremy at the university in Boulder. After the holidays, Jennifer called to tell them she had work at two theater groups, one with a national reputation. Jeremy changed his major again, to chemistry this time. Connie was planning college visits with Mike, so Steven sold some of his stocks. He had Annina's hatred of debt, an eccentricity at the end of the Second Millennium. His arguments with Connie almost always centered on his fear that some calamity, personal loss, or devastation could sweep all of his stability away and leave them wretched. Fear, she said, was keeping him poor in outlook.

Jeremy was one of Steven's worries. His interests had always had a pack rat quality—intense but random; he took things up, burned with them for six months, and then let them go without sorrow or any sense of loss. Steven thought his range was too wide: bonsai at twelve, Chinese writing at thirteen, and at the university, he had gone from geology to anthropology and from math to chemistry. Jennifer was dramatic, intense, quick, and labile emotionally. Steven had seen her off for Chicago and her theater work without realizing how intensely he would miss her. She was doing so well there that every contact she made and all the reputation she built were only working to keep her there indefinitely. Mike was the most considerate of the three, but all of them were alive in a way Steven had never experienced for himself. "Mexico. When we were going up to Callan, Jen was talking about Mexico."

Connie smiled at him. "You were so busy surviving, your experience doesn't give you much background to deal with these kids, who have so much. Jen may still come back, and Jeremy, too, will settle down."

Steven thought of the word *settle* in its legal sense and smiled. "Some settlements are hard on everyone."

Annina's apartment had been cleaned out. The four Capodimonte pieces were in the back of Connie's cupboard—until such time as Jennifer would take them—the jewelry distributed. The leather valise was in the tiny attic, where they kept boxes of memorabilia and the kids' outworn hobbies. They had taken a carton of cooking things, bedding, and towels to send to Jennifer, and it pleased Steven to think about her, in Chicago, using the dented pots and chipped plates he had grown up with in Annina's kitchen.

Steven's practice took him to ski areas all over the state, trips that were two or three hours each way. He used the travel time to hear notes on relevant cases. He had put these on tape. He was listening *to* McDougal v. Gold Flume Corporation, and he was on his way to the ski area for a meeting.

Ashley McDougal, sixteen, skiing out of bounds at Aureole's Whiplash, had noticed the abandoned miner's cabin and skied to it. In the cabin, she had fallen through the rotted floorboards, breaking her leg. She had spent the night in the cabin.

At first, Steven had thought she had no case. He would have to explain to her and her parents where the world's responsibility to her ended.

On the following morning, she said, ski patrollers had been alerted by her calls and had rescued her, but they had ignored her leg injury in favor of treatment for hypothermia. The case might be one of substandard care.

He had begun *McDougal* with key questions for the ski patrollers and was now reviewing their responses. Then, somewhere in the intricacies of the case, he lost the thread of his thought and saw himself in the apartment and looking again into Annina's leather valise, finding a hidden pocket or a false bottom that held the records, pictures, letters that would tell him about his father. Even though he had told Terry that Annina might have torn up the death certificate, he knew she would never have done so. She'd had the immigrant's terror of losing any official document. Why was there nothing relating to Alonzo Howe, not a picture, a news item, nothing after his arrival in the United States, discharge from the service, and signa-

27

ture on Annina's citizenship application. If her life with Lon Howe had been unpleasant, why were his own memories so golden? Even children of four or five hear their parents fight, suffer the brutality of their rages, remember scenes and screaming or silence and turning away. Surely he'd been aware enough to gauge the emotions in a room, to sniff the air as he came from school and opened the door. Surely he'd learned the child's survival alertness that reads danger even before words give it form.

He remembered a boy in college who had a war-bride mother. "They split up pretty soon," the boy had told him. "He fed her wind about the ranch his family ran in the great West. She came here and found five acres and an old trailer. I think lots of those war brides got snookered that way—handsome soldier, big and rich, walking tall in Italy and France, Morocco and Algeria: 'Come to my five hundred acres in New Mexico, my emporium in New York'—the desert and the candy store."

The boy'd had a wry take on his mother's experience. "What gets me," he'd said, "was that the five acres were in Black Hawk, and if she'd hung on, my father would have drunk himself to death anyway, and she would have been left with five acres that are now worth a million an acre. She showed it to me, once; the land was right in town."

Annina had conveyed no such anger or bitterness to Steven. What he felt growing up had been her sorrow. Perhaps she grieved over the death of a loved young husband, over poverty and friendlessness, over the Howes, who'd been cold and had dissolved the family bond, moving away from their stagnating town.

With an impatient and dismissive click, Steven reran the tape and pushed the play button, trying to concentrate on the picture of Ashley McDougal lying

28

thrashing in the snow. What did they see at that first look? What did they decide?

On his return from Gold Flume, he played the messages on his answering machine.

Three contained routine scheduling details. The fourth was from Terry Shannon. "Lo, Steve. On a whim, I did the trace on Alonzo Carl Howe. He didn't die in Colorado and he hasn't been listed as missing. Keep on, or what? Should I try to get links in other states—Kansas, Wyoming?"

Chapter Five

Jennifer called home from Chicago. "Don't worry—
I'm okay."

"I'm so glad to hear," Connie said. "What's
wrong?"

"I—uh, I had an accident. I'm in the ER, and they
wanted me to let you and Dad know. I'm covered by
my group insurance, but they said I should tell you."

Connie motioned to Steven to pick up the other
phone.

"It's my knee. I don't think anything is broken."

"I'll be out there as soon as I can get a flight,"
Connie said.

Jennifer argued, but Connie won. She called Steven
the next day. "They're going to do some surgery on
the knee, and the doctor says the problem isn't major.
She'll be up in a day or two, but with a brace for a
while. Her friends are helping. There's something
else."

"What else?"

"The medical report said that she walked into a fire
hydrant, walked into it so unaware that it tore up
things in her knee and she couldn't walk. The doctor
called it a 'suspicious accident' and he started asking
questions and tested her. He thinks Jen has a vision
problem. He said she didn't walk into the hydrant
through inattention; she didn't *see* it."

"I can't believe that. Of course Jennifer can see—she
was reading to me when she was here. Don't you

remember? She's a little clumsy; she's always been clumsy. She fell when we were at the projects. And she's excited and full of her own ideas, and she gets inattentive."

"The doctor says she's been moving defensively, that her visual field isn't normal."

"What does he say to do?"

"They'll fix the knee and then we get a complete eye exam."

"Will she get the tests here?"

"She says no, but she's angry at the doctor and at me. She's defensive about walking into things, but she knows something's wrong; I can tell. I talked her into letting me stay, and I'll go to the exam with her as soon as she can manage."

"Wouldn't we know if she couldn't see? She's not some neglected kid no one has cared about."

"We'll work on this bit by bit," Connie said, "as it comes."

Steven told Mike the news over a TV dinner. Mike was incredulous, but in the course of the evening, he moved, like a big ship changing direction in a quiet sea, degree by degree. " . . . 'cause except when—there was that egg, Dad. She had it at the edge of the counter and I thought she brushed it off with her sleeve, but what if she didn't see it?" Then he peered at Steven and said, "Why not let me cook for us tomorrow? If I'm going to be a man of the new millennium, I should be as good in the kitchen as any woman. What if she has a brain tumor?"

"Oh Jesus, Mike!"

"Well, could it be that?"

"I don't think we should speculate about anything until we know. We're just scaring each other."

Connie was away for six days. She called every night with the day's events. Jen had been given pain pills on her release from the hospital and a sheet of instructions about rest and exercise. She had a brace and was being helped by all her friends.

"They're a good group, Steve, her theater friends—fun and so attentive to her. I had planned to shop, but it was all done when we got back to the apartment. I feel so much better leaving her when the eye exam is finished, knowing they'll look out for her."

On the next day: "We did the eye exam. I'll be home tomorrow; Jen will be coming in with me. We've been arguing and she wants to tell you about it herself."

Eye problems—cataracts, maybe. Steven had heard that they could appear at any age. The surgery would be one eye at a time; it was a common operation, overwhelmingly successful, but he spent a restless night.

"Look," Jennifer said as they walked from the gate at the airport. "I'm not leaving Chicago. I'm not coming back here. I'm not going to die of this and I'm not going to be living dead."

"This comes before 'Hello'?" Steven asked. He could see that Connie had gotten enough of Jennifer's defensiveness. "Let's wait till we get home," he said, "before all three cats get out of the bag."

Jennifer was limping slightly and looking ready to begin part two of an argument. "I'm only saying—" Then she bumped into a man hurrying to his gate. Connie jumped forward, but Jennifer shook off her arm, hissing, "Oh, shit!" and began to cry.

The man harrumphed, "Well, excuse *me*. Are you blind?" and moved away.

"Here, let me—"

"I'm telling you, Mom, I'm all right."

When they were in the car, Connie said, "Steven, Jennifer has a—"

"Wait," Jennifer said. "It's what *I* have. I get to say it in my way and I want Mike and Jer to be there so I don't have to say it all over again and again. I have a

32

way I want to say it, and things I want to say about it."

"Your vision . . . how bad is it?"

"I am seeing; I can see. I want us all together. I want to talk about *Macbeth*, which West Wind is staging and for which I'm doing the costuming. After that, *Raft of the Medusa*. After that, *Skin of Our Teeth*."

And she did, her face relaxing into its expressive beauty, a glow, as she described her ideas. "It's why I won't be able to stay past the weekend. We're starting on Monday and I shouldn't be here at all. Everyone always goes dark with *Macbeth*, but remember when Duncan says, 'This castle hath a pleasant seat'? They were normal before the witches got to them. They had a nice castle, good servants, nice clothes. The designers always put Mrs. Mac in black and show her as being about fifty. In our production, though . . ."

She went on about Macbeth, surprising Steven. "He's not a bad man in act one. You watch him go wrong. What would the costumes be for showing that? What would the hairstyles be?"

Steven shrugged. "I guess I never notice things like that," but he was thinking, Eyes, she sees.

"If the production is good, you wouldn't. It all emerges as a feeling. Oh, yes, and our witches are a little girl, a ravishing young woman, and a crone, all dressed very sumptuously."

"Listen, Jen, it'll be tomorrow evening before Jeremy might get in from Boulder. Can't I know something about what's going on? This isn't a drama where we all need the suspense."

"Yes, it is, Dad. Mom swore she'd wait. It's my problem, and I don't want four versions of it floating around."

He turned for help. "Connie—"

"I swore."

33

Steven spent the next day in his office, working on several cases, but every so often he would think about Jennifer, and what she would tell them.

He had done the discovery on *McDougal*. He didn't look forward to conferring with the girl and her parents, telling them that their case was weak, and that if they pursued it, they would lose, and that they would be paying a lot of money to lose.

To his intense relief, good sense prevailed. Ashley threw a screaming fit, but at last, he said, "You can choose to see yourself as a crippled ex-skier who was mistreated, or you can choose to see yourself as an athlete who is somewhat handicapped, who made a mistake but then responded with courage and perseverance. Which is it to be? You get to choose."

As they left, he comforted the mother, who was embarrassed. "Her temperament may modify, and the courage will still be there."

Chapter Six

At seven o'clock, the Howes were all sitting in an artificial silence at the dinner table, to which the food had not yet been brought. Jennifer told them she wanted to wait until after dinner, but Connie said that enough was enough. She would serve while Jennifer told them.

"You've worked us up, so we're thinking this is something fatal, at least," Jeremy said, and was hissed to silence.

"I went to the ophthalmologist," Jennifer said, "and he dilated my eyes and shone the light into them and said there were irregularities. He did some other tests and said I would have to go to the hospital for a specialized test that would confirm what he thought."

"So what did he think?" Mike asked.

"Oh, shut up," Jeremy said.

"Did the tests hurt?" Mike asked.

"No, some were fun, sort of, seeing colored lights and things moving in and out of my line of sight, telling him when I saw them."

"She has tunnel vision," Connie said.

Mike began to laugh. "You didn't need an eye exam to tell us that."

"Shut up, dimwit," Jennifer said. "It's true that I don't have the peripheral vision you have, but within my field my vision is twenty-twenty. My biggest problem is night blindness. I'll have to carry a big flashlight. The good news is that I've already lived with this for years. It's crept up on me. The doctor said it must have started when I was eight or nine and slowly progressed."

Steven thought back to the series of still pictures he had of Jennifer's growing up, memories of Jennifer: falling, walking into things, losing things, her excitement making her inattentive. It had rendered her vulnerable and dear to him.

"The bad news is that I have this thing," she was saying, "and it's eight syllables long and they can't cure it and it's genetic and it's progressive, but that means it could be slow and never move past where it is right now, which means I carry a big flashlight at night and keep designing theatrical costumes for a long, long time."

She said all that at double speed and spoke without feeling, as at a line reading, impatient to get to the wished-for part. Among the torrent of words that washed past Steven, three lay like alligators submerged except for a barely seen ripple in the water: "Can't cure" and "Progressive."

"It's called retinitis pigmentosa," Connie said.

"There must be some treatment," he objected. "Every condition has *something* that can be done."

By a strange process, all the air had been taken out of the room.

Jennifer said, "There are canes with electronic beepers; there are *things*, but I'm not nearly that bad."

Connie said, "And there are also groups, they told us, support groups."

"There's no drug, Dad, no exercise or operation, no replacement of anything."

"And progressive."

"It hasn't progressed to legal blindness yet."

He thought, Oh God. "You mean it could leave you with no vision at all?"

"Tunnel vision, and the tunnel can get narrower and narrower and it can close up."

They sat stunned into silence, even Connie, who had heard it before. "I'm nowhere near that. I may go on as I am for years. He said 'moderate.' I'm moderate. There are people my age who are stone-blind, but I'm moderate."

"How do you know how bad it's going to be?" Jeremy asked.

Mike said, "You don't smoke or drink a lot. . . . You could give those up."

"They don't know what affects the rate of progress. This is a rare condition and has two forms, dominant and recessive."

"Genetic."

"Yes."

"But that's crazy," Mike said, seizing the contradiction like a rescue line. "None of us ever heard of this thing. How can it be genetic? There are no blind people in our family."

Steven knew that Mike was seeing all the family he knew moving past him on parade, all of them seeing, eyes front, here and there with the sun glinting off glasses that corrected the normal forms of visual problems to crisp lines and full depths of field.

Jeremy said, "How can we know without genetic tests? If the thing's rare, the families don't have enough kids, that's all. In the days where there were twenty kids in a family, you'd see these recessive conditions. I learned that in genetics class. If you have only one or two kids, the chances are you'll never know what your genetic weaknesses are until the laws of chance get you in the short ribs." Everyone was silent. "What's it called again?" he asked.

"Retinitis pigmentosa," Jennifer said, "and I've had it since grade school, only I never knew. How can you know what someone else is seeing? You assume you're normal and seeing what other people see. Remember, my vision is twenty-twenty."

Steven found himself breathing more deeply to compensate for the lack of air and the sudden closing in of the walls. He noticed that outside it had begun to snow, a desultory, undecided snow falling straight, illuminated by the lights from other houses. There was no wind, or not yet. "Do you have classes tomorrow?" he asked Jeremy. "Maybe you'll want to stay over."

"Who's heard the weather report?"

"Let's wait for the ten-fifteen."

These comments were made in flat voices, as absentminded as the snowfall. "I've got a heavy day and a lab class to prepare for," Jeremy said. "I'll start at ten-thirty if they don't predict an immediate howling blizzard."

They talked more—they talked without listening. Connie served dessert and herb tea. The weatherman said light snow. Jeremy put on his coat and left for Boulder. Mike asked a few more questions about night blindness and went to his room to finish his homework. Jennifer said, "Nothing's changed since last week or last month. I'm no blinder than I was then, and I want to go back to my apartment and my job and my life without your nagging about it. Mom wants me to get hooked up with support groups and RP networks right now and start being a 'survivor.' I'm not a survivor yet and I don't need any banner to march under. I don't want to be organized or processed or put on anybody's list. Not yet."

"But you fell."

"I fell. I know why now. I know there are things I don't see, and because of that, I'll have to learn to sweep around, turn, move my head. When I go out at night, I'll take a flashlight the size of Brazil and not be embarrassed."

38

He wanted to forbid her to return to Chicago. He wanted to keep her in the house, safe. He knew that this idea was ridiculous and beyond his power to effect. The war in him between wish and reality rendered him silent.

They went up to bed. "Steve, I'm so sorry. What you said about treating, about cure—the doctors say no, but I'm going to research this all I can." He was sitting on the bed, making no move to undress. She came in from the bathroom, where she had been speaking while she brushed her teeth and washed up. Her definiteness, a matter-of-fact strength, cheered him somehow. "Con—"

"I know. I wanted to tell you that night, but Jen needed to do it this way."

"It's awful any way it's delivered."

"Yes," she said, "yes, it is."

Jennifer was at the museum the next day, and the day after that, she returned to Chicago, turning down Connie's help and maneuvering her way alone through the crowds and the complexities of Denver International Airport. She was wearing her knee brace and she was still on pain medication.

At the office, Steven tried to forget the problem, but questions and arguments kept intruding. He hadn't asked how much of her field of vision had been darkened. He hadn't asked about the mechanical aids she had mentioned, the electronic technology that might be used. That night, he had a dream in which an army of locusts was advancing on a city, and he realized on waking that the dream referred to Jennifer's blindness, pictures his fear had taken in its laboratory of metaphor. Farms and open country had been swallowed up, the outer suburbs covered by darkness.

Connie's response to the problem was aggressive. She threw herself at it. On the day Jennifer left,

Connie went to the university's medical library, and that evening, she checked on the Internet. There, she fell into the tidal ocean of fact and wish. There was information about the dominant and recessive forms of retinitis pigmentosa, and an array of aids to mobility. There were definitions of legal blindness, and of research being done and of research being planned.

And there were the "cures" and the "alternative approaches," anecdotal and miraculous: cabbage diet, lemongrass, vegetarian diets, head standing, rocking, megavitamins, acupuncture, acupressure, chakra stimulation, stress reduction, transcendental meditation, LSD, herbal eye drops.

"I don't think any of the alternative stuff has been tested," Connie told Steven, "but there is some good research being done, a drug to slow the condition down. Maybe Jen could go to Houston." And the next night, "They said that by stimulating the retina at its points . . ." Later, she called Jennifer with the things she had learned, and was disappointed when Jennifer sent back an E-mail:

> I knew this would happen. It's why I haven't told my friends yet. They'll all want to help and so do you, but I want to do what I'm doing. Tell me what the Internet says about any kind of velvet that hangs like velvet, looks like velvet, and in which actors won't sweat like stevedores. Tulle scratches—please advise. My actor is chunky; I want to play that up. The production benefits from her chunkiness—she hates me.

Steven was also amazed to hear Connie talking about it as he came into the kitchen the next evening

40

and heard her on the phone. "Well, no, they haven't found a cure yet, but there are at least three places where work's being done. . . ."

"Who was that?" he asked when she hung up at last. He was trying not to sound critical.

"Oh, that was my mom. She asked about DNA testing, if the family should be tested. I told her it wouldn't help."

"I know Barb and Tony have to be told. I guess I wanted you to put it off for a while, until we got used to it ourselves."

"Talking about it—it's a woman thing, I guess. I need to tell people—family, friends, people I love."

"What good does all the talking do?"

"I can't tell you that; I can only say that I need to do it. And Steve, when the truth came out, if Mom and Dad hadn't known it, and my friends, at least the closest ones, they would all see it as a betrayal."

"But how can they do any more than suffer themselves?"

"They can't, but not to tell means leaving them out. We're a family, and we have friends; they have to know."

"It feels so raw. I wish we could have waited until we knew more. I'm not ready to talk about it, to deal with it, not yet, not until I know how slow or fast, how soon—"

"But we won't know that for years, perhaps, and all our behavior with them will be closed off and artificial. We'll be sealing ourselves off."

"And sympathy—I don't want sympathy."

"You'll have to tell Paul, Terry, and Jack soon."

"I guess so," Steven said wanly. "I don't want to. I want to wait until I'm ready and I know what will happen and when, and when I can take it all in—when the time is right."

41

"Paul had to tell you about his son and Terry about his daughter. What do you think they'll say when they find out you've held out on them for a year or two?"

"I guess they'd think I tried to put one over on them."

"It would be a betrayal of friendship."

"No, it's a power thing."

"Where do men get that?"

"It's part of the kit."

"I never understood that part," Connie said, "because what happens is that you're silent and strong and alone and then you wonder why you're lonely and why no one understands you, and why you're mute."

"Do I seem mute to you?"

"Yes, sometimes you do."

It gave Steven a pang to remember that in all the upset over Jennifer's condition, he hadn't told Connie that Lon Howe, his father, might be a missing person.

Chapter Seven

He told his friends at the monthly lunch. He told them quickly, clinically, remarking that Jennifer might reach old age without much more handicap than she was facing now. He defined tunnel vision. He allowed himself to complain briefly about Connie. "She's disappeared into the Internet and come out dripping wet somewhere north of Zamboanga. She wants to know all there is to know."

He caught Terry's quick look. They hadn't talked since the phone message about there being no listing of his father in the recorded deaths.

Each of his friends reacted characteristically: Paul was silent, listening intently; Terry had questions about the doctors. Who'd made the diagnosis? Were they sure? Jack displayed his need to cover unpleasantness, especially the pain of a friend. He got off several witticisms and changed the subject, which by then was a relief.

After lunch, Terry walked Steven to his car. It was the mid-February Chinook, a false spring that opened coats in the middle of the winter, a break before the biggest of the snows, which would come in March.

"It was tough telling us, wasn't it."

"Connie tells everyone, family, friends, passing birds. Sorry—I'm not being fair to her. Some women need—"

"Maybe men do, too. It was good for me to tell you when the world caved in on me."

Steven suddenly knew what Terry was thinking, that his own daughter's fatal accident had broken up his marriage a year later and that Steven's marriage might be strained by what was happening.

"I apologize for not getting back to you after I got your message," Steven said. "You went to some trouble to trace my dad's death dates."

"I didn't do that much, but if you or Connie really wants to locate your side of the family, or if some doc needs the genetic stuff for the other kids, or if you just want to find some relatives, let me know. I've got programs that will do all that with no effort at all."

"If finding a dead relative could give Jen one more degree in her range of vision, I'd do it in a minute. Otherwise, I don't know what good it could do."

Steven realized that Annina's death had closed ways to the past that he had never thought of venturing into until the venturing was no longer possible. Jennifer's condition, with its genetic secret, ignition from a match struck long ago, had made him ask questions he had never posed before.

Connie knew how ambivalent he was. She needed to call friends and to study the genetics of retinitis pigmentosa, but she carefully arranged to do those things when he was not at home, and in doing so, she had to take part of herself away from him.

He was escaping into his work. He'd always imagined the law as a refutation of fatalism, the idea that in injury or injustice, nothing could be done.

A skier might go up the lift, laughing with friends, eager for a day on the slopes. Later, he might be retrieved on a sled, shivering, broken, changed in every way he would have to live from then on. For some of these injured, the law could provide compensation that allowed for care, training, and support. His inquiry into the history of the incident, its physics, its responsibility, its blame, was minute and detailed, but he couldn't understand inquiry into a condition for which there was no actionable cause. Still, he thought, there was the mystery of genetics, identity.

Annina had been a fatalist. All surprises were bad, and death alone ended the potential for worse evils. He fought his clients' despair with possibilities and choices. He was sure that had Annina lived to know of Jennifer's condition, she would interpret it as an obscure fault in her lineage, surfacing now as a curse against a beloved granddaughter, the result of sin eternally punished under an evil star.

Connie was calling Chicago no more frequently than she always had, but Steven was more sensitive to Jennifer's need for independence, even as he yearned as much as Connie did to know that she was safe. He thought he heard the impatience in Jennifer's voice, and when they spoke, she pleaded with him: "I'm no worse than I was last week, last month, probably last year. I'm having a great time. I don't work at night when I don't have to, and my friends look out for me. How are you doing?"

He said he was fine and joshed with her over the phone. He knew he was spending too much time worrying about her, seeing her in danger, wondering how much she was hiding from them. Worry left him with a feeling of malaise. He wished he could trade his depression for Connie's energetic research.

Connie had told the Scott grandparents, and for two or three days there had been phone calls and flurry back and forth. As if to defend against an accusation, they had undergone the expensive DNA testing. There was no RP, Barbara Scott said, but they had learned other things. There was both Native American and Jewish ancestry in their pasts, enough to interest, Steven thought, not enough to trouble. Connie's people were proud enough of themselves that any humbling piece of DNA would surely be overlooked by them, a single small blemish on an all but perfect lineage.

"I'm glad we were tested," Barbara told Steven. "I think it's important for Jeremy and Mike to know."

"Neither of them is affected, and if it were potential in them, so what? How would unearthing my missing uncles, aunts, and cousins help? Does it really matter whose family has the gene?"

"Don't you care? Don't you want to know?"

No, Steven thought, goddamn it, no.

Connie began tracing the Italian Massachettis. Steven realized that she couldn't stop. She was working over genetic information because there was no treatment available to help Jennifer, no specialist, no surgery, no drug, no exercise. She was fighting depression as the cheery Scott family always had—with action.

Their twenty-fifth anniversary approached and Jennifer said she would come in for the weekend. She arrived, only a little slower of movement, and glowing with youth and health, finding him easily among the many people at the airport gate.

"I'm doing *A Man For All Seasons*," she told him as they drove home. "Did you know that Thomas More was said to be the *wittiest*, most urbane man in England? No way will I dress him in those burial clothes, the ones they gave him in that film." He delighted in her enthusiasm. Nothing was pro forma for her, nothing unquestioned. She studied for each play, going through all the characters with a fresh outlook, and Steven thought that from now on he would notice the clothing worn by characters in the plays he and Connie watched.

"I talked the director into trying my idea."

"What idea?"

"Making *Macbeth's* Banquo feast into a real 'We Have Arrived' blowout. It should be full of glitz—her overdressing will be a sign of their sickness. Where was humanity without Velcro? Quick costume change? Little buttons? Nope. With Velcro, you tear it open neck to crotch and you've got your change for the next scene in four seconds."

"Jen . . . come down a minute."

She faced him straight on. "I am all right, and I have quit faking it, pretending I can see at night and getting lost on my own block. If a guy wants to take me out, it has to be okay with him if I pull out my flashlight to see the menu in a dim restaurant and even to find my way to the ladies'."

"I wasn't trying to corner you."

"Yes you were, but it's okay."

He noticed that she moved her head more often and bent her neck to look down carefully when she was on stairs or walking. When she caught him checking on her, she laughed. "Standing still and just looking, my vision's better than yours. See that elk on that mountain? See that skier—oh, look, he's gone over on his ass!"

Later, Steven was sitting by the TV, watching the recap of a football game. Connie disliked the noise of football, but seeing the game with low sound seemed to take something away and his attention flagged. He was passively eavesdropping on the conversation Jen and Connie were having in the kitchen, enjoying their casual, companionable talk.

"Not that much garlic."

"Oh—and yes, I did see that piece drop on the floor."

"Sorry, Jen. I keep wondering . . ."

There was silence and then the sound of a food processor and then the sound of oil sputtering on a skillet.

"Let the oil get very hot. Wait, though—not all at once."

He heard something being poured into the hot fat followed by an aroma that awoke his appetite.

"Dad isn't all that keen on your looking up the Italian part of our family, is he?"

"No, but I can't stop now. It's like a big mystery. I liked Annina—no, I loved her, but she wasn't what you'd call giving or open. I know she liked me and I know she loved you. She was afraid, terrified of something, and it closed her up."

"Daddy has some of that secrecy in him, doesn't he?"

"It's a man thing," Connie said.

Steven found himself smiling. It's a lawyer thing, he thought.

"When Nonna talked about Italy, she made everything seem terrible—all that poverty and hunger."

"Well, that was the war, bombing and the invasions, and the country was poor even before that."

"All I could drill out of her was that she had four brothers and four sisters but that five of the eight died before they were grown, and that her grandmother was killed by a bullet that ricocheted off a wall two blocks away. One uncle sold candy from a big tray he hung around his neck. He walked with that for miles, through all the sections of the city. There were two aunts in a convent. That was about it."

Steven sat there, amazed. Jen's sketchy information was twice what he had been able to elicit from Annina all his life. Aunts in the convent? Candy dealer? He did know about the sisters and brothers. Preserved in his childhood's bath-time ritual was a chant Annina had created for him of their names: "Celia, Bernardo, Paula, Carlo, Laura, Julia, Tillio, Io." The joke came when he would end with Tillio, Io, and she would be washing him and would give a rub with the washcloth and say, "No, *tuo*, ma *Io!*" When he was old enough to wash himself, the chant was lost, only to return on the day he washed Jennifer as a baby, and to his amazement, found himself murmuring it as she squealed with delight. Thereafter, he had chanted it to all three children in the bath, but they hadn't known that the words were the names of great-aunts and -uncles.

Massachetti. How common was the name in Naples? How much older were Annina's sisters and brothers? One of the pictures showed them much older than the frail teenage bride. Now, they would be in their upper seventies, at least.

What if he told Connie the bathtub-chant names? Would she go right away on the Internet and find the right Massachetti family? If there was a blind person there, the hunt would be over, but once again his family would be the one diminished. He turned the sound up on the game.

The anniversary party went well, although a little too managed for Steven's taste. Some of the professionalism of Ring and Wreath was reflected in the family's private parties, but Connie's events did bring out the combination of excitement and relaxation in her guests that he didn't always see at other evenings.

This was a large affair and included his friends of the Witty Committee and their wives or significant others. Jack had begun to plan the yearly guys-only ride to the casinos at Black Hawk, and for a few moments the four went to their calendars to block out a Friday afternoon. Tradition held that they all went to that occasion in modified cowboy costume, worn denim jackets, and old hats. Jack, whose day it was, always wore fringed leather and his Stetson, and he lost more money than the other three combined.

"Twenty-five years of marriage," Paul said. "These days, that's quite a feat."

Steven tried for graciousness. "We haven't had the kind of trauma that sinks a marriage," and he could see Paul thinking, Until now.

Paul said, "They say that suffering is supposed to bring a couple together, but not in my experience."

They heard a burst of laughter from the other side of the room. Paul said, "Jack's new girl is getting relaxed."

"Well, it's certainly not Steve's booze," Terry said, and they laughed. It was a traditional teasing about Steven's stinginess. "Cheap stuff in small glasses."

Jeremy was explaining something about chemistry to friends of Connie's. Steven noticed Mike standing alone, so he went over and joined him, surveying the buffet. Jennifer came by, talking to three women. "Look at that. She really glows."

"Dad, I've decided I want to go to Metro."

"Why Metro? It's a big city school, no campus, no college life."

"You didn't have any college life."

"I'm sorry I let you in on so much of my bio," Steven said. "It's the reason I want a full college experience for you."

"They have a work-study program there that I think will work for me."

"What program?"

"Rehabilitation."

Steven's heart sank. "You'd be working with uneducated people, poorer people."

"Not exclusively."

"Is this about Jennifer?"

"What doesn't she see, Dad? What's her world like, and can the limitations she has be pushed in some way? I want to know what's happening to her. Maybe my field will be blindness, maybe something more, but I'm really excited about this."

"Well, at least Mom will love having you in Denver."

Mike laughed. "And you won't?"

"If you stay at home, you can cook when she's away evenings."

"There's more. I signed up to work this summer at a camp for handicapped kids." Mike was grinning at Steven. "I wish I had a picture of you right now. Why do you look like I just shot your dog?"

"It's a class thing, I guess, a snobbishness I never knew I had. When a person leaves something he hates, he doesn't want his kids back in it. Rehabilitation isn't highly paid, either. I can't say I'm very grateful to you for showing me this part of me, but I guess I'll learn to get past it."

"I should have a good apartment off campus, then, shouldn't I, something with built-in appliances and a view?"

"A snob isn't an idiot. Don't push your luck."

They looked out at the party guests, Connie moving in and out among them. "I see her hovering over Jennifer," Mike said. "Did you know Jeremy broke up with Bettina last week?"

"Who's she?"

"The recent throb. Mine are year to year. His are month to month."

"Don't envy him. Sometimes I think your brother is a bit callow."

At midnight, they had a small ceremony, a cake, champagne, and toasts to twenty-five more years; there were some comic gifts. The party began to wind down. People left and those who stayed talked more intimately, which Steven always felt was the crown of the evening.

After they left, the family surveyed the mess. One of Connie's laws was that parties, no matter when they ended, left no traces. Everyone began picking up.

51

Jennifer, a tray of dirty plates in her hands, was moving into the kitchen as Mike was about to take the empty champagne bottles to the recycling bin. They collided and she went sprawling, sending plates skidding off the tray and onto the floor. For a moment, everything stopped and Jennifer cried out to them, "Leave me alone; I'm all right. I want to get up by myself." Then she began to cry, pounding her fists on the floor. "I've always been the clumsiest, the klutz. It wasn't fair. It was because of going blind!" Steven pulled in his breath at the word. She sat up, but didn't try to stand. "Remember when I tried out for the soccer team and they wouldn't let me play at all? *It wasn't my fault!* Remember when I designed the whole fantasy fashion show in senior project and they wouldn't let me model any of the outfits because they said I'd get dizzy and fall? 'She's such a klutz.' Even the teachers laughed, and one said, 'Well, we can't all be Lady Di,' and it wasn't my fault. 'Oh, Grace, how's charm school?' Why didn't anyone see or figure it out? They all *saw*. Why couldn't they see that?"

Chapter Eight

The Witty Committee casino trip took place at the beginning of April, between snows. Jack liked to gamble and the others went along for the day out. Every year, they spent a day in one of the Colorado gambling towns. Steven enjoyed the beauty of the rides up and back without the pressure of work at the end. They went in jeans and flannel shirts and avoided shop talk. He was an anxious bettor, afraid of any urge to surrender his rational self and succumb, to bet all he had, even though he knew the percentages to be overwhelmingly skewed for the benefit of the house.

They wound into the mountains on roads never meant to carry the numbers of players now eager to lose money at altitude. Steven, as usual, carried no credit cards and only fifty dollars in cash. Jack was driving, and by the time they turned off the mountain road and into the town, they were singing.

Here, the casino motif was of garish faux-1860s gold mining. Steven could tell from Jack's ebullient mood that the outing would last until his friend was well past his limit. The day was mellow, with sweet mountain air and a warm sun. Steven was loath to go into the noisy, windowless casino.

"Listen," he said, "I need some air. Why don't you guys go and start and I'll join you in half an hour."

Jack pretended annoyance. "You must hate losing so much, you'll sit outside and freeze your ass off."

"I'm a secret drinker," Steven said, "with bottles hidden all over town that I need to check on."

He left his friends at the entrance, then climbed the narrow mountain street to a level place where the bones of an ore breaker stood on a mound of tailings, the left-to-stand quaint reminder of the town's past. Noise from the lower streets drifted up, but this area was bare, and Steven took a deep appreciative breath as he sat down and looked out over the town. Clouds overwhelmed the view to the west and hid the mountains, but the sky above him was Colorado drop-dead blue and absolutely clear. He was conscious of a feeling of perfect relaxation, of being completely at leisure. A light breeze came up and the sounds of talk, car motors, and movement that had risen from the streets below were carried away on it. He thought he would stay until he was chilled, and then he would warm himself with the walk back to the casino. From far away, a buzzing separated itself from his daydream. As he waited, the sound identified itself as it became louder, then separated into several sounds, familiar and exciting, and he was wide-awake as the two motorcyclists jounced over the incline at the far side of the mound on which he was sitting and then stopped on the level twenty feet from him. The bikers were in black leather vests, studded with patterns of steel beads. They had heavy leather gloves and high cowboy boots. They turned off the motors of their BMWs and straddled the bikes. They were young men. He could tell that from the fluidity of their movements. The first biker lifted his helmet and stretched, then the second. The first rider hung his helmet from his handlebars and pulled his cycle around. His move revealed the second rider more fully.

That rider was Steven's father. For a long moment, Steven stared, taking in the lithe, powerful body, the ginger hair, the tanned face. How wonderful it was to see him after all this time. His father smiled and stretched.

Only the fiercest logic stopped Steven from struggling up from his seat and climbing the mound to his father, crying out to him, telling him about the years, about being married, about their children, the law, his mother's death. The biker, who was now joking with his friend, had given Steven a brief glance and turned away, unconscious of Steven's fascinated stare. Alonzo Carl Howe was telling the friend that money was too hard-earned to throw away down there, and then, to Steven's shock, said what his father had said to him years before, "Use your head, boy!"

My father isn't twenty years younger than I am, Steven's daytime mind, his lawyer's mind, spoke to him out of his dream, and the illusion was gone. The mind that knows wordlessly, that sees in a crowd of hundreds the single wished-for face, was still speaking to him: He's come back for me; I need him, and he's here.

He'd seen his father in dreams now and then, but with Annina's death had come to the knowledge that all the ways to his past were closed. He'd begun to dream of barricaded roads and borders he couldn't cross. What this vision signified, he thought, was simple grief. He had been so taken up with Jennifer's problem that his orphan self was haunting him.

On the few occasions when Annina had spoken to Steven about his father, she would tell of his handiness, how he built things wherever they lived, to make life easier. He made little toys for Steven, too, and, of course, kept his motorcycle in perfect, harmonious order. Whenever Steven had asked about Lon Howe's work, she would say, "A man works where he must. Your father, he always had a job, yes." When he asked what the jobs were, or where, she would go gauzy, her replies vague. "Many places."

"I remember living on a ranch."

"Yes, a big house."

"When I was in first grade, was that the ranch?"

"I don't remember, but maybe yes. You came home on the school bus, a big yellow bus."

"When did he die? Was I in third or fourth grade?"

"Oh, that time was sad—so sad."

She'd never told him to stop the questions; she'd simply removed herself when he asked them, and by the time he was in his teens, his questions had stopped. It was only in the law where questions yielded answers, elicited truths, provided reality, and opened ways. His legal briefs and depositions were done with elaborate care, turning on the finest points of language, context, and connotation.

He rose from his place on the bank and stretched, forcefully turning his back on the ginger-haired man with the wrinkles from sun squint at the corners of his eyes. He made his way down the hill, talking to himself. "What were they like, the sisters and brothers, the aunts and uncles? Why did we leave them all behind to drift away out of reach?"

Back at the casino, he wandered the periphery of the room, desultorily watching for his friends. Now and then, sounds like a factory of machines whirring, clicking and ticking overwhelmed the cries, groans, and chatter, the mutters and cheers that rose in the windowless captivity of the huge room. He found Terry first.

"I've had enough for a while," Terry said. "I wouldn't kick if we availed ourselves of a nice late lunch and got back by four. I'm auditioning for the editor in *Our Town* that Westside is doing, and it would be nice to spend some time thinking about it. Did I tell you? Our Pete is auditioning for a role in it, too."

"I'm glad," Steven said. "Tell me when it plays and we'll all go."

Terry's son had been distant since the divorce. It was good that they were doing something together.

"Let's hunt up the others, then, and tell them we'll need to be careful of the time."

After lunch, Jack and Paul drifted off for some more play. Terry and Steven walked around the town. Steven found himself avoiding the street that led up to the breaker and the level piece of ground.

"We gave them one hour," Terry said. "Let's hold them to it."

"Jack's the problem. Paul's running on empty."

Terry gave Steven an appraising look. "I'm tapped out, but you just seem otherwise involved."

"I am. Connie wants to trace my part of the family, and to test my DNA. I think it's a waste of time. It's not going to help Jennifer, but I know why she's doing it—she needs to do something and there's nothing she can do. I stew. She follows leads to find people who may not want to be found. My mother was reticent to the point of muteness, especially about Dad's family, about who they were and why we moved and how and when and where he died."

"Listen, Steve, if he was shipwrecked off the coast of Zanzibar, my programs would be able to find out how and why." Terry stretched. "Computers don't make us smarter, just better informed."

By the time they left the casino, it was twilight. Jack had won a thousand and lost fifteen hundred. Paul had won slightly more than he had lost. Terry and Steven had spent their limit. The three friends were indulging in replay while Steven sat silent, disconnected from the moment. He was thinking about the biker, trying to recapture the timbre of the voice that had said, "Use your head, boy." He thought, I'll never see my father old, feeble, senile. He'll always be

57

younger than I am now. What a heart rise he had felt when that rider had appeared up the bank of the hill, stopped for a moment, and become his father.

Terry called two days later. "Alonzo Carl Howe's not on any of the records we have of people who died in the years you gave. I've got his army number and Social Security number. I know the date he separated from the service, and I'm sure of the man I'm hunting. He's not some other Alonzo Carl Howe. He's the guy, and he's not missing, and he's not dead."

Chapter Nine

H i, Mom, how are you?"
"Let me get Dad on the other line."
"Hi, Dad, what's new?"
"Nothing much, I'm happy to say. The committee and I had our day out in Black Hawk and I actually won some money."

"Great!"

"Say not 'great.' Say modest, modest pelf, and I'm spreading said pelf, diluting it, as it were, by causing a distribution among the female constituency, who will dispense, disperse, and otherwise fritter away said lucre and pelf to the hands of an army of retailers. You yourself will, with the next mail, acquire and receive a substantial portion, which is to say a percentage of said pelf."

From the time she was a little girl, he'd amused her with the game they played together, a sort of W.C. Fields-Mae West game. He knew he was trying a shade too hard, imitating an easier self. She played anyway. "A grateful recipient thanks you. The well-appointed lady should never be without her hat pin, her derringer, and a bankroll equal to the GNP of Peru."

"Did you get the fibers catalog I sent you?" Connie asked.

"Yes, and thanks. There are some great things. Dad, a ski case hit the papers here. They didn't mention your name, but the article said it was precedent-setting."

"Do you remember the name of the case?"

"I have it here, somewhere—*Pugh v.* . . . . I'll send it along. Does Mom have a scrapbook on you the way she does on us?"

"No, I have a file at the office. Jen, is everything all right?"

"I went to the support group. I'll tell you about it when I see you."

"That's wonderful, Jen. I'm glad you went."

Connie was pleased. She had been nagging Jennifer about going.

Steven hadn't told Connie that Terry's research had yielded no place or date of death for his father. Lon Howe must have fled his family, abandoned the two of them and left the country. He might be in England or Canada or Mexico now, and of course he would have gone there on the motorcycle, not the rusted truck they had sometimes been driven in. Lon had been good with his hands, capable. People had sought him out for work. He would have found a need anywhere he settled. Of course, Annina had told Steven that his father was dead, sparing both of them the shame of being left, cast off. He couldn't tell Connie what he didn't know—when or where his father had gone. That Lon had deserted them explained Annina's silences, her fearfulness, her hesitancy at anything new, even if it meant something better, and perhaps all the moving they'd done before the final disappearance. This knowledge changed everything for Steven, but nothing has changed. Why talk about it at all? The loss had happened long, long ago.

Two cases were reaching their golden time, that interval six weeks before trial, when it was most likely that respondents would agree to settle. In one case there was some evidence that the respondent had ingested alcohol at lunch: two rum cappuccinos. He was from Texas, and the rarefied mountain air might have increased the effects of the alcohol and blunted his consciousness.

In *Kinear v. Jones*, Steven had learned that Kinear had not been eleven years old at the time of his accident, but nine. The parents had lied to him, thinking the case would look better if the boy were older. A jury would ask why parents would allow so young a skier to go off on his own. Steven had recently become aware that clients were lying more frequently now—full lies, not simple misperceptions. Some of them were trying to cook their cases. "They lie out of what they think is necessity," Steven told Paul, "and necessity knows no law."

He always took time to visit the scenes of the accidents, skiing down to them himself and watching other skiers navigating the territory. He tried to match weather, snowfall, quality of the snow, all of which changed from day to day throughout the season. Novembers tended to be colder, with short days that preserved the dryness and lightness of the powder snowfall. Later Colorado snows were heavier, carrying more water, creating the ice, which melted and froze again, and then packed deep from a base. Later still came the heavy snows of spring, longer days, warmer sun, and little beads of "corn snow," which were more like the falls in New England and the European resorts. Each of these conditions, along with weather and skill, challenged the control of all but expert skiers.

Steven was driving up to Vail to meet with the counsel on *Stinson* and to take a deposition. On his return from court the previous afternoon, Connie had greeted him at the door with the news that she'd contacted a relative of the Naples Massachettis. "On the Internet, and some of the family is still in Naples, although most of them are scattered. The brothers and their families went north to Turin years ago, and the married sisters went to Greece. The old people, Annina's parents, died in the 1960s. I asked about blindness that wasn't in old age—if there were any young people with poor vision."

"Do you think anyone would tell you? It's not a thing people might want to reveal," Steven said.

Connie shook her head. "I think people are more open, more forthcoming on the Internet."

"It seems to me they also have more opportunities to try to please, to impress. . . ."

He knew that Connie lacked the sophisticated trace programs that Terry used, but since he had come to the knowledge that Alonzo Howe wasn't dead and had realized what that knowledge signified, his feeling of defensiveness had grown and deepened. He didn't want his family to be the carrier of retinitis pigmentosa to Jennifer. He felt protective toward the Massachettis and the Howes in their poverty and narrowness. He wanted to spare them, even if all he remembered of his father's people was the sparse welcome he'd received at his grandparents' house in Callan. He'd just seen the smallness and shabbiness of that house. He remembered only shadow figures, shapes of people moving inside it, a cool cheek he had to kiss, a harsh whisper to be quiet, someone with a beard, someone who'd hit him, someone who had given him piñon nuts. His father's moves had begun when he was too young to remember and seal the identities of the faces of aunts, uncles and cousins, or to make clear their confusing relationships.

Some of his memories, he realized, were of people he'd confused with family, people who were not related. There had been a man and woman at a ranch, people he called sir and ma'am, vigorous, hearty people with whom he'd felt secure and happy. They'd called his father AC. He now understood that they'd been his father's employers. Years later in Denver, he'd asked Annina about some of the places and people. She hadn't remembered from his descriptions of them.

During their courtship, he'd told Connie about all the moves they'd made and the loss of family, and she'd been incredulous. Everyone has a family, she'd insisted, and the amazement seemed to be oblique criticism of Annina for not staying close to the Howes or keeping in touch with the Massachettis.

So it was that Steven sometimes took a perverse pleasure in providing Connie with examples of the undersides of family life that he came upon in his practice. Relatives feuded over settlements: divorced and separated spouses re-appeared, revived with the elixir of large judgments. One woman told Steven she'd been able to raise the dead—great-uncles and long-obscure cousins who had come out into the light, blinking with renewed life. "And to think that all I had to do was have a ski accident."

After the deposition in Gold Flume the following day, he found himself back on the highway and nearing the Callan exit, changing lanes precipitately and pulling off there, smiling to himself at how quickly the six-lane freeway gave way to the rutted dirt road.

A surprise awaited him as he rumbled over the Ute River Bridge. A large detour sign guided him in the opposite direction from the old Callan road and there were three yellow earthmovers gouging at the upslope on the far side of the river. He was forced to follow the detour away from his street and he began to mutter to himself. The decision to come back to Callan was ridiculous. The detour became a road that hadn't existed when he'd come up with Jennifer, Jeremy, and

Mike. The road ended at his grandparents' house, now demolished into a heap of boards to be carted away. His own house was gone, the ground leveled raw.

The sight left him dumb, and after sitting in his car for some minutes, he turned around, his tires slewing in the softness of the newly cut road. He returned to Main Street.

There, at least, the landmarks were more or less as he remembered them from their last visit. A sign on the post office said it had moved. He stopped in at the hardware store. "Condos." The man behind the counter gave a nod for emphasis. "Town's building up, and they're putting in a whole interchange, three new roads in here. Ask why? It's where all the service people for the ski areas'll stay. Land prices are out of sight so near to Gold Flume. This town is going to be for transients and service workers, that kind of place."

"Who owned the old house up past Sixth Street, on that new road?"

"You mean the old Anderson place?"

"Where are they now, the Andersons?"

"Oh, they sold out two months ago, made a pile, too; the houses are demolished, but they had ten acres. I heard they went south, Albuquerque. You don't shovel no snow down there."

"And before the Andersons?"

"I don't know. . . . They was here when I came, thirty years ago. I thought it was their old family place."

Steven drove back to the highway, feeling bereft and chilled. All evidence of his father's people was being erased. Soon, his own memories would have no objective reality; people, house, yard, tree, the very configurations of the ground would be changed.

His cell phone buzzed as he was driving home. "Hi, Steve, it's Terry. Steve, where are you?"

"Passing Bluebank, on my way home. What can I do for you?"

"Well, I have some more info about your dad."

Steven had a moment of dislocation and almost said, He may be in Mexico and the house is gone, but instead, he said, "Oh? What is it?"

"Well, it's speculative, some of it, and I want to see you so you can decide about it."

"Can't you just tell me?"

"Not really, and it's personal, which I'm not comfortable talking about on a cell phone."

"I'll have to call Connie and tell her to hold supper."

"Tell her I'll take care of your dinner."

"You'll cook?"

"Are you crazy?"

"Chinese?"

"Sure. Spicy."

Chapter Ten

The weather had turned mean after its mild stay in the valley. Over Victory Pass, the temperature sank and visibility shut the mountains away long before darkness fell. Snow began to move behind Steven, following him down, overtaking him on the pass, and down again into Denver. He made Terry's house near Park Hill ten minutes before the world went white.

Terry's divorce had left him the house and shared custody of his angry teenage son. The house was neat—Terry employed a cleaning lady—but its spirit had fled. Steven remembered to ask Terry about whether he and the boy had been given the parts they had auditioned for in *Our Town*.

"I tried out for the editor," Terry said. "I got the drunk. Scott got the lead, George. I'm happy about that."

They ate their takeout on the Spode and Danish flatware of another life. Terry showed Steven his new laptop. "I used to think these machines were miraculous—work anywhere, no wasted time on airplanes or in doctors' offices. What's come is a twelve-hour workday. No more casual chat. I used to like meeting people on planes or in the courthouse, waiting for a case to be called. Now we all open the eternal laptop and zombie out."

"Terry—"

"Listen, it's coming down ugly. Why not stay over?"

"Is this about Alonzo Howe?" Why didn't I say, "My father"? he wondered.

Terry began at the beginning. He described how he had chosen the program he was using.

"Terry—"

"Yes, I'm getting there. The name Alonzo Carl Howe isn't common, luckily. It didn't appear in any of the data banks as deceased—not in Colorado. I also checked Wyoming, Nebraska, Arizona, New Mexico, Kansas, and Montana."

"You told me before that there was no record of his death—"

"Let me do this my way, Steve. I had the VA data banks available. So I got his service number and ran that. I want you to know how this happened. I thought, I'll just look there, and one thing led to another."

"Terry, will you tell me what this is about?"

"Please, let me tell you how it happened. I had the idea that you were together until you were eight years old. I started to think about separations other than death—illness, disappearance, that kind of thing. The programs are all there, just a five-digit number. I kept going: hospitals, nursing homes. You mentioned biking, that he had a bike. I thought he might have been hurt riding and was left a paraplegic or brain-damaged."

Steven began to tell Terry what he had realized, but he noticed that Terry's voice had become louder, that something was coming that had upset him. "What did you find?"

"I went too far."

"What did you find?"

"He's not in a hospital."

"What did you find?"

"He's alive, Steve. He's in Cañon City."

"Where?"

"In the penitentiary."

"Why is he in the penitentiary?" Steven hadn't let himself think about what was being said. He was speaking automatically.

"He's a convict."

"What was the conviction for?"

"I don't know; I stopped then."

"How long has he been there?"

"I told you, Steve, I stopped, I didn't go any further. It would have been prying after that, and I didn't want to risk our friendship. His—his problem's none of my business."

"Are you sure it's my father?"

"I'm sure."

"And he's not working there, a guard or something—you checked?"

"Very carefully."

They sat looking at each other and then Terry rose stiffly and turned off the lights, for which Steven was grateful. They watched the snow, white against the streetlight and muting the traffic noises and distancing them from the world outside.

"I'll need time to get used to this, before I spring it on Connie," Steven said, "but she's on the track of it without knowing. She doesn't have your equipment, but I'm afraid she'll get there, and I want to tell her first."

"I don't think she'll find it. She has the Internet, but none of the skip-trace programs or anything for scanning populations that I have. I'm not saying her getting the information is impossible, but it isn't likely."

"Our families have always been . . . unequal—her big bunch and me with just Annina, and here's one more dark spot for mine."

68

"I've heard you on this subject before, Steve, and you know as well as I do that the bigger a family is, the more chances there are of having the off note sounded here and there. Some families can hide their problems and some can't."

"Connie is very big on family."

"Is she likely to go down to Cañon City with a fruit basket?"

Steven began to laugh, and then both of them laughed.

"The reality of this hasn't hit you yet," Terry said, "and it's a mess out there. You're not in the right shape to navigate it. Why not call Connie and tell her you're staying over? We can watch the fights on TV and drink beer and scratch—"

"He'd be—seventy-seven now?"

Terry's answer was lost to Steven as a weakness came over him, a dislocation and the unreality one has in auto wrecks and earthquakes, sudden deaths and reports of terminal diagnoses. Alonzo Howe, who had died young in an accident, on his motorcycle, perhaps, and who had been mourned by his son in quiet pain for years, had abandoned his family, but not in the way Steven had imagined, and was indeed living another life, a daily existence that didn't include him.

He heard Terry say, "I'm sorry Steve; I picked a fine time to open this up."

Steven shook his head. "Annina was the villain, here. Her bad timing in death started this whole thing, and I've got a good mind to cut her out of my will."

"Just don't cut *me* out of your will. I know your boys get the cuff links, but I hope I'm still top of your list for the office chair."

"Not until I get it done in purple Naugahyde," Steven said.

The banter was to convince Terry that things were all right, so he could go home. The roads were closing fast but still drivable, he guessed. He wanted to be alone to explore whatever feelings would come to him, because now all he felt was a hollow incredulity.

"Terry, I've got a cell phone if I get stuck, and my tires are good. Thanks for the offer, but I need to be alone now. Later on, I'll want to thank you for all this work you did and for stopping when you did."

"I want it to be all right."

"It will be."

He was three blocks from Terry's when he realized that trying to drive home had been a mistake. The snow had fallen in the last warmth of the day, had melted on the roads, then frozen into a thick black ice, on which additional snow acted as a lubricant. Even where the roads were sanded, traffic crawled, some cars slewing out of the line to crash weakly into others. The side roads were skating rinks.

He drove, skidded, recovered, slewed around, and recovered again until he found a road on which the cars were moving more easily. Visibility was so poor that he followed the lights, coming within inches of other cars skidding out of control.

He arrived home an hour and a half later, to find a worried Connie. "Terry called. You left your briefcase there, and he wants you to call and tell him you're safely home."

Steven's jaw was sore from clenching his teeth and his diaphragm ached with held breath. "Con, will you call Terry? I want to take a hot shower and relax. It's been a long day."

He thought that after his shower he might go down to the living room, sit with her on the couch, and tell her, but his confusion was still too great. He thought that he might tell her just before sleep, when they lay side by side in the dark. There had been many confidences shared there, but when she got into bed beside him, the moment passed. The next morning, she was out early, and the next evening they were to be with friends. It might be best to wait for the right moment, a peaceful moment, with lots of time to come to terms with the hard fact.

Chapter Eleven

Four skiers were missing in the same storm that had blown over Denver and caused the power outages and fender benders on the ice. Steven heard the news the next morning as he shaved. The storm had broken just as the lifts had closed for the day. They had been five, skiing together, seen by the lift operator as they were going up to expert runs. After the lifts had closed for the afternoon, one of the skiers had come in and reported an injury and that his four companions were trapped by the storm.

Steven had discoveries to do in Gold Flume, and some filings at the old courthouse in Aureole. The snowplows would have been through by now and travel there was possible.

News of the missing young men wound in and out of the local report as Steven drove north. The four were being searched for, the reporter said, directed by the fifth, who had made it to the bottom of the hill.

For a while, he calculated the problems of skiers being lost in a whiteout. He'd been in such weather often enough to remember that when vision is so curtailed, the only way for a skier to ascertain direction is by gravity. If you slide, you must be going downhill. If you stop, you must be on a level; if you slide backward, you have been facing uphill. A person stranded in a complete whiteout might get some definition by trying to stay close to trees, but that might lead into rocky and dangerous woods, sudden drop-offs, cliffs, long falls. The best choice would be to stop, wait for the wind to die and sight to be restored, make a snow cave, hole up in it, and wait for help or clear weather.

Arriving in Aureole, he could see the grayness that indicated a storm still hanging over the pass. All the mountaintops were obscured, while to the south and Prospector Mountain, the sun was shining on pristine powder snow, the sky a blameless blue, with the pines and firs standing against it in motionless propriety. Amazing. Thirty miles away and one mile up, people might be fighting blizzard winds and blowing snow, lives being decided and time an implacable enemy.

The road to Callan had been cleared and he made good time. He would be meeting with four attorneys: two from the ski area, two from the insurance company. The corporate presence of all this counsel was meant to intimidate, but Steven had had many good wins and knew that juries tended to favor individuals over organizations. He was also aware that some of the potential jurors in the state weren't friendly to big ski areas, the new land-grabbers. Knowledge of these things made his walk into the corporate headquarters of the Gold Flume Company easier and he smiled at the soaring skier logo that dominated the back wall of the entrance. Artistically, the logo was beautiful—the shining image's uphill arm drawn far back, his right ski slightly raised, and his left a gleaming lance of steel, tilted downward, but in reality, if the skier kept that posture, the poor sap would land splat, skis and poles in the ten-yard circle the kids called 'a garage sale.' The logo always amused him and he had once mentioned it in a meeting, to a general chill.

He went into the meeting room, all blond wood and rounded edges, all slickly finished, the chairs tastefully covered in textured fiber, never upholstered enough for comfort. They were all sitting, waiting for him, a ploy, since he was on time.

Steven was meeting in the matter of *Harmon v. Aurole Corporation.* Todd Harmon, nineteen, had been taking a lesson and was standing on a beginner's slope in a group of novice skiers when the group was run down by a ski patroller on a snowmobile. Harmon had been seriously injured. The ski patroller claimed that he had swerved to avoid two other skiers on their way down the crowded hill and had hit a rock and lost control of the vehicle. Witnesses claimed the rock had been flagged and that the snowmobile was traveling too rapidly in an area full of skiers. The slope, they said, had become icy with use. The patroller had also been injured.

Although the stated reason for the meeting was a disclosure of information, a sharing of fact and a setting of the case's venue, there was also opportunity for a certain amount of jousting. Steven enjoyed the subtle feeling out of weaknesses in opposing counsel and in their case. It was at discovery that he saw his possibilities and conceived his strategy. He had spent time and effort developing a gracious and generous attitude about winning.

He emerged from the meeting outwardly relaxed and easy. The company wouldn't want to take this case to court. Even nonskiers on a jury would feel sympathy for a novice standing still, no matter how urgently the snowmobile operator had shouted his warning. Warnings are useless if the skier lacks the competence to respond in a useful way. He would argue for high compensatory damages.

But at some time during the give-and-take in the conference room, Steven found himself caught in other thoughts. When would he tell Connie that Lon Howe was a convict, a lifer, in prison? Would he tell her at all? The fact seemed so outlandish as to be no fact, nothing he need credit or remember. Three days ago, his father and mother had been dead and his

74

responsibility had been mourning for his mother and saying good-bye to the cut ends of his family. Beyond learning about one or two genetic facts, Connie had no special interest in the Howes or the Massachettis, and he could understand why. The Scotts were family enough. Both the Howes and the Massachettis had been poor in ways far deeper than being without money. "And a decent life," he had said to the opposing counsel, "takes more than money." They stared at him. "A decent life" had sounded a false note, and what were they deciding but financial recompense? Steven covered his lapse by explaining the possibilities of a lifetime handicap. He had lost focus when he should have been fully involved with Todd Harmon's case. He hadn't done this before. The loss of concentration rattled him. He didn't want to face Connie, who would see that something was wrong.

He arrived in Denver after six o'clock, called, and told her he had one more stop—a visit to Todd at his rehab center.

The atmosphere there was of struggle and earnestness. None of the furniture matched, telling the visitor that it had all been donated, and that the center's money had been spent on staff and equipment. The floors were bare, the walls scarred with the efforts of walking and the mistakes of wheelchairs.

The dinner hour was over, and the residents were watching TV or huddled at computers in the lounge. He was directed to a small room from which overloud music was blaring. Todd was standing in the arms of a young woman, working at a slow dance in which he moved blockily, with a slight drag in his left leg. Was the blockiness his ineptitude at dancing, shyness, or his injury?

"Todd?"

The boy stopped and took a long minute, placing Steven. Was it a pause anyone might take, seeing someone not well known and out of context?

"You're the lawyer. . . ."

"Steven Howe, that's right."

"Do you want to talk to me? Is it a legal thing?"

"Nothing serious—just a chat."

"Let's go to my room." Todd smiled, and Steven saw a difference on one side of his smile, a contraction of a sort, but one that could have been seen on many faces. His friend Paul's smile was slightly askew, and Steven didn't know if Todd's smile had been skewed before the accident.

"How are you doing?"

"Okay, I guess. They make you do lots of exercises. They encourage you—you know, 'Come on, Todd, you can do it!' But sometimes when I'm on weights or doing pulls, I think, What's all this about? Why do I have to do twenty-five? What if *I* got to pick how many?"

Was this statement the dull question of incomprehension or the acute one of reasonable protest at the loss of self-direction and independence? "Do you think you're improving?"

"Sure, in my ability to do pulls." Steven laughed. "Is that what I want to do?" the boy asked plaintively. "Pulls?"

"What was your life like before you had the accident?"

"I was skiing."

"I mean, were you in college or working?"

"I was skiing—it was at Prospector. I was having a lesson. It was my second time on skis."

Steven let his breath out slowly. How deep was that literalness? What had Todd been like before? If the settlement wasn't sufficient and the case did go to trial, it would be his job to reveal that literalness to

76

the jury, to bring out Todd's frustrations with both dancing and abstract thinking.

Todd's parents had been with him at the first and second conferences. The elder Harmon was a geologist, his wife a physical therapist. They had thought the pressure of the necessary evaluations would be too great while the boy was still recovering. He would have to impress on them that there were limitations of time and validation, fogging of witnesses' memory. He already had depositions from all five people in the ski class, and a statement from the instructor. The case was strong and he would have pictures of the location, doctors' reports, prognoses, et cetera. He expected a good judgment with enough money to supply all of Todd's needs even if he was unable to work again.

They chatted for a while. Todd said that his ability to play the trumpet hadn't been affected, and that he had begun to feel clearer in some of his thinking, though he still had no memory of the accident. Steven assured him that no one would require him to testify about the accident itself. By the time he headed home, Steven's mood had lifted. Connie was tucked up before the fire. It was a blue category day—no burning restrictions, though the wind that had cleared Denver's pollution would cause their wood supply to be quickly eaten up in the permitted blaze.

"This is inviting," he said, coming in, thinking that perhaps after dinner he might begin to talk about his father, give her the little he knew.

She smiled up at him. "Take a seat a minute. Dinner is drying out in the oven, Mike's upstairs studying, and I have no meetings to go to. How was your day? How was the boy?"

"The boy's recovering, but the final word on his brain damage is pending. Con, I was up in Gold Flume at the conference, talking about him, and all of a sudden I was thinking about being an orphan, about

77

what real poverty is. I skipped a couple of beats and said something inappropriate. I covered more or less, but it was very upsetting. It's happened before with clients—confusing one with another, momentarily but never a loss of focus like that. It's a loss of control, and I hate that."

She moved closer to him on the couch and put a hand on his shoulder. "It must have been awful. Let me get your dinner—I'm sure you're starved by now. We can come back to the fire later and sit here and stare at it. There's information from Italy. Jeremy called, and he says that he will definitely change his major. I've reached an understanding about that, too. I'll tell you what I think is behind it."

"Sure, and then do we get to sit and stare?"

"All you want."

Connie was a good cook, and Steven knew it stung her to have to bring him a dried-up, overcooked dinner. He said, "This is okay, really, and the holdup was mine. Don't feel bad."

"River, stop flowing," she said. He laughed at the familiar answer. They took their coffee back to the living room.

"So, about Jeremy. . ." Steven said.

Connie sat down and began. "He was always more physical than Jen or Mike. You notice how hard it is for him to wait, just to stand around waiting, or to sit for long periods?"

Steven had been aware of Jeremy's impatience, but Connie's mitigation seemed more like an excuse. The career jumping was, he thought, more an annoying weakness than a part of Jeremy's personality. Steven's own personality, his caution and dislike of surprises, made Jeremy's dilettantism upset him more than it should have.

"I've lost you," Connie said.

"I'm sorry. What were you saying?"

78

"That the professions college trains people for are mostly sedentary, and that's why he gets turned off them all."

"How did you come to this idea?"

"It was one of those mental leaps. I started thinking about Jen—if her vision worsens. It would be tragic, I thought, because the things she wants to do are all about vision, about how things look, what people see. Then I thought about Mike and that losing his sight wouldn't be such a terrible blow for him, because in two years he'd be mastering survival skills and in three he'd be counseling or teaching mobility to other people. Then I thought about Jeremy and it struck me that the worst thing Jeremy would face in blindness would be its limitations on his movement." She rose from the couch and took the coffee cups back to the kitchen. When she returned, she was grinning.

"I've got news myself. Another one of Annina's relatives surfaced on E-mail. She says there was no blindness that she remembered in the family. She wants to come here. She asked if we were close to Disneyland. I had to tell her it was sixteen hundred miles away and I think that cooled her ardor." Steven had begun to laugh.

They heard a shout and a crash over their heads, a thump—a body fall—muffled by the carpet, then silence. Connie cried out. Steven was up from the couch and taking the stairs. At the top, he saw Mike, rolling on the floor in pain. Blood was oozing from a gash on his chin, but the upper part of his face was covered by some sort of mask or device, obviously homemade and attached with strings. Steven drew close, knelt beside him, and saw that the mask consisted of a pair of tubes—the gray cardboard tubes from toilet paper rolls. Mike had Scotch-taped them together at their far ends and widened them near his eyes with a cube of Styrofoam.

"What happened?" Connie cried behind Steven. The arrangement on Mike's face was blocked by Steven's body. "Mike, are you all right?"

"Wait. . ." Mike gasped. He was clutching his leg. " . . . till I catch my breath. I'm all right. I just—just give me a minute."

The wait gave them time to understand what had happened. Mike must have been sitting at his desk wearing the contraption. He had risen, turned, and probably caught his foot on the leg of the computer table or become entangled in its heavy wires, gone forward, overturned the table, and fallen on top of the computer and table, knocking the wind out of himself, gashing his chin, and bruising his leg. Then he had tried to disentangle from the mess and made it to the doorway. From his writhing, Steven thought his injuries must be painful but not serious.

"I thought," Mike gasped, still trying to gather air enough to speak, "I thought I could . . . could find out what she was seeing, how things looked to her. Connie stood staring down at him. Steven was kneeling close. "She wouldn't be falling like this all the time. I just got sidetracked and forgot. I swore I would spend the evening wearing this, so don't ask me to take it off. I've learned a lot already."

"Are you really all right?" The device looked ridiculous, something a child would create as a costume mask for an alien. Mike got to his knees.

"I'm fine—well, I'm hurting the way it must be for her sometimes, but what you do is to treasure the light in the little circle, and every bit of energy goes into that. You don't think about the dark all around it. I was thinking she should be learning Braille, doing blind stuff, getting ready, but I see now why she won't. She won't be ready for Braille, or for mobility lessons, or for anything that accepts blindness. She won't be ready when her vision narrows to the width

80

of a gunbarrel, then to pencil lead. She won't be ready until she's stone-blind. She'll want to pour every bit of energy into looking at that little circle of light, until the light is gone and she knows it's gone for good."

Chapter Twelve

In June there was a short break in her work and Jennifer came home. She had arranged her flights for early in the day; she was very careful. Steven picked her up at the gate.

"Dad, I could have made it to the terminal."

"Pursue your independence in other venues," he said. "Relax and enjoy the invigorating ramble through the airport, luggage lurch and wrestle, another ramble to the parking lot, and with each of these activities, a chance for light banter or deep talk. It's up to you. I'm warning you, though—your mother thinks you look like a refugee and will take you clothes shopping. I think you look like a refugee, too, but that seems to be the style young people are wearing."

"How are you, Dad?"

For an instant, he thought of telling her about his father, her grandfather, of describing Mike lying on the floor with toilet paper tubes taped in a contraption before his eyes to simulate her visual field. He could share neither of these subjects with her just now, even though either would have meant a great deal to her. Instead, he found himself talking about Todd Harmon and another case he had. She told him about the drama scene in Chicago.

"It sounds like a good place for you, lots of work," he said, "but I'm afraid that as your contacts build there and your reputation gets made, you won't want to leave, to come here, for example."

"Dad, stop campaigning."

"Be realistic. You'll need help as time goes on, although maybe not a lot. You'll be more likely to get that help from family, and that has nothing to do with your creativity or with success in your field. I'll say no more, but think carefully."

At home there was a party. Mike and Jeremy had invited two cousins over for the evening. On Saturday, the three of them were out all day and then went to a rock concert after dinner. It was Sunday morning before Steven and Connie were able to corral Jennifer for some talk.

The five of them sat around at a late breakfast, reading the paper, the kids arguing over which parts they wanted. Connie was wearing the taffeta housecoat that Steven had given her for Christmas, a deep blue with bands of light green that brought out her delicate coloring and green eyes. He wished he had given Jennifer one like it. He said, "Are you still going to the support group?"

"What support group?"

"You told us there was one in Chicago."

She thought for a moment and said, "I went once— I'll tell you about it. I got the address on the Internet and showed up there on the Thursday they met. It was a church basement—just what you'd expect. I didn't know there'd be so many people—RP is rare, after all, but there must have been thirty people sitting on the usual folding chairs. The place smelled of wet winter clothes and those shoes with the heavy rubber soles. Sure, I thought, blind people need to be very careful of their footing. I've been called clumsy myself," she said, and looked pointedly at Jeremy.

"Oh, knock it off," Jeremy said.

"Hey, Jen," Mike said.

"Anyway, they had used this place for monthly meetings for years, but it made me depressed. There was the old serenity prayer and the standard form of the introductions. It all made me think of the AA meetings my friends went to, the one difference being the lighting. No AA meeting is held in a glare like that.

"I'd expected an older group, but most of the people were young and some had older sighted guides—mothers, sisters—mostly women, which tells you something."

"What, exactly?" Jeremy asked.

"Let her talk," Steven said.

"When the introductions came around to me, I told them I'd just received my diagnosis. I wanted to say that I wasn't sure I was ready to be in the group, that I didn't believe much in support groups, and that until I was forced into the RP straitjacket, I would struggle with ordinary life, but as soon as I said 'diagnosis,' there was a kind of recognition sigh around the room. After that, everyone in the circle told about the day when the bad news got said."

"Wasn't it a relief that people understood," Mike asked, "that they knew without being told what it was like, getting the news?"

"I guess, but it seemed artificial to me, rehearsed. I looked around the room. One woman said that when *he* heard her diagnosis, her husband left her. Then her children disappeared. It was the prospect of caring for a blind woman that did it, and she found herself five years later, living a life radically different from anything she could have imagined."

"Wow!" Jeremy said.

"Still, they all gave off that fake cheeriness, and her story was obviously no news to the group. Everything fitted a rhythm that was form, familiar. They all kept their faces turned to the speaker, all their expressions accepting and encouraging."

"What's wrong with that?"

"Nothing, Ma, it was. . . . well, drag-ass. The whole thing was so relentlessly upbeat and cheerful, I wanted to do something that would make them drop the act. It brought out the worst in me."

"But you stayed?" Steven found himself using the half statement, half question he used in court.

"Yeah, I stayed, and I heard all of it. Some of them were fully blind, and their problems were about mobility and consistency of response from caregivers, nightmare stuff, and there was all that about talk *independence,* over and over, like a mantra."

"You use that word all the time," Mike said, "and when you're not using it, you're screaming for us to leave you alone."

"All right, I'm big on it, but coming from them, it sounded fake, wrong, like independence was all there was, the only thing, and—"

"And what?" Connie's voice was thick and Steven could see she was struggling with tears.

"They call themselves 'consumers,' not victim, patient, client, survivor, handicapped. They have these special *words,* like passwords. So that, God forbid, I'd have to learn the lingo to belong. The guides had their little words, too, *enabler* was one, but all the time there was that cheerfulness, but careful, no being sentimental. At the end of the formal part of the meeting, the man who seemed to be leading said that this was his ninth anniversary with this group and they had all helped so much after his wife's death and blah, blah, blah, 'Your strength keeps me going.' Something about him did seem more authentic than the rest of them. And he was nice-looking, a big handsome guy."

The brothers set up a series of whistles and Steven wanted to stifle them. "Would you continue," he said, attorney to complainant.

"He seemed more open, less patterned, but, of course, he wasn't a 'consumer' or even a sighted guide. His name tag said C.T. He encouraged me to participate. When the meeting was over, people broke into groups and went to the side table for coffee and cookies. Someone stumbled against a chair and everybody laughed and someone yelled, 'Who's the klutz?' and we were all laughing. Just then, the group seemed okay to me and I could see why it might be good to join—there was so much we didn't have to tell one another."

Connie took a breath to speak, thought better of it, and waited.

"He came over to me and I told him I was sorry to hear about his wife. He had a nice way of saying it still hurt. He said he wanted me to meet the lady who was pouring coffee. She did it the way blind people do. C.T. said she was the bells and whistles woman, a one-woman band of assistive paraphernalia. She said, 'I heard that,' and they started to joke around.

"I didn't want to meet people; I wanted to be out of there, but I couldn't be rude, so I let him lead me over. I knew she would have to tell me that her blindness didn't mean she wasn't getting the most she could out of life. Bullshit. I have things to do, a career to make. I was on my way somewhere else—I *am* on my way somewhere else and I have no time for blindness. At the meeting, she had called it 'an inconvenience.' It's a goddamn catastrophe."

Connie was weeping silently and Steven was fighting tears. Mike said, "RP people must take enough beatings from the outside. That group would get together to hear words like *inconvenient* rather than *hopeless*."

Jennifer said, "I don't want to sit in a doctor's office while he measures the degrees of loss, side to side, up and down. Let them send me a list of which streets have the best lighting and which restaurants I can go to where I won't be stone-blind in the romantic glow. The people, I can do without. C.T. asked if he could take me home. I said I was okay. He asked if he could take me to dinner sometime. He laughed and said McDonald's is one of the few places where the light is good enough. What a date. He said another RP experience is the local hospital cafeteria. Spectacular lighting, he told me, and French cuisine. One of the cooks is named Delorme. I said I would think about it. I told him I had a play, so I wouldn't be free for another three weeks. He had all the good blindness manners. He didn't just leave, but said he was going to talk to some other people.

"The room was clearing. I was putting on my coat when the coffee lady moved in close and asked if she could talk to me. She said it was about C.T. 'He'll call you,' she said. 'He'll ask you out. You'll date. He'll fall in love with you.' I laughed. She said, 'No, this isn't a joke.' She'd dropped the cheery tone. 'How long do you think C.T.'s wife has been dead?' I said I didn't know. 'Six years. What's he doing here? He's dated every woman in this group below the age of fifty, including me. It's a glorious ride, let me tell you. He understands it all. He's kind and patient and funny and wonderful, and the more helpless you are, the better he is.' I told her . . ." Jennifer's voice had begun to break. "I told her I hadn't said yes. She said, 'I'm not saying don't. I'm saying look and listen. We saw you together. We thought you should know.'"

Chapter Thirteen

Jennifer came out of her room wrapped in a piece of fabric and pulled a swoon with lots of twitching and declaiming. She was demonstrating a problem to Connie. "It's rumpled; it looks like you slept in it."

"The fabric needs to be heavier," Connie said.

The women were fussing with the piece, chatting easily. Jennifer's flight left at three o'clock and Steven had cleared the time. He went into his study to work on a case. He had suffered some disappointing judgments recently, especially galling when he thought he had an obvious win. When a case went to trial and the jury found for the other side or gave what he considered insufficient compensation, he was driven to work harder to nail everything down with more details. When he lost cases, the failure often resulted in a depression, a darkness lifted only by the next win.

He never closed the study door. Years of living with noise had unfitted him for quiet. He worked best in an atmosphere where activity was going on around him. When he and Connie had first been married, they lived in a tiny apartment in Aurora, where she had tried to mute the noise of the neighbors and the housework. His concentration suffered until he realized that the silence was drawing attention to itself and away from his thought.

The women were in the front room with materials Connie had brought from Ring and Wreath. They were talking about tiaras. Steven wasn't sure he knew what a tiara was. He finished working on one case, and before he started on another, he sank back in his chair and listened, amused, to the two of them. He heard Connie speaking for some time before he realized what her purpose was. She'd been describing some of Ring and Wreath's recent weddings, telling Jennifer how much more elaborate and expensive they had become.

"The old 'married in the living room, catered dinner buffet for twenty' has all but died. We have weddings on skis, skydive-weddings out of airplanes, weddings on ships, scuba weddings. People wear bikinis and parkas. They have elaborate garden productions, weddings in the woods, all-white weddings and day-glo weddings, and now the grooms are beginning to leave the tuxedo behind for a whole range of choices."

Jennifer must have felt the tug before Steven did. "Ma . . ."

Connie had obviously rehearsed what she was saying. "We could give you steady employment as the designer for complete wedding outfits of the major participants. We already have one or two designers who do this work, and it would save effort and money for the customer if we did the designing in-house. We have a woman doing alterations, so you wouldn't have to sew."

"Ma, I'm a costume designer."

"Wedding outfits are costumes and getting more so. Weddings now have themes. . . ."

"You want me safe in Denver, close, doing semi-professional work, where I'll be looked after. I'm getting ready for New York or L.A. or San Francisco, for theater and TV."

"With the Internet, being in those places may not be so important. Soon you'll be able to send designs—"

"When that happens, I'll think about it."

"Please consider the offer."

"I would if you were the Smith and Jones wedding service in another city, but don't you see, if I went with Ring and Wreath, I could never know if I was working for you because I was gifted or because I was family, wounded, needy family, to be taken care of."

"We're in business, Jen."

"But I would never *know*. Would Uncle Bry fire me if I didn't do the job he wanted? Would the other workers feel that I was being hired because I was the battered bird seeking shelter under your wings? How marvelous would I have to be to overcome that thought in all their minds?"

Steven turned his chair to face the window and looked out at his professionally tended lawn. He sympathized with Connie, thwarted in her plan, but he was proud of Jennifer. Everyone was reaching to help, for which she wasn't ready. Perhaps there would come a time when the offer of a job at Ring and Wreath would be welcome. He heard Connie begin to argue, so he rose and went to the kitchen for coffee and asked them if they wanted any.

Jennifer left for the airport without concluding their argument. He left her at the security check but stood back and watched her go through and the watched her walk easily down the long gate corridor and away. She seemed so normal, so healthy and vigorous, even though every now and then she swept the area with her gaze, locating.

On his way back to his office, Steven saw a biker, a man his own age, and for a moment, thought that it might be fun to be a biker himself. He realized that the father picture, the image of Lon Howe the biker, was gone.

Because Alonzo Carl Howe was not young and was not dead. He was living, an old man, in Cañon City, in one of the many prisons making up the Colorado Department of Corrections, and when Steven thought of this, his urge to know more was overwhelmed by a greater need to retreat into muteness and learn nothing. Even as he decided to wait before he told Connie, he realized how futile his passivity was. The longer he waited, the more dangerous his waiting became. The truth was hunting, ambling along, nose down. When its quarry had been singled out, it would center, perhaps from the computer, perhaps by coincidence, its glowing eye on the sea of possibilities and people, aim, fire, and somewhere in the world, a single individual would be blown into light, caught, blinking. This time, it would be an old man, a lifer.

Steven's wish to create a defense for his father intruded into his dreams. In one, Steven stood by as Lon slammed into a free-for-all bar fight. The dream surprised him because his sense of his father had always been of a quiet, self-possessed loner, who never entertained or socialized with friends over for dinner. In another dream, he was fighting alongside his father as sidekick in a Hollywood B movie shot in lurid Technicolor. When he woke, he thought the dream might have captured some reality of his father's situation. Maybe Alonzo's being a loner had occasioned a fight. There was a shotgun in the dream, a long, blue-black-barreled gun, broken for loading, and primitive in looks and handling. It was the dream shotgun that made him remember such a weapon in his father's truck. The gun and the truck—what had happened to them?

From the dreams, memories were evoked, places, people, discontinuous and holding little meaning. A man leaned inside the truck window one time. "Hey, Lon, I see you got your boy here. . . ." But who the man was, or what they spoke about, was gone. "You

91

workin'?" That was from a store owner, the hardware man.

"Yeah, I got work till October."

"I got somethin' needs doin'."

What thing? Steven wondered. Where? It was all gone. Another memory: words behind his back. "She's Eyetalian, quiet. Quiet? She don't make a peep."

"I wish my woman was like that." Laughter.

"No, you don't, Charlie. A man wants to come home to a house is got some life in it."

As far as Steven could remember, that fragment of talk was the first time he'd been aware that his mother was odd, different. How old was he then—five, six?

He'd seen Terry at the monthly lunch and knew that his friend was keeping his secret, although wondering, perhaps, if Steven had gone on, learned more, knew, maybe, where Lon Howe had been imprisoned, for what offense, and for how long. The dreams all said the offense had been fighting; maybe it was the killing of a man in a fight or because of a fight. . . .

Steven's waking days were full of work and pressure and the need for a keen and focused intelligence.

"Mr. Howe, I do general practice for the Malin family and I'm calling on their behalf. Their son, Peter, was one of the five boys skiing at Gold Flume back in April."

"I heard they built a snow cave and did all the right things."

"The boys claim they had been skiing at Prospector late in the day. Peter was injured, and while waiting for help they saw the last sweep done by the ski patrol. I think there's a case here. The boys say the patrollers were fooling around on their way downhill, not looking for skiers. The boy who made contact at the base said there was time for help to be deployed if the system had geared up immediately, but key people had left early and others were incompetent."

92

"Would Peter be the sole client?"

"Yes. He's lost a leg below the knee."

Shortly after that call, there was another. "Mr. Howe, I'm calling to see if you'll take my aunt's case. She was skiing at Steamboat, and this young guy came by, knocked her down, and skied away."

"My aunt skis on a senior pass. She has a shattered pelvis. I got the guy's name and called him. He said, 'Just my luck. I had to run into a museum piece. Why don't they keep those antiques off the slopes!'"

Steven took both cases, raising his active load to fifty-two. Cases wove and braided through one another often in complex configurations. He checked the accident report from Gold Flume on the Malin case and went scrolling down to subsequent events.

A few days after Peter Malin's accident, a snow-plow operator at Gold Flume noted the absence of visibility into the Not for Grandma run, the run on which the boys had been trapped. The problem had been caused by expedient, unwise banking of the snow to improve a more popular intermediate trail. The snowplow operator's name was Carl A. Howe. Steven saw the signature jump out at him and looked again. There it was. If Carl A. Howe were a relation of his, a son or nephew of the Callan Howes, he might learn about the family without ever touching the old man in Cañon City. His inquiry might not be about blindness only or what Lon Howe had done. Steven didn't even know if he had cousins. Were there any relations left alive here in Colorado?

Carl A. Howe lived in Gold Flume. He answered his telephone with a single word: "Howe." Steven introduced himself and began his questions. The man was hesitant at first, but Steven was experienced in eliciting information.

"The A in my name is for Ambrose, my mom's people. I grew up in Wyoming. My dad died when I was

93

twelve, but I'd always been told that his folks came from back east somewhere."

Steven wanted to say, They tell us lots of things, but he only asked, "Do you remember any mention he made of a Howe family having lived in Callan?"

"No, I know there was another Howe family up there, because when we first came—that was back in the eighties—people would ask us. There was a Lonnie Howe or a Lon Howe, but something bad happened—I don't know what it was. I had the impression it was trouble—you know how it is, what people don't say but hint at."

Steven's heart had begun to announce itself, and he thought that Carl A. might hear it pumping through the phone. His voice lacked its usual smoothness. "I'm not asking this idly. There's a—we have a genetic problem in our family. We moved away after my father. . . died, and my mother never told me about his people." He took in air, pulling with difficulty, as though it were water and might drown him. "My father had sisters and brothers; that much I know, and Callan was where they had their ranch. The name of his mother's people was Kendrick. Does any of this sound familiar to you?"

There was a long pause while the stranger thought. Steven's pulse slowed and he thought that for some people a pounding heart is a stimulant, an aphrodisiac, and that excitement and stress call out the same battery of chemicals pouring into the brain. That fighting might have thrilled his father. Wouldn't he have seen bruises if his father had fought? Not if his father had been skillful enough, and had killed by mistake, must have killed, to be imprisoned for so long, or, having been imprisoned, had gotten into other fights while in prison, heaping up other sentences along the way.

94

Carl A. Howe was trying to pick threads out of his own frayed family cloth—cousins, yes, but he didn't seem to know who they were or where they had been raised. A name or two surfaced, which Steven took down. They might have moved to Callan, Carl Howe said, but had never heard any mention of them living there.

"Those other Howes—was there any talk of what that scandal was?" Steven asked.

"No, and I only guessed at it because of what wasn't said or the way people reacted when they heard our name was Howe."

"You're walking along and all of a sudden you fall in a hole," Steven said.

Carl laughed. "I guess so."

They ended the conversation with mutual good wishes. He's not my cousin, Steven thought, but he kept the three names Carl had given him.

The five young men involved in *Malin v. Gold Flume Corporation* seemed to fill the inner office, which Steven kept small and dull. He liked to sit close to clients, unobtrusively noting their body language and moments of hesitation. He used a table and offered the clients coffee during the early conferences.

In most instances, details decide whether there's a case or not. Clients don't usually provide the relevant points, and many clients have no memory of crucial moments before an accident and need to be encouraged, supported, or disproved by the physical details on the scene. ("You must have been thrown at least twelve feet, because your ski was *here*; your other ski came off *here*.")

The client, Peter Malin, had been skiing with his four friends on the expert farthest-west run, called Not for Grandma. It was a chute whose northern rim was woods, the boundary line of the area.

It was the last run of the day; the young men had skied aggressively since morning and had gradually descended into that overtired state in which accidents happen. A light snow had begun to fall, but they all swore that visibility was still good. Peter had stumbled among the large mogul bumps of the run and shattered his knee. They sent Alan to ski down for help, but they knew that it was almost time for the area to close for the day. The sweep, the patrollers who did the last run, would be coming. The patrollers did sweep the area, but the didn't take Not for Grandma. They stayed on the easier slope and in the trees beside the run. The boys cried out to them as they skied on past. Steven knew from Carl Howe's report that large sections of Not for Grandma were invisible to skiers on the other run because of woods and the high banking at the edge.

Then the wind had picked up and the snow became heavier. In another half hour, there was a whiteout and the boys decided it would be best to carry Peter to the far side of the chute, up to the shelter of the trees. Once in the woods, they used their skis and poles to frame a snow cave, where they holed up, keeping warm by huddling on the raised bed inside it. Peter found that if he kept his leg cool, the pain was lessened. The boys used one ski pole as a splint.

The fifth boy, losing time in several falls through nervous exhaustion and deteriorating weather, finally made it to the bottom of the hill and alerted the patrol. By then, the snowfall was heavier, but visibility was still passable. By the time a sluggish response was initiated, the storm had produced a whiteout and a rescue was impossible. It was well into the next day before searchers could be sent.

Steven outlined the case again and asked the boys for verification. He now needed specific information from all of them, as minute a timetable as they could give, a trip back to the area to locate exactly where they had been so that pictures might be taken, and a step-by-step time line of the hours they had spent on the slopes, in the gully, and in the woods.

Steven had skied Not for Grandma. It was a difficult run, a steep, narrow chute at the very edge of the ski area. He had asked expert skiers how weather and season affected it; he studied reports of other accidents there, and the chute's propensity to catch wind and funnel the cold and snow down its length. It was believable that some members of the ski patrol might fudge the run, especially in bad weather, skiing easier ground and detouring to the rim of the gully only now and then. He made more notes.

Research took him to the Aureole library. Many of his cases were centered in the county and he had found it useful to check the local newspapers for details not always supplied by the ski area during discovery.

The Not for Grandma run was relatively new. The western boundary had previously stopped at the intermediate trail, which was easily monitored. He was flipping his microfiche reader quickly through the news accounts of the first acquisitions of land for the area in the 1950s, scanning the sheet and absorbing the ads, announcements, and other stories, the ambience of the time. God, there it was:

CALLAN MAN PLEADS GUILTY

He didn't read the article consciously. His eyes took to the page without volition, flowing over the words.

> Alonzo Carl Howe has confessed to the molestation of six area children and the murder of Mary Mangano.

The print went so small that Steven couldn't read any more. His head roared and sickness welled up in him and turned the room askew. Holding on to chairs and the wall, half blindly, to the men's room. His body had gone cold and pulpy and he heaved up a lunch he thought had been past returning.

It was more than half an hour later—when he had stopped trembling, rinsed his mouth, and washed his face—that he was able to return to the carrel. He sat down shakily and read the article.

Alonzo Carl Howe, the convicted child molester, who had savaged at least six children in and around the Ute Valley town of Callan during the winter of 1956-1957, had been caught, had pleaded guilty, had been convicted and sentenced. The conviction had not been because of a bar fight, or a robbery gone wrong, a theft meant to feed him and his mother; it was not a macho need for revenge that took Alonzo Carl Howe out of the sunlight, away from Steven's sight and into custody and then into prison.

Even as he read the article that had at first contained too much and now too little, his lawyer's mind wondered what the legal process had been. The article had been published in April 1957, when the *Ute River Voice* was a two-page paper, featuring legal notices and social notes. It also reported the first plans for the construction of the two ski areas that would revivify the Ute Valley. He rose and went to the desk to request all the 1956 and 1957 editions of *The Ute River Voice*, *The Aureole Prospector*, and *The Rocky Mountain News*. The afternoon moved across the windows in the world where he sat but was not present.

The *Prospector* had a picture, and Steven's first emotion was a primitive joy at recognition. That's Dad—Daddy—there he is—and then the letdown, looking at the details of the picture, past his father's face. Lon Howe was being led away out of the courthouse in Aureole in handcuffs. The Callan jail, the paper said, had been flooded at the time. It was his dad, with the same apologetic, kind of smile he had worn in one of the army pictures that Steven had seen in the scanty collection in Annina's old valise. It was a youthful, pleasant face, with no exceptional features. An actor with that face wouldn't play the lead, but the lead's kid brother, the sidekick, or the victim. He gave the impression of both litheness and frailty; his nutmeg hair was long for those days, giving him a boyish look. There was no beard.

This pleasant-looking man had abused, molested, killed.

The accounts in those days were weighted with euphemisms and a standardized protective language for kitchen-table reading. The words buffered the horror and gave no description of what Lon Howe had actually done to these children. None of the victims was named, and Steven's lawyer mind poured his defenses into the void. What precisely had Alonzo Carl Howe done? Of what precisely had the state of Colorado accused him?

Chapter Fourteen

There followed nights of broken sleep stippled with sudden waking. He had bad dreams. Hands emerged from nighttime foliage to pull in a child; one dream was dark, with only the sounds of a panting chase, running feet, screams. In the daytime, the horror faded to a dull half-sick feeling, pushed aside, blessedly, by daily needs.

With a surreptitious caution, like a boy reading thrillers behind his schoolbooks, Steven began to research the Howe family. He went to the Aureole Courthouse and spent the day there, studying tax records, a Callan town history, the local newspapers, and the memoirs of an "Uncle John" Pierson, who had kept his journal from young manhood to great age and had willed it to the town on his death. After 1958, the Howe name disappeared from the Ute Valley. He didn't research Lon Howe's offense. He approached his father like a hunter on a circuitous trail from the beginning of a Howe presence in Colorado.

Malvern Howe had come into the Ute Valley in 1888 as a rancher, after the gold and silver chimeras had blown away and people were able to look at what was in the valley, rather than under it and under the mountains surrounding it, and see the abundance that had fattened generations of buffalo, deer, and elk. His son, Asa Howe, had been twenty and had married in the valley, to Serena Buoninsegna. Steven was amazed at the coincidence, the Italian thread in his lineage.

Seeing the name, a thought flashed by: wait till I tell Connie about this. The Buoninsegnas had been farmers, lured by the valley's abundance and beaten by its cruelties—hail, freeze, drought, and grasshoppers. There had been four sons and three daughters. One of these sons had died in France in 1917, one in the 1918 influenza epidemic. One left the valley. The girls had grown and married, two staying in the area, ranching in Bluebank and Granite Creek until 1939. Alonzo Carl Howe was born in 1922, the oldest of the three sons and five daughters born to Anson Howe and Martha Rule Howe. The brand of the Howe ranch was

AH

The family lived on the edge. Land taxes were paid on the last day of the grace period. Mortgages were barely settled when new ones were taken on. Sons-in-law came into the operation optimistically, discovered its realities, and left, three formally, two by night, as it were, leaving no forwarding addresses. The ranch to which Annina Massachetti Howe came in 1947 had been denuded, pinched almost to bloodlessness, its tenants despairing. In 1958, the bank foreclosed and the family scattered.

Where did they go? He remembered uncles, aunts, cousins, and the old people. He didn't remember family closeness or family parties. The grandparents didn't like Annina. This was only a feeling Steven had, no more hint than a sigh as she passed, the turn of an eye, a silence, a shrug.

More memories came—one outbuilding, comfortable for his size. He'd called it "Home House." There was also a sense memory of sun slant through seams warping a barn roof. He remembered his first day of school and his father saying, "Here's a little man in school!" and lifting him up.

Lon Howe wore cowboy clothes then, a western shirt, velvet-worn denim jacket, boots, and a thick belt. In the background, Steven could hear his mother's sounds: "Oh, come and eat." "You are so tired." "Oh, how cold it is." She feathered her world; she smoothed what was ruffled, making nests of small feather-soft sounds. Her gestures were of straightening and patting smooth. She blunted anger with feathers of apology.

The motorcycle: a whine, a buzz that was heard from far away. Lon Howe brought excitement home on his clothes, in his hands, in his eyes, smiling, laughing.

And now and then he allowed Steven to help him work on the delicate, shining mechanism of The Motorcycle. What, besides the wind itself, could be so powerful, yet so fragile? There was a hubcap dish of nuts and bolts soaking in solvent (something that *solves*). Lon said, "My daddy told me: 'Never show a fool half-finished work.'" He conveyed these words of tradition in his slow, matter-of-fact voice.

Because his words were rare and because Steven had heard them spoken when all memory is long-term memory, he felt sure he could re-create every word his father had chosen to speak to him. "And don't neglect your tools. I hate mechanics who think slack ways and dirt show their skill."

How many moves had the family made? One morning, he murmured to the face in the bathroom mirror, "The moves weren't about work. Maybe he was caught, or about to be caught, or just afraid. He was a scared man, running away."

He'd last seen his father with the eyes of an eight-year-old and had no idea of what the man was truly like. Did he have a temper, a rage that was the dark side of his energy? Did he drink heavily? Was what he did to children done under the influence of drink or rage? Did he collect and cherish injustices, keeping them close?

It was useless to demand answers of the child he had been, memories with nuance and detail. It was easier to cover the newfound trail, to hide it. Howe, he knew, was the Saxon word for hill, and how many people in the eleventh century gave their names to the Domesday Book as Thomas Atte Howe or John Farmer Atte Howe. There were hundreds of Howes not of his lineage at all. That, he thought, might be the salvation of his secret—not too few, but too many for Connie, looking for the lead to one mystery, only to be ambushed by another.

When he had a memory stumble again, smiling at Connie as they sat at the dinner table and about to say, "It's Ma's birthday next month; let's take her out," instead of sorrow, there was a surge of relief. No one could get to Annina now to make her tell what she knew. Had she been at Lon Howe's arrest and trial? Had she understood the legal words they used to describe what he had done? Had she realized why they had to keep running? The relief lasted only as long as it took Steven to understand that he'd loved and grieved for the loss of a man he'd never known.

Jennifer's calls and E-mails were uniformly upbeat and cheery, to the point of falsity, Steven thought, and this caused him more worry than if they had darkened in tone. She was designing for a musical with some dancing. Then there was to be a kids' show with lots of colorful animal costumes. "How are you really doing, Jen?"

"I'm okay. I'm surprised how okay I still am. I haven't fallen over anything; lately, I haven't walked into anything. My directors and coworkers respect me and I even go out on the occasional date. If I ever do

Hamlet, I'll have the whole thing ready to go, swatches and all."

"If you ever get mad that your forebears did this to you, gave you your problem, remember, too, that they were people with a lot of courage."

"They were good people, but I wouldn't call them courageous."

"I don't mean the Scott side of the family; I mean the Massachettis."

"Nonna? She was dear and sweet, but I don't think she was courageous."

"A world fell on her and she picked herself up."

"You mean her coming over here, or after your dad died, Grandpa Howe?"

"Both. It was both I meant."

"Maybe, I guess. What about your side, the Howes?"

"I wish I knew more about my folks, but from the magnificent example you see before you. . ."

"Oh Dad!"

Bishop v. Chambers was settled for costs and $165,000. Steven accepted *Lyons v. Viking Ski Company* on the locking of a binding at $135,000.

Jeremy had fallen in love with a girl in his chemistry class earlier that spring, and his dying passion for chemistry had been rekindled into a radiant incomprehensibility. He no longer spoke English, but a kind of chemo dialect, and he displayed his stained fingers with pride. His calls and E-mails had been as ebullient as an unknown compound fizzing and bubbling in a laboratory beaker. Did Steven and Connie know that new elements and elemental relationships were being discovered every day? "The new element," Steven told Connie, "will be called Jeremonium. It will glow very brightly and then change color and go out." Sure enough, a month later, the girlfriend moved in with another student, a bio major, and the heat sank in Jeremy from white to blue and then faded. He had been less than a year studying chemistry, about average for his enthusiasms. As he prepared to leave for a summer job at a mountain conference center, Steven and Connie convinced him to take some interest and aptitude tests.

"I've seldom seen a set of scores like this," the psychologist said afterward. "Your son is worried that his interest hopping is making you think of him as a lightweight. He's very bright, as you know, and his aptitudes and interests are very high on almost all the scales."

"Isn't that good?" Steven asked.

"Not necessarily," she said. "When you walk down a hall of doors and every one of them opens easily and in every one is a guide beckoning, which door will you choose? The happiest people I see are those with one or two very high aptitudes and interests and many very low ones. They can follow a road without being sidetracked and without regret for the road not taken. Jeremy has been attracted by all those interests and disciplines in an increasingly anxious search for the limits, the boundaries to his talents. He hasn't found any yet."

"Can we help?" Connie asked.

"Let him know that vocation isn't a substitute for selfhood and doesn't represent the sum of what he is."

Steven met his friends for the monthly lunch and told them about the tests. They began to kid him and one another about who would pass and who would fail each one. Steven was relieved that their joking was back and the careful self-censorship was over. He relaxed and enjoyed the conversation, the gossip, war stories, and shoptalk, in the old, easy way. Even Terry was himself again.

They began to talk about vacations.

"I still want to make that Italy trip some time," Steven said, "especially to Naples, but my immediate desire is to spend a whole week at home, doing nothing. Oh, did I tell you? *Malin* is going to court."

Paul said, "Isn't that the case of those five skiers lost on the mountain?

"I was sure Gold Flume would settle, but they're sticking on weather. Everything I've got tells me that there was a window of opportunity there, and the patrol could have made a rescue. On my side, I have a well-spoken client with four clean-cut friends; they're not idle rich folks, and the boy lost a leg."

"Well, good luck," Jack said. "I hate jury trials. I'd rather go back to the crap table. It's more of a sure thing."

Steven had long since crystallized trial mode into a set of behaviors and a strict routine, part for focus, part superstition, for luck. He had a "trial" suit, a pair of lucky shoes, and a lucky key ring. His measured behavior before a courtroom appearance went at a ceremonial pace, and his breakfast was small but high in carbs, for quick energy. When he left for court, he went loaded with displays and a full briefcase. These he delivered early; then he went down again to the street and walked quickly around the large courthouse block. He breathed deeply, readying for combat.

Chapter Fifteen

Malin v. *Gold Flume Corporation* had been called for the 8:30 opening, but it wouldn't actually get started until 10:00, with jury selection from a pool of largely unwilling veniremen called to serve. Steven's first job would be to overcome this unwillingness, the impatience of having been uprooted from a daily routine to be dumped into a stranger's problems.

The defense would ask whether the five had been skiing beyond their competence, when they were tired. The rapidly degenerating weather would be an issue. When did the heavy snow commence?

Two of the skiers had gone up with a photographer before the area closed for the summer and she had taken a series of photographs of the chute and the blind spots in the gully where the four skiers had waited—showing the universal sign of distress: skis raised and crossed.

In the June courtroom, receiving its first benediction of air conditioning for the season, Steven would try to re-create the scene of downslope cold and upslope wind, ice, shrinking visibility, and an injured boy gritting his teeth at the sensible move up out of the gully to the shelter of the trees. With his laptop and projector he showed ten Power Point slides and diagrams detailing the spot where Peter had fallen. It would be good to have skiers on the panel, but he doubted that P.J. Bowles, Gold Flume ski area's trial lawyer, would pass them. He and P.J. had often opposed each other in court and had long practice with each other's weaknesses and strengths. Both were on a committee of the Colorado Bar Association and were acquaintances of long standing. Steven had won the last four cases he had argued against P.J., but he had the advantage of being able to choose his clients, while P.J. was a company gun.

The introduction of his case and the selection of the jury took the first two hours of the morning. By eleven o'clock, Steven was into his foundation and first witnesses. He led Brad, one of the boys who had stayed with Peter, carefully through his testimony about Peter's injury. "He couldn't even get up or roll over," Brad said. He told of their wait for some other skier to come by, of waiting to alert the patrol on its last sweep, how the sweep had come and how they had heard the voices of the patrol above them on the ridge, how the five of them had shouted for help, how they had followed the ebbing of the voices here, here, here, pointing to the diagram of the ridge and then down and away. There was light snow by then, which they noticed as the voices faded.

After the break, Alan testified about going for help, and of finding no one at the lodge who would listen to him. "The managers had taken off. A worker told me to ski over to the patrol shack. I thought he would call over there and alert someone, but he didn't. It took me maybe three minutes to ski there, and no one was in the room. I finally found the patrol members in the lodge, having drinks. By the time we came out and they got started, half an hour had passed. It was snowing hard, but you could still see. There was an argument over which patrollers should go. By the time they started, the wind had come up and then we were in a whiteout."

On cross-examination, the boys resisted making impulsive statements or falling for loaded questions.

Steven saw that the jury was feeling the boys' frustration—the four on the mountain, the one sent down as he went from place to place for help.

The case was going well. His client's friends were well-spoken; they had acted courageously and sensibly to help Peter and had come through an experience that might have resulted in their friend's death instead of an injury that would leave him an amputee.

The other two friends gave corroborating testimony. The day ended. Steven went to the fitness center to work off the tension. Later, he walked to the park and watched some kids play baseball. Connie had a meeting, Mike an orientation class. On court nights, he followed another ritual: silly films. He had a collection of them, and he took W. C. Fields' *The Bank Dick* downstairs to the basement family room and let himself laugh out loud. Then he went back to polishing the case.

Juries, even in the heart of ski country, were usually composed of nonskiers, many without the money for what could be an expensive sport. Steven would be working to modify any perception in those jurors that the five boys were overprivileged young men, skiing beyond their capabilities and being missed in the storm by ski patrollers who were working under deteriorating weather conditions. A bad weather report, Steven would argue, was all the more reason why a prudent patroller should have skied Not for Grandma, where he would have come upon the scene well before the heavy snow began and while there was still a good chance of a successful rescue. Weather reports showed that the full storm hadn't hit that part of the mountain until 5:00 P.M. Question: Were the patrollers on the final sweep skiing together for fun, laughing and talking on their way down?

The next day, Steven kept the pace moving. He brought on the local weatherman who gave a careful account of the changes that day, including a welcome bit about the sudden cooling that had iced the north-aspect slopes, which would explain Peter's fall. There'd been no ice until 3:00 P.M. or so, and by 4:00, the sun had gone and the low spots on each mogul had begun to freeze. Such a trail, challenging but skiable at 2:00 or even at 3:00, might have been near impossible by 4:00.

The third friend stood up well on cross-examination. "You didn't go down as soon as Peter was hurt?"

"We know now one of us should have," the boy said, responding with the puzzled sound that gave his voice sincerity, "We thought it would be only a few minutes before the ski patrol came. They've got radios and they would radio down to the right people. We tried to make Pete comfortable while we waited."

"When you saw the ski patrol, you didn't all call out to them together? Surely five voices raised to the maximum would alert anyone. Sound does rise."

"I don't know why they didn't hear us. They were skiing the woods in and out, uphill of us, up on the ridge."

"You knew they were patrollers?"

"We saw their jackets once or twice, the red color, in and out of the trees, and they were moving down the slope, talking and laughing. We thought we heard a third one go past on one of the runs, yelling something, and they laughed."

The laughing would do it, Steven thought, that little detail that stood for a whole attitude and behavior. People often laugh under stress. Soldiers joke before battle, but in the quiet courtroom, the mention of it signaled careless inattention. The jurors, sitting helpless in the gully, would hear that laughter on the ridge. Steven kept his face carefully neutral.

110

The fourth boy testified to their response after the patrollers had gone. "We knew we couldn't stay where we were—the snow was banking in the gully and the wind was making the cold even worse. We decided to go for the thick woods up the gully. We tried to package Peter"—he bent his hands in a wrapping motion— "but things were so bad, we ended up just dragging him up behind us.

"We got to the top of the far side of the gully and the trees there helped to break up the wind. We saw it was doable."

"What was doable?" Steven asked, moving the boy toward telling about the snow cave.

"Staying alive," he said.

Bingo. The testimony was making the jurors aware of the danger and an intelligent, courageous response to a life-and-death situation.

"We set up our snow cave on the lee side of a big tree, where the snow would be softer. We had left our skis back in the gully, but Pete had some avalanche cord, so I used it for a belay. I went down there three times and got the skis and the poles and brought them up, and they were very good for helping to make the cave. We used one pole to splint Pete's leg. We knew the break was bad and so did he. He was shivering."

Steven didn't want to break the narrative with a question. He could see that the jury members were scrambling up that bank and heaping snow up for the cave. A few of them had brought their arms up in the late-spring courtroom, crossing them for warmth.

"We got the cave dug and slid Pete into it and he was lying inside, trying to help by sculpting the cold trap. I know it must have hurt him to move at all. By the time we were done, it was dark. We ate our dinner—"

"Dinner?"

111

"I had two candy bars I'd saved for us to share on the ride home. They were pretty well sat on with all the work. We ate some snow and then we all curled up around each other, switching places through the night. We let Pete have an inside place. I was scared for him."

"About his leg?"

"Well, about hypothermia. We were all moving a lot, warming ourselves, but he was still and colder than we were. We got rescued the next afternoon."

"And how well was that rescue done?"

"Very well. Alan had made it down and told the patrol where we were. Later, the ski area people told us they had no responsibility to us because we were out of bounds."

P.J. objected again, but Steven was feeling a good balance to the case. Its architecture was in place and well made.

The cross, with objections and two sidebars, took two hours.

Steven re-called Peter for a final testimony. The young man had been fitted with a prosthesis below his knee but wasn't yet experienced enough with it to be free of a cane. His testimony added the colors of fear and pain, of blacking out and being cold with shock. Steven had already introduced testimony from the surgeon. The injury itself wouldn't have resulted in loss of the lower leg had rescue been timely. Testimony by a physical therapist told of the kind of treatment Peter had undergone and what he still had to undergo. With practice, he would walk, dance, ski, but he would still be an amputee.

P.J.'s cross-examinations were competent, but mostly concerned with small inconsistencies, differences in time and weather for the skiers and in differential diagnoses in the medical reports.

Day three: plaintiff rested; defendant began. The patrollers testified that the snow was falling heavily when they left the top of the mountain. They had not been laughing or talking and they had continually skied over to the edge of the difficult gully to look into it. Wind would have carried any cries away from them. Steven's cross-examination pitted this testimony against the information he had from the weatherman, and he managed to make several telling points about the laughing and talking of the patrollers, who, if they had been in a low-visibility situation, would certainly not have been skiing easily, "socializing their way downhill." Why had the patrol leader been in the lodge instead of the patrol room? Were the patrollers indulging in some après-ski relaxation? Had some of them gone home? If so, it spoke to the fact that they had known a storm was coming and had left before the end of their shifts to beat the weather.

Perhaps the patrollers doing the sweep were not consciously lying, Steven said at summation. Perhaps they truly believed they had looked into the gully. Not for Grandma was unappealing at the end of the day, and icy, and there was a knife-point wind whistling upslope, so why not ski the top and just check by looking over the edge here and there. They had missed the five boys crouching, the crossed skis signaling for help. This was the nub of the case. The slack half an hour had made the difference, and a bad injury had been worsened. Delays and a failure of communication had closed the twenty-five-minute window of opportunity that had existed before the storm had broken on the mountain, isolating the four young men and giving the fifth a nightmare of frustration and anxiety.

Summations, instructions. The jury was out for three hours. Steven had brought a laptop and brief-case full of work. He had warned the clients and their

113

families that the wait might be long, and they stood watch in shifts with cell phones.

Judgment came in for the plaintiff in the amount specified by the documentation from doctors and hospitals and physical therapists, tuition for missed school, legal expenses, and fifteen thousand dollars for pain and suffering. Steven was appalled.

He sat in the cleared courtroom silent and shocked. What had he not explored, shown clearly to the jury? What point had escaped him, or them? He had made some points theatrically, but there was always need for some theater in a trial. What could the trouble have been?

"Mrs. Hendry, this is Steven Howe, Peter Malin's attorney. I'm calling about the trial today. Now that the case has been decided, contact between us is perfectly legal, so I would be very grateful if you, as a juror, could tell me why you awarded a judgment for my client that was so small."

Her voice was hesitant. "We wanted to tell you about that. We all did, but we thought it might not be right to do."

"What was the problem?"

"The *problem* was those boys. You were working so hard for them and making all those points, and we did give him all his medical care and rehabilitation, but the boys . . . well, each one came in all nice and polite and well-spoken and you questioned each one on the witness stand and they were all respectful during the cross-examining by the other side. Then they left the court. They were together with us when we were riding down in the elevator for our lunch break, kidding around, and we saw them in the parking lot, and there they were, mimicking the judge and the bailiff and capering around and laughing at the whole trial. Later, they came up after lunch, and they were

114

still acting like it was all for their entertainment. We thought you must have told them about wearing suits and speaking respectfully, but when they were on their own, we saw they were just five spoiled rich kids."

Steven sat in his study off the kitchen, feeling thwarted and depressed. He hadn't seen the need to warn his clients about their out-of-court behavior. He had been blindsided, caught.

He thought that Annina's death had caught him also, taken him unawares. His grief had been shadowed by a sense of being balked and closed in, caught in midstride. Jennifer's stumbling clumsiness had been revealed as suddenly, from ambush, as something much, much worse, and a loved and grieved-for father stood before him, from hiding, the stock villain in a thriller.

"What do I do now, get drunk?" He was muttering, moving his fists against each other. "Go upstairs and pound holes in the wall of our bedroom? Get in my car and tear away someone else's life? I'm so damn cautious and so damn scared."

Blindsided. Tunnel vision. He felt an overwhelming desire to go somewhere, to act, and not simply be acted on, to make a statement of selfhood. Where was he to go? To Cañon City, to where his father was.

Chapter Sixteen

As he drove south, Steven mumbled to himself while the tapes of case notes he had planned to study droned meaninglessly in the background. Once he'd made the decision to see his father, he kept struggling to find a justification for the visit. Annina's death? The news could have been sent by letter. The way to get in would have to be the family problem of genetics—Jennifer's condition. He didn't like to use that lever. He'd always had a superstitious fear of making capital out of a family tragedy, but what else was there to do?

What had years in prison done to his father? Surely, at seventy-seven, the man would be changed, weakened, made humble by age and illness. Steven had never practiced criminal law. The prisoners he'd seen in his life were all in the movies, innocent men, or savages, killing one another to play out fantasies of revenge.

The man might be anything but passive and burned out. He might be a madman by now. He might be bitter, full of hate; he might be clinging and dependent and demanding. Steven had called the prison and been told by a professional female voice of his father's location, that visiting would be permitted, and that the prisoner had a right to accept or reject visitation. He'd listened to instructions concerning what he was to bring with him, how and where he was to be checked and searched before the visit, how the visit

116

was to be monitored, and how much time would be allowed. What was his relationship to the inmate? Steven couldn't say "son" or "He's my father," although he considered saying, "He was my father." He equivocated. "I'm a lawyer."

"The inmate's attorney?"

"No, this is another matter."

"Oh, I see," and the woman sailed off into a safer set of assumptions. She went easier, using a pleasant, less formal voice.

And he still hadn't told Connie any of this, allowing her to assume that this trip was one of his usual meetings. He heard himself saying to her, at some later, safer time, "I wanted to know enough before I told you, to have facts, not guesses and mysteries. I wanted to be fair to him and to you, too."

Back in September, before all the bricks had fallen, before Annina's death and Jennifer's stumbling, before Jeremy became disgusted again with his major and Mike fixated on Jennifer's blindness, he had come upon Connie standing at the mirror and muttering to herself. "What's up?" he'd asked.

"I'm getting a double chin, see? Look at these wrinkles. I'll have to have my ears pierced."

He'd laughed, and, laughing, had told his friends about it at lunch, and they had all chuckled at the perfect example of the screwball psychology of women, their incapacity to frame thoughts logically. Now he saw into that moment and recaptured the idea, realizing it was shorthand for Connie's very logical thought process. There was no way to erase the wrinkles and she didn't want surgery to correct the double chin, but some change was needed, a small adjustment, because none of the bigger ones would bring the return of youth.

He said to the steering wheel, "Connie, I can't remake five adolescent witnesses or go to Naples or pierce my ears, so I'll have to go to Cañon City and visit my father."

He had been given directions to the "facility." The facility was not one big prison, but a prison complex with separate buildings, each with separate requirements for security. He realized that without the directions, he would have been hopelessly lost.

His destination wasn't the new complex, but the old territorial prison, miles away from the newer buildings, although itself expanded. When he pulled into the parking lot, he sat in the car for a while, gathering his thoughts.

Eventually, he got out and went up the walk to the door.

He was almost oblivious to the check-in procedures because he kept looking at anyone passing, trying to see his father, afraid he would miss him. He signed in, left his attorney's license, and was then taken through a series of halls and then through another door to a room that but for the barred windows could have been any nursing home dayroom. Here old men shuffled, sat, or dozed in the hot June sunlight pouring through the high barred panes, or gazed at him from their places without interest.

Here and there, guard-orderlies walked about, and it was by one of these that Steven was directed to a nursing station. The odor was quintessential nursing home, its strength increased by the warmth of the June day. The staff seemed to be unconcerned about time, having taken notice of him and then letting him stand for some minutes before they looked up again and one of them said, "You wanted someone?"

"Alonzo Howe."

There was an instant's puzzled look and then the staffer said, "Oh, Lonny—I'll go get him. You're one of the shrinks?"

He couldn't make himself say "He's my father" or "I'm his son," both of which he had practiced on the way down. He opened his mouth and out came, "I'm a lawyer, but . . ."

Surprise. "Oh, I see. We don't often get people still working cases here. You'll have to meet with him in the dayroom or—Angela's office isn't being used just now; you can go there. I'll bring him out."

Steven looked around. Some of the prisoner patients were helping others, feeding them or pushing their wheelchairs. The ubiquitous TV rose and fell behind them, its sound swallowing the moans, grunts, and shuffles, and the automatic muttering of senile dementia.

The man came in walking, slowly, looking around. For a moment, Steven stared at him, thinking this man was only another patient, but when the man was through the door, he gave a turn of his head and at the same time a slow blink, and with a jolt, Steven remembered that habit and how his father said, *"Well!"* as he sat down to eat. The short, compact body was his, and the face, half the face regular in feature, recognizable. But beginning at the hairline top left to bottom right at his chin ran a heavy scar, like a downed power line.

"Listen, Lonny," the staffer said, "the doc's going to be in soon, and you'll want to get this over with before he gets here."

"Sure," Lon Howe said in a voice that Steven didn't remember.

He motioned Steven to a chair and said, "TV a problem?" Steven nodded. The staffer said, "I'll go unlock Angela's office," and they followed him. Steven studied his father from the rear. His steps were slow but not fumbling. The office was plain, small, a table, four chairs. The staffer said, "I'll come for

Lonny when it's time." They sat, Steven facing his father.

Lon Howe looked at him. "I have no lawyer; what's the deal?"

"I *am* a lawyer," Steven said. "I'm Steven."

"Steven who?" Then peering close, he said, "Stevie?" and then, "Well!" and Steven felt the move in his throat where weeping begins. He conquered the urge. The unremembered voice said, "So, uh, what brings you out today?" as though the visit were routine.

Steven couldn't say "A bad verdict."

"Mama died in November," he said, beginning at a place he hadn't planned.

"Oh, yeah? What was it?"

"Heart. It was very sudden. It was a big shock."

"Did she ever tell you about me?"

"She told me you were dead."

"Figures. So, how did you find me?"

"Computer, and you had no death certificate."

"Well, not yet I don't."

"How did you get that scar?" Steven asked.

Lon Howe leaned back in the chair, pushing it closer to the wall. Then he tipped it back and looked at Steven through half-closed eyes. This freedom, Steven thought, the back-tipped chair, the half-humorous look, must be rare in here. Lon Howe was taking advantage of a moment's relaxation of the rules. "We got air conditioning back in the seventies because the guards wouldn't work here without it. They turn it on to suit themselves." He touched the scar at his upper lip. "Not everyone in the facility approves of what I did that got me in here. You wouldn't remember, but there was a bad riot right after I got here and one of the guys took the opportunity to express an opinion. You came here to tell me— what?"

120

"To ask you something."

"What is that?"

The question came too soon. Steven felt the amused glance of the man whose turf this was and who, paradoxically, had all the power on his side.

"Well, first I want to say that I have three children—we have three children, my wife, Connie, and I."

"Does this Connie and these three children know about me?"

"Not yet."

"You'll tell them?"

"Yes, of course."

"When?" The eyes were evaluating, still amused.

"Soon."

"So, you're a lawyer."

"Personal injury. I specialize in sports injuries—ski injuries, principally."

Lon Howe leaned his head against the wall and laughed. Steven remembered the sound of it and at that moment knew that he was seeing his father. A wave of longing broke over him and forced tears out of his eyes. One fell on his hand. To hide them, he sat forward and put his elbows on his knees as though in thought. Lon Howe, still absorbed in his own merriment, didn't seem to notice. Steven took several deep breaths and regained control.

Years in prison had taught Lon different manners. He made no attempt to excuse his laughter or to mollify Steven. He chuckled, "Don't that beat everything? Lawyer. Have you studied my case? Is that it? If you did, you'd know I had no lawyer and no way to get one. None of the times."

Steven said, "But I haven't—I'm not familiar with your case at all. Mama told me you had died. We moved to Denver. We were on welfare. I see now that she must have been terrified of being deported. Her

121

strategy must have been to keep quiet, to be invisible. She seemed so afraid all the time, even after I started earning enough money to move her out of the projects. She never asked for anything, even from me, and she rarely went out, except to shop." He looked up. "Did she know what the crime was that sent you here?"

"I'm not sure how much she knew," the old man said. "She was in court a few times, but who knows what she made of the legal lingo. I'll bet she never spilled to a priest. She didn't go to church, Annina, not after me. You didn't grow up with rosaries, did you, candles, statues around the house, any of that?"

"No."

"Naples, a girl from there, you'd think she'd Ave Maria herself inside out praying me out of purgatory. She was never religious, I'll give her that. When the boat sailed out of that harbor, so did she, right out of that world." He was still for a while and then said abruptly, "What did you want to know?"

"It's something about your side of the family. I remember aunts and uncles, when we lived in Callan."

"Are you making a family tree, trying to find a winner somewhere?"

"Do you have any family?"

"I guess everyone does."

"I don't."

"I forgot that. When I got sent up, they all dropped me. No letters, no visits, no Christmas cards, but yeah, I had two brothers and five sisters, aunts, uncles, the whole shootin' match."

"Were any of them blind?" Steven asked.

"What?" Lon's face still showed its cool amusement. Steven realized that the only facial expressions prisoners could allow themselves were the blank-faced no-look and the cynical half smile.

He repeated the question.

Lon chuckled. "I'll say this for you, you pitch a terrific curveball. It must help out the lawyering. Ski law. I'll have to share that one around."

"I need to know," Steven said.

Lon shrugged. "Is there some blind guy named Howe going to leave you a fortune?"

"The blindness would have shown up in their twenties, but you were away at war. It might not have shown up in your brothers and sisters until you were gone. Do you know where any of them are living now?"

Lon shook his head. "We were never what you'd call close. You get your folks, your sisters and brothers, luck of the draw. Sometimes some of them like each other, sometimes not. We didn't."

"So you don't know where they are?"

"Get real, sonny. I did what got me in here. I did what got me *this*." The scar on Lon's face had reddened with his annoyance. Steven thought, that scar must betray him all the time, going pale in moments of fear he might wish to keep from others, reacting beyond the control he keeps of his expression. It was a body language immediately readable by his enemies, and in this place, who wouldn't be an enemy?

The guard's head poked through the open door. "Hey, Lonny, Doc's here."

"Okay." And Lon Howe rose and, without any of the lubricating looks or words necessary in normal society, began to move to the door.

Steven rose and took his father's arm as he passed. "Were any of them blind?" In a sudden turn of the head, he received an icy stare and felt his father pull away quickly. *"Were any of them blind?"* Lon left the room without further words.

The guard reappeared at the doorway and came in. "Quite the feller, ain't he?"

123

Steven hadn't corrected the impression that his visit was professional. As a lawyer, he possessed a status he'd be lacking as a convict's son. "He doesn't seem as feeble as most of the others here."

"You got his good day. He's a renal case, and there are other things they treat him for—I'll ask doc to see you, if you want. It'll mean a wait; doc's pretty booked up." In the hesitation that followed, an expression of curiosity appeared on the guard's face. "He's fighting release, ain't he? I don't blame him, after all this time."

"This is another matter," Steven said. "Something concerning another case."

"And he was uncooperative. . . ."

"Very."

The guard sat down where Lon had been sitting, tipped back as Lon had, and motioned Steven to the other chair. He took out a pack of cigarettes. Both men were aware they were in a smoke-free area. The guard offered Steven one and when rejected, lighted up himself, took a long pull, and sat back in a satisfying cloud of blue smoke.

"Ain't everything is as advertised. They took your smokes away, didn't they?"

"I don't smoke." Steven and most of his friends had stopped years before, but the look of ease and completeness he saw in the guard made him regret the loss.

"They get difficult, very private, most of 'em," the man said mildly. "In this facility, it's so many years since they did their offense—it's another life. What he did, Lonny, the compulsion—the docs say they never get over that, but I think it burns out of some of 'em; they get old and they're not so hot for that thrill any more."

"Can the rest of us afford to wait around?" Steven's tone was dry.

124

"I ain't said it was nothing, molesting kids: I only said they're not that one thing alone. I meet 'em younger over at the facility they got for sex offenders and they're smart and dumb, decent men and assholes, family men and loners. Your client's not a bad guy. Some of 'em you get here are con men or abusers, stone evil. You probably know Lonny's history, but things look different when you're inside, and like I say, Lonny's not a bad guy. You want me to tell doc to give you a few minutes?"

Steven rose, shook his head, and turned, and the guard reluctantly rose, too. "It's Lon's call whether he wants me to know his condition, and my bet is that he doesn't," Steven said.

The guard nodded. "I'll take you out. Trip was for nothing, then. Sorry."

"It happens."

The guard motioned Steven ahead. "You might try again. It works like that sometimes. They don't get much choice in here, like I said, and saying no is one way to make the most of what little they got." He put out the cigarette and dropped the butt in his shirt pocket.

"I'll keep that thought," Steven said.

They went through the maze and out the main door.

The rain began as he drove north, a fearsome gully washer that blinded him and forced him to the side of the road. He had chosen to drive the back way up toward Cripple Creek and almost to Denver before rejoining the interstate. His idea had been that the serene, still-pristine beauty of the land would quiet his spirit, but instead he was sitting stopped in his car, fogged in and contemplating the chances of being washed away in the mud or rock slides that now and then closed these small roads.

He had known that Lon Howe was alive since April and he hadn't told Connie. He had known that Lon was in prison and he hadn't told Connie. When he'd learned the reason for Lon's imprisonment, he hadn't told Connie. He came from a generation that held honesty in personal relationships as the prime virtue, secrecy the prime evil. Watch TV, and there are people confessing everything to everyone and confiding their horrors as though they were everyday events.

He sat in the besieged car and thought of ways to get the words said and wondered why it was impossible to say them. He knew he should have gotten past the twinge of shame he still felt at the differences between his family's tight scarcity and the abundance and ebullience of the Scotts. "Connie, we've lost one family member and found another." "Connie, I went down to Cañon City, to the prison, to find out if there was blindness on my side of the family, but my father wouldn't tell me." "Connie, my dad, my shining black-jacketed dad, is a sick, stunted old man whose clothes and food and shoelaces are issued by the state."

He began to weep and then to sob, but, with the pounding rain on his car's metal roof and hood, not loudly enough for him to hear.

I was at Jen's sixth-grade commencement, at all their graduations, at Mike's plays and Jeremy's ball games, cheering the team on and taking everyone to McDonald's afterward. There were years of such celebrations, without a single memory of having had one myself. My mother didn't go to my college graduation. By the time I graduated from law school and had one of the Scott parties, I was grown. For whom am I crying?

His clients had provided him with many examples of self-pity, lack of balance, denial of objectivity, and even a simple thankfulness at a good settlement. He didn't admire that weakness in his clients and his vanity wouldn't allow him the emotion once he had

126

identified it. Self-consciousness muted him and stopped the tears.

It was an hour before the rain ended as suddenly as it had begun. The road back to the highway was a challenge to his driving skills. He was two hours late.

"I was getting worried," Connie said, "and you didn't call."

"I almost drowned," he told her, recounting how he had been forced to sit in the stopped car until the storm had gone on. There were places where hills had blocked his cell phone and kept him from calling. No rain had fallen in Denver. He wanted to sit down with her at the kitchen table and begin telling her about Lon Howe, but the words wouldn't come. Soon the evening interruptions began, the phone calls, social and business, E-mail from Jennifer and from Jeremy, who was now well into his summer job at the conference center near Estes Park. He lacked the stillness and peace that might have moved the words forward. The moment passed, the evening, a day, another day, and the secret hung in the closet like a suit he shoved away on its hanger every morning as he took down the one he would wear to work.

Chapter Seventeen

Jack called Steven and told him that the Long Branch, their usual meeting place, had closed for remodeling. "They'll remodel the prices, too," he said. "Let's change. Paul wants to try an Indian place near here."

The Tamerind was a five-table family restaurant and people at the other tables looked Indian. Paul admitted that his brother had invested in the place. They ordered combination plates and enjoyed the redolent aroma.

"I hope the management isn't saving as much on food as they do on lighting," Jack said.

The dimness was a relief to Steven. "Do you remember when Dave Eisner told us he was going to the doctor for a backache and how the tests showed cancer?" The others nodded.

"Well?" Jack asked.

"All that came out over lunch, didn't it?

"Yeah, I guess so," Terry said, and nodded almost imperceptibly at Steven.

"What about our other bad news?" Steven asked. "We didn't meet after work or at night, or sit by the fire with brandy and cigars and confide. We talked at lunch, right in the middle of the workday."

"It keeps the thing in perspective," Paul said. "When our Joe came out as gay and I was terrified of his having AIDS, I told you over lunch, because the time limit kept me from going overboard."

"Hey, Steve," Jack said, "this isn't about you being sick, is it?"

"No, not about me, not directly."

Paul murmured, "It's not Jennifer, is it?"

"No, it's about my father. I need to talk about my father."

Steven had a sudden sharp picture of the biker, leg just being thrown over the glistening barely hooded engine that was sputtering with the wish to burst into motion. Beside him Terry let out a breath, probably of relief.

They listened. Food came and they ate, and Steven, spoke between bites of food he barely tasted but which seemed to impress him subliminally, so that long afterward he remembered the cubeb, pepper, and cumin flavor when he remembered what he had said.

They asked some questions, lawyerly questions, when Steven realized would not have occurred to others. In which particular institution in the system was Lon Howe imprisoned? Had he had a lawyer? When Steven mentioned the year of Lon's conviction, they all understood that the trial and sentencing had occurred before 1963 and the *Gideon v. Wainwright* decision establishing an accused's right to counsel. His friends didn't argue or advise. Mostly, they listened, and Steven was relieved not to be cornered or pressed about what he did or didn't know, even as their tidying legal minds worked at the strings and cords of the case.

Paul and then Jack reached for cell phones to call about running late.

Terry asked, "Did the papers say who the judge was?"

"No, and I didn't look it up. It would have been in Ute County. I saw my father last week. We talked for almost an hour, but I didn't go into the details of the case; it would have been pointless."

129

"Will you see him again?"

There was silence after Terry's question. "Yes. He didn't tell me what I needed to know. He didn't act it or say anything, but I think he wants me coming back."

"He must have been glad to see you," Paul said.

"Maybe he's simply bored. Prison is incredibly boring, and I'm a break in the routine."

"Nothing more?"

"Probably not."

It occurred to Steven that were Connie confiding in her friends now, they would ask her to describe her feelings. His friends, of course, didn't. Their sympathy was expressed in noting the long distance Steven had to travel to get to Cañon City and back, the traffic on the interstate, the inconvenience his visit imposed, the humiliation of check-in procedures and being patted down by guards, officiousness and bureaucratic stupidity in the making of meaningless rules.

At the right moment, Terry stretched, looked up, and said, "Well, I've got to get back for another peak moment in American law." They all rose.

On his way out, Jack stopped Steven. "You've had quite a year, haven't you?"

"I hope it's over."

"I guess I was envious of you, that picture-window family, complete with dog. You always seemed to be trying too hard, pushing."

"We all push, and the dog died three years ago."

"I had my marriage blow up on me, I was drinking too heavily, and until very recently, I had a woman who didn't give a rat's ass about me. And there you were—"

"Fat, dumb, and happy?"

"Happy, anyway, yeah."

"I guess a little quiet enjoyment of a friend's comedown is normal enough."

"Normal doesn't mean I'm proud of it."

"I'm not innocent."

"I always thought we should get another word for half the uses we make of that one—'innocent civilians.'"

"Say 'uninvolved'; nobody's innocent."

"I'm sorry, Steve."

"It won't go on your personal record."

In the telling, the secret had lost some of its size; it no longer dwarfed him, and he was relieved to be able to return to work.

He spent the afternoon on three cases, one of which was a consultation with a prospective client. She had precipitously gone into labor on the slopes and delivered a cord-strangled baby in the aid room. "A jury will ask why you chose to go skiing at the very end of your ninth month of pregnancy," Steven said, keeping his voice neutral. "Because of this, I don't think you have a case."

"I've always been athletic. I wanted to be in shape for when the baby came," she said.

He looked hard at her. "You had fallen, hadn't you?" She nodded unwillingly. "How many times?"

"Three."

He tried to look sympathetic and to hide a tired impatience.

He told the story to Connie that evening. "You're wondering where her good sense was," Connie said. "When I was pregnant, I had lots of energy right up to the end. I also knew that those moments were precious and that it would be years before I would be as free again. I sometimes think that life's peak moments show people at their best and their worst. Your ski accidents remind me of the weddings, the best and the worst. Bronson-Sullivan is the one I think of as a best."

"Remind me."

131

"Five hundred guests at the reception, and the best man had a seizure at the altar. Paramedics came and took him to the hospital. The bride, the groom, the parents, and the minister all went down to the ER and held the ceremony there, gown, veil, train, and all, and they did it without a break in stride. Today, it was Russel-Jones."

"Not your finest hour, I gather."

"She was apoplectic about her flowers not matching her peach and gray color scheme. The decorations on the cake weren't exactly the same tint as the ribbons held by the bridesmaids. She had a screaming fit."

"Peach?"

"Everyone's idea of *peach* is different. We spent the whole afternoon trying to comfort the little dumbbell. You want to please the bride and groom on their wedding day. You hope they'll tell their friends about how great the experience was. That little twit works for a mutual fund, somewhere in the same world I inhabit. She shops, eats, undergoes the daily hoo-ha without throwing fits. I figure it was the wedding that did it—changing her into Medusa."

"And my parturient skier lost her mind trying to beat the clock."

Connie smiled, a hint of softening nostalgia in her expression. "That and clinging to her identity as a girl maybe just a little longer, not entirely wanting to give that up for being a mother."

"She still has no case." Then he walked over to where Connie was peeling a cucumber, a vegetable she smuggled into his salads, and embraced her. She turned and, with the peeler still in her hand, kissed him.

Right now, he thought, he might let go, share everything, even his picture of the quiet, laconic man in the room with barred windows, the man made vulnerable by the scar bisecting his face. Steven took a breath before speaking. "Annina told me that my father was dead," he began.

Connie said, "I'm glad she didn't know about Jennifer's condition. She'd assume that Jennifer would have to stay single." Connie went on and Steven let the easy topic flow, pushing him along and away from the secret.

What was the secret, really? It was only one visit to a bitter old man, a man who had given nothing, who hadn't answered his question. One visit hardly constituted a relationship. He wasn't even sure he wanted to see Lon Howe again.

Chapter Eighteen

His second visit to Cañon City was two weeks later, on a day of sporadic rain. The Colorado earth pulled in the moisture, thirsty in scarcity. This time, as he filled in the required forms and received the pass, he became impatient, and the guard at reception shook her head. "Mister, if you were entering a maximum facility, the check-in would be twice as complicated. We go easy with the geriatrics and the sick. You're not checking into college, y'know."

The building itself looked squarer, harsher than it had on his previous visit, although lilac and snowball bushes, kept small, were meant to soften the effect. On the way in, he had seen a squirrel drinking from the cup of a leaf. Under the lilac foliage in absolute motionlessness, a striped cat was promoting the squirrel. The eyes of the cat never wavered; its stillness was a thrum of tightened muscles. Steven's presence, his walk up the strip of concrete to the door, alerted the squirrel, which, turning from its drink, saw the cat. The cat realized that circumstances had changed and sprang too suddenly. The squirrel exited easily, its tail like a banner on parade. The cat, from its graceless end spring, looked up at Steven with a hiss of temper. "Oh shit!" Steven said sympathetically. The cat shook itself out and began to perfect its stripes with its tongue, then, regaining its insouciance, trotted away. Steven entered the building and was guided again into the ward.

The odor there was worse than the first time because of the rain, and the closed windows, opaque with condensation, imparted even more of a prison feeling.

Lon Howe, moving slowly, came in behind the guard. This time, they shook hands and stood waiting. Around them, a circle of wheelchairs surrounded the TV. Lon looked sideways at Steven. "The environment getting to you, is it? They'll get us into our private office soon." Steven looked around at the room and the other inmates. Some were very old and had wheeled oxygen tanks with them. Others coughed resolutely, one after the other, trying to breathe around their asthma or emphysema. Two generations past, people had come to Colorado for their lung problems, bringing with them the trees and plants that had sickened them.

The guard came and motioned to them, leading them down the short hall they had walked on his first visit, past the office and to a much smaller room, equally nondescript, furnished with two small folding tables and four mismatched chairs. In this poverty of choice, Lon played host. "How's this?"

"Fine."

"Coffee?"

"How good is it?"

"Choice Colombian, grown on the north-facing slopes of the Andes."

"No, thanks."

"Wise choice. Oh, and don't be surprised if Feeney watches you when you leave. Believe it or not, we've had some petty theft around here lately. Feeney'll be looking out for those chairs."

There was a window in the room and they both sat silently, looking out at the rain. Steven said, "I think I owe you an apology. Last time, I wanted to know something and I forced my agenda on you."

Lon took a breath. "Of all the things that happen to someone down here, what happens to privacy is the worst. Psych students come, penologists, Bible-bangers, people writing books: 'Tell me about your crimes,' they say. They get deep and serious—lots of eye contact. They want to hear it all. You give, maybe because you're bored. Sometimes you even think giving might do some good, help some other dumb slob, prove you're not scum, but it's the same anyway. They take, they go, and they leave you feeling you've been had. You get raw, sensitive." They were silent again. Lon said, "You did tell me Nina died—"

"Last November."

Steven found himself describing the Thanksgiving party and how they had all been sitting at the table, laughing and joking, and how they had missed her dying moments because she had gone so quietly. "She always made a panettone to bring to the holidays," he said. "It was the only thing she made well."

Lon chuckled. "I know. She kept trying and it only got worse. I couldn't take it out on her—they were so poor over there. She used to get bread, soak it in olive oil, and fry it up. That didn't work with American bread. She couldn't cook American spaghetti, either; it came out doughy. I guess I thought she'd go back home, be Italian, take you and raise you there."

Steven was amazed that Lon would think so. Had Lon forgotten Annina's fears and neediness? "She never would have done that," he said, "as poor as we were, things were better here. Also, there would have been the shame."

He had blundered into the word, thinking of Annina alone, saw there was no change in Lon's face, so composed that it might have been that of a corpse. "I meant the shame of returning a failure, a single woman with a child. She told me how they had all gone down to the pier to see her off. 'Good-bye' meant 'Don't come back. Give us one less mouth to feed.'"

"I guess you're right."

"Did she see you after you were arrested?"

"You're asking how much she knew. I told you last time: I don't know, but she was at my arraignment, at one of them anyway, '*The State of Colorado v. Alonzo Carl Howe.*' She yelled then, you know, howled like a wolf. They had to take her out. I was in shackles and that was hard for her. I was glad she never came again. It went bad for me that she wasn't there. The judge took that in."

"So, you never had a jury trial."

"No. I pled guilty. I told you. I was making too many of them scared, and it was getting worse, too. I was getting angry with them, beginning to hate them. That's scary, being afraid of what you could do."

"Angry with *them*?"

"The kids." Again, no change in the face.

Steven wondered how this quiet man could be saying such things. A feeling of unreality enveloped him. His hearing distorted and the words sounded far away.

"Are you going to puke?" the distant voice asked.

"No," his own distant voice answered, "I'm all right. Just give me a minute."

Silence. When Steven next spoke, he sounded normal. "I wondered how you could sit there and say what you did."

Then there was a change in Lon, a ripple of expression that moved around the scar. "Look, people don't understand. I've been questioned and interviewed to death by two generations of psychologists. I've gone into it, said it, relived it. I've had electrodes measuring every response, including erection. What's shocking to you is common run to me."

Lon had been speaking without using a single foul word. Steven said, "You don't sound like . . . uh . . . a prisoner."

"Like the prisoners in the movies? Some of the long-termers, when they're seventeen and they've proven themselves at Lookout Mountain and Buena Vista, they get here, and they're deeply impressed with themselves. Every second word will be garbage. The image calls for it. It's that image thing that makes the young guys so dangerous. When I came in, it was the same. But five years go by and then ten, and some of us get tired of that pose, that talk. Maybe we've read a little or talked to some educated prisoners. Steve—this is my life. I can make it better, or"—a grin, his father's long-ago, familiar grin—"I can fuck it up."

"You seem different this time," Steven said, "easier, maybe."

"I didn't think you'd come back."

"You were a biker, weren't you?"

Lon's head came up. "I had a bike, I rode a bike, an old Indian, but I wasn't a biker. I didn't have a club or go on any trips. There wasn't money for that."

"What happened to the bike?"

"Nina must have sold it."

"And the outfit, the leather jacket with the fringes and the leather gloves and the boots."

Lon's mouth worked. "That leather came off no cow on earth. The boots were leatherette. I don't figure she got five bucks for the whole outfit."

Lon talked about work he had done in prison, in the print shop, the best of his placements. "I was in the mail room, too. Lots of different jobs. What was all that blind business you were asking about last time?"

"My daughter has retinitis pigmentosa. It causes what they call tunnel vision—there's no peripheral sight and the tunnel hole gets smaller and smaller and the light. . ."

138

Where did the sudden tears come from? All with no warning or chance to collect himself, to hold on to some inner rein that would stop the tears, speech and breath betrayed him. His eyes were brimming and his throat narrowed. He knew the tears weren't for Jennifer alone. He saw Annina watching her husband being led away. He saw himself reverently placing the motorcycle's screws and bolts into the solvent for his father. Lon made a quick *hmm* sound. "You wouldn't last ten minutes in this place." The words weren't said with any special vigor, but the scorn was evident.

"I've noticed," Steven said, "that suffering often makes the sufferer arrogant." He pulled a Kleenex out of his pocket and blew his nose. "Jennifer's condition is genetic," he continued, "and when I found out you were alive, I saw an opportunity to trace the familial part—Kendrick, Howe—you might have seen people who had it. Was it slow or fast with them? Were they completely blind? Did it take sudden leaps, or was it steady and gradual? You understand, there's no treatment and no cure. We can only try to ready ourselves."

He reached into his inside jacket pocket and brought out two photographs. One was of their last Christmas group, the three young ones and Connie, standing self-consciously beside the tree. The other a wedding picture. Lon took them, stared at them briefly, and returned them without comment. Steven tried to look at his father without the scar to see if any of the three in the photograph took some quality, some feature from the man who sat facing him. Jennifer had Annina's coloring but Connie's features. Mike was pure Scott, but in Jeremy, there was the curve of Lon's eyebrows, the set of Lon's jaw, the nutmeg hair that would thin later.

He began to work at describing his family. He told Lon about Jeremy's too many peaks of interest, about

Jennifer's finding her career, only to have it threatened by her dwindling vision, about Mike's decision to go into work with the blind and his and Connie's trepidation about the choice. Lon listened quietly, and when Steven came to the end, he said, "What do you want? I don't think you want me to be grandpa. I went away in 1957. That's a lot of years. Things were done to me down here and I made the man I am, and it works for me. That man doesn't include being anyone's dad or grandpa. This cut down my face was the least of it. There's hate by other cons and hate by guards and allowances made for what they do, because of what they think we are. Whenever I think I'll have some peace, the therapy folks come in with something new, or prison rules change, or someone shows up, and"—he made a flicking motion against his thumb—"gone."

"Were any of your people blind? Did any of them have diminished sight?"

Lon rose and sighed. "I got some medicine to take," he said, and went to the door, knocked, and was let out. He had sounded casual, but there had been the flicker of pain lifting his lower lip, just for a moment before he could cover it.

Steven wondered about the illness. Most of the other men in this place were older-looking than Lon, sicker-looking. What was the condition that was giving him the privilege of this part of the system?

Steven was out of the building before he began to sift the reasons why Lon hadn't answered his question about blindness in the family. It was certainly possible that the withholding was a way of bringing Steven back. Lon might be holding out, favor for favor, or he might be playing with Steven, amusing himself, or he might be trying to establish trust. He hadn't been a malicious man in Steven's childhood, but prison changes people, and need twists them.

140

Steven saw the striped cat napping under the lilac branches. Did it know it was striped, that the sun and shadow of underbrush was perfect camouflage? "I don't know enough about him," Steven said to the cat. "I've been too afraid."

The records had been kept in a basement flooded in the big storm of 1982, when filthy water had washed down the Aureole courthouse's red stone steps. It was still possible to visit the now-deserted structure and tell the depths of the water that had swirled through the rooms by high-water marks. A plaque in the new courthouse recorded that volunteers had come, at great personal risk, to save the records and carry them to safety.

The following year, the records were transferred to the new location. Many were in water-stained boxes, wrinkled and mildewed. The librarian was young and pretty, but one eye seemed to wander out of her control. "I'll open the window for you and that might help with the smell."

He began with the originals, starting with 1932, and hoping for any mention of the Howe family.

Sheriff's call notes, handwritten in a grade-school printing that, though water-stained, was regular and pleasing to read:

> May 1935: Got Lonny Howe sent over by Principal Jennings for showing himself in girls' bathroom. Talked to him. Sent him back to Jennings for discipline. Spoke to Elisha about it. Apology. Nice boy.

Lon would have been thirteen then.

July 18, 1937: Arrest: Lon Howe for
luring Martha Mae Johnson of Bluebank
into barn and mollisting her.

The sheriff had misspelled *molesting*. What exactly
was the molestation? Was the contact violent?

The sheriff then was Neil M. Foster and no doubt he
took Lon out back of the jail and beat him senseless. It
was the way they handled juvenile crime in the county
in those days.

What does constitute molestation? Is it touching?
Fondling? Penetrating? Is it raping? Did he rape this
girl, or other girls? His urge was an early vocation. At
the age that Edgar Allan Poe was writing poems and
Albert Einstein was contemplating the space-time
continuum, Lon Howe was moving past habit and
toward compulsion.

In 1938, a minister sponsored a youth group and
enlisted a Ronnie Howe as a leader. As the group
consisted solely of boys, the town perhaps imagined
them safe. Had one not confided in a friend, the
silence of children and the claustral nature of their
world would have protected Lon. In 1940, Alonzo
Howe, eighteen, was sentenced to three months for
"indecency." What was that? There was no record of
counseling.

Pearl Harbor provided the county with a neat
solution. Send the boy to war. Many young men
would die or disappear abroad, and why not Lon, with
any luck at all? Steven understood that Lon's years in
the service had probably included incidents not in
these records, but those might be with the army. The
hero of hard combat, of landing beaches and mountain
hideouts, the lucky, clever, intrepid soldier, the man
who smiled out of the photograph in Naples, was by
then a habitual molester of children.

142

Why did he marry? Was it to hide? Steven tried to remember anything that had seemed false or devious about his father. There was no hint of it. His memories were of eager anticipation of his father's return from work, the comfort of his presence, the motorcycle, the excitement his father tried to convey in their moving to all the different houses. On one place, there had been horses. His father had ridden, and, yes, the place was a ranch. Mama was a maid there, and there were five other people. They were all hands or servants, he thought, but the owner, the boss, was seldom present.

Steven remembered that suddenly it was time to pack up and leave the ranch. Was it because Lon had done something again, hurt someone, had been caught at it? Where did they go from there? He had stopped scanning sheriff's records and was staring intently at the wall, so intently that if his eye had been an auger, it would have drilled a window.

In 1956, Lon Howe was arrested on a charge of child molestation when found in flagrante delicto with Jancine Carter, age six, in the show home of a newly built development in Aureole. He was released on a technicality. Two months later, he was discovered at the riverbank park by campers with Lirra Driver, five. The girl ran away from him and up the bank into the campground parking lot, where she was hit by a car and killed. Howe pleaded no contest to the charges of kidnapping and felony murder, causing a death in the commission of a criminal act.

What did he do to the girl, to all the girls, and to the boys at that camp? Did Annina find out? Did she understand any of the proceedings? What was she told? Did she try to get a lawyer for him? Was the sentence appropriate? Was there anyone to suggest psychological or psychiatric treatment? Under these questions was a deeper, more primitive thought: Why did he leave me for all those other children? I might

143

have satisfied him and he could have stayed then, and been my father, too. And if he had hurt me, it would have been worth it, despite the pain, but then he'd be my father and I would have protected him and never given him away and we would have been a family. This idea horrified Steven. Lon might have believed he was saving his son, but Steven and Annina had been forced to live without him, without his grin and his light, his support, his American presence, his sense of protection from the world's dangers and hard judgments. They had been poor without him, cold, hungry, pinched, dried-out.

Lon must have let his victims go afterward. Did he threaten them? If he did, was that the worst part of the abduction, the fear? How did he get the children to go with him? Did he use charm or force? If force, what did he force them to do?

Chapter Nineteen

On his third visit, Steven checked in at the security area and was directed to another floor of the same building. It was a small room where eight men lay in loungers, each next to a machine, each neighbored by a medical standard hung with bags of fluid and coils of plastic tubing.

"Welcome to the dialysis unit," the aide told him. "Your Lonny's down at the end there. We don't usually allow visits here, but being you're a lawyer, we ain't about to shut you out. Wouldn't want no hassles with the ACLU, now would we?" He made a sarcastic pull of his lip.

Steven began to speak. "All these men . . ."

The aide thought he knew what the question was and shook his head. "We're a rich country, mister. We can afford to run dialysis on murderers and monsters like your client over there, look out for their little blood-sugar levels and monitor their little heart problems."

Steven thought that by now people must know he was Lon Howe's son, and that the aide felt free to tease him, playing, as a way of equalizing some social distance between them. "Come on down!" the aide said, in the TV game-show voice.

Steven walked past the three men on his side of the room. He was surprised at the fragility of two of them and the relatively healthy look of the third. This illness seemed to have no correlation to age or even

145

general physical health. The aide, who had changed his mind about accompanying him, came to his side. "They can turn this treatment down, you know. Some of 'em do; three, four years of it, they get tired, don't want to keep it up, but you got death row guys come in, extra guards and all that to dialyze a guy who's supposed to die. All of it costs more money than I'll see in a lifetime, and I'll never figure out why they treat any of these guys, the government paying all that money out for it." He raised his head and gave the pulled-lip smile. "Hey, Lonny, here's your legal eagle."

Steven saw the same arrangement of tubes and pouches, the same medical standard holding them, the same machine connecting him with gleaming plastic tubing, other tubes carrying the blood being washed into and out of the machine. The room was cool, but summer-cool; he was surprised that the patients had blankets over them. The hum of the machines was low, changing in tone now and then.

Two of the patients were talking from couch to couch. Steven wondered if even here there were some hierarchical order dictating who could laugh or speak first. Two other patients lay still and expressionless on their couches. One was reading. Two others seemed to be asleep.

His father lay with his eyes closed, but when the aide called to him, he opened them quickly and made a gesture of greeting. His arm was burdened with its tubes. He seemed surprised by the visit, even though he must have known about it. The aide brought a chair, checked some of the dials on the machine, adjusted something, and left.

"A bastard, that one," Lon said. "One of the worst things about being in what they call a 'structured setting' are the people who have control of you."

Steven asked, "How did you get a life sentence?" The question had come to him on his way up the stairs. He wondered why he hadn't asked it sooner.

Lon's eyes widened. His expression didn't change, but the scar was livid under the fluorescent light.

"That opening sure beats the standard 'Hi, Lon, how are you?'"

"It's a long way down here. I don't have time to chat." He hadn't planned what he would say. The sight of Lon being treated changed the intensity of Steven's need. Lon was old and frail and might die as suddenly as Annina had, who took her secrets with her.

Lon said, "Well, then, are you going to ask me exactly what I did and how I did it?"

Steven thought, He likes having the edge, playing with me. This place, prison/dialysis unit, is his turf, more comfortable for him than for me, and he's playing.

"I know some of what you did, but maybe *why* should come first. You were in the army, you had a pretty, loving bride, and the gratitude of her whole family, and then—"

"You've got it wrong," Lon said. "I thought the army would stop me. I was glad for the war. There are no kids in the army, no little boys or girls. I liked being free of all that." He paused, breathing hard. "I liked being with the guys, earning respect there. I was in the landing at Salerno. Did you know that? I did good things for my men. I got to be a sergeant because I was good. Guys who were near to bugging out, deserting, killing themselves or us, guys who were close to going nuts, didn't, because I was there." His voice had risen from the dead level, not louder, but more animated and lacking the sullen tone of someone busy in his justifications. He raised his free hand. "Don't look for medals. I didn't get any, and they

147

busted me down afterward because we were in Naples and there were all those kids, filthy, orphaned kids, kids who offered themselves to us for anything, just to get a meal and a place to sleep."

"And you took advantage of that."

"Sure I did."

"You raped them?"

"No!"

"What did you do, then?"

"I never hurt any children. I loved them too much as they were, when they smiled and were happy. The kids over there were starving and half-naked. They wanted food and safety, and I gave them that. They wanted someone to love and I loved them, but I never entered their bodies. And I never *hurt* them."

"What did you do?"

"I worked on myself when I held them. When I was done, I kissed them and gave them the food I had or the blanket, or whatever they needed."

"And the army found out."

"More than once. You understand," he said quietly, "that in here, in the sex offenses unit, where they had me before my kidneys died on me, there are people who murdered kids, raped and murdered them and made them do terrible things."

"And you never hurt any of the children."

"No, never."

"How do you know you didn't damage them? You never admitted how you hurt me. Not all injury is physical. You abandoned us, Mama and me. What was that little girl running away from? Did any of those kids beg you to let them go? How did you get to the kids? Did you promise them rides on the bike?"

"What got me in here wasn't nice. I did what it took. I tried to be good to them, to be gentle. There were things I swore I'd never do, and I didn't do, even

148

when the feelings were so strong that I thought they would tear me apart."

"Why didn't you kill yourself over there?"

"Back then, I thought I could beat the devil, use willpower. I was young, and a guy doesn't think about suicide when he's spent four years putting everything he's got into staying alive. I was into trying things, too, masturbating as often as I could, cold showers, praying. . . ." Lon looked up at Steven. His voice was low. "I've answered dozens of questions from shrinks and I stopped feeling anything. You show up and it all hurts again. What do I say to you? It was awful and I did it and I hated it."

"Was it about sex?"

"The need was stronger than sex."

"You married."

"Even that wasn't what the shrinks said it was, that I did it to hide, even from myself. The army didn't like you to marry back then. If you got a girl knocked up, they would transfer you way up the map. I didn't want to leave my outfit, the buddies I had, what was left of them, but I thought it would be good to be married. When I was with Nina, back then, I didn't need to be with the kids, to see them cry—"

"I thought you said they didn't cry."

"Some didn't cry."

"You were courting Mama, you said."

His eyes, which had closed, opened, and he made a snorting sound. "Courting." He pulled in a breath. Steven studied the machine.

"Does that process hurt?"

"Yeah, some. Mostly, you feel like you're dying. You know, what the docs call 'discomfort.' You wonder what they think is pain." He took two or three breaths and then said, "Courting back then meant bringing the girl and her folks bits of the food the army wasted every day, getting medicines, blankets,

149

khaki shirts. Half of Naples was in fatigues. They would have given us all their women for three cans of beans and some DDT. I'll tell you, DDT saved Europe. Now it's a big villain. It saved lives; I saved lives."

Steven was becoming annoyed. Why didn't Lon cut the excuses? Sometimes, in an interview, he would listen to skiers who had chosen to go out of bounds and then found themselves in trouble. Now and then he derived a certain wry pleasure in informing them that they had no case.

"Nina was a good kid," Lon said, measuring some wider space with his gaze. "She was like a kid, too—sweet, innocent." Steven shivered. "She was small, skinny, the way those hunger kids are. And the family made me feel like a king."

"She had a picture of you standing there with her family."

"Yeah, a buddy took it. I know what you're thinking, that I got her because she was like a kid and kept her that way because I needed to have kids. Why is that so bad? Look at the women we're supposed to think are sexy in the movies. Why do so many of them look like boys? Annina—you saw she was undeveloped. That's what war does to kids. She had a way about her that was like a little girl, too. She would laugh easy and cry even easier and she was scared of thunder and would run to me and put her head into my neck to get away from it. I thought I could stop loving the kids then, like I told you, and I did for a while."

"Loving—don't make me laugh. You knew what you were doing was dirty, disgusting. It was evil."

"Of course I knew, and I knew how dangerous it was. I've got the scars. You think I didn't want to be like other men, have a woman and a family, stop having to move all the time, stop being ashamed of myself?"

Steven felt blood pulsing around his eyes. "Then all those times you made us move, all those packing boxes scraping across the floor in the dark—sounds I learned to hate—all that was about your—"

"Need, sickness, compulsion."

"Evil."

"I want you to know I fought against doing what I did. I didn't let it ride over me, not till the very end. I want you to know that."

"All right, so what happened?"

"Life happened, and getting worn down happened. She got here, and for a while it was great. She was so bug-eyed and scared, and I was her protector. Then she learned enough English for jobs, cooking, cleaning places. We couldn't live with my folks—my dad wouldn't have that. So my brother let me stay in a place he owned."

"It was in that house in Callan near the old folks."

"You remember that?"

"I hunted it up after Mama died. I took the kids there. It's lucky I did, because both houses are gone now. They're under a big new highway interchange and a development." His father's face was expressionless. "I'm sorry—go on."

"I thought I'd whipped it, the need I had. When it came back, I tried different things, praying, fasting, getting away on the bike. Nothing worked. I knew a guy who cut his own balls off. I was afraid to do that."

"I can believe it."

"I was afraid it wouldn't work. Yeah, well." Lon shifted on the couch as the sound of the machine changed. "When this is over, I'll have to go to bed. It wears you out, dialysis, and you're dog meat all day and into the next. Then there's a regular day, and the day after that you start dimming down. I'll do this again, the day after that. Twice a week. Every three months or so, I have to have transfusions. If I turn any

151

of it down, they send a psychiatrist in. Bobby over there, he turned it down and said they should let him die. The psychiatrist said that meant he was nuts, so they put him on all kinds of drugs, which his kidneys have to handle." He was looking at a large black man across the ward. Next to him lay two men who were handcuffed to their couches. "Those guys are nuts, but if the state doesn't keep them alive, there'll be screaming from all of our protectors."

The aide returned and heard what Lon had just said. He began to turn off the machine. "What are you grousing about?" he said testily. The two were silent. With no particular gentleness, but competently enough, the aide disengaged Lon from the machine, checking, winding, hooking and unhooking. He turned to Steven. "Help him up, will you? They're woozy afterward, and I've got all these others to do." He pushed the machine back against the wall.

Steven shrank from physical closeness to his father, but there seemed to be no choice. The aide, on his way to the next man, pulled Lon's sleeve down over the bump in his inner elbow, where there was an implanted shunt to take the twice-weekly needle. Lon looked at Steven. "I can get up on my own." He put one leg over the edge of the couch and then the other, prepared to swivel himself around. Seven bent over and took the thin arm, squeamish because of the implant. Lon turned his body and clung to Steven until he could get his feet under him. They moved without grace; Steven, unused to the technique and unwilling, was clumsier than he thought he could be.

They were standing very close. Lon was a full head shorter. Steven felt the flesh of Lon's upper arm beneath the thin shirt, pouchy and hanging where the loss of muscle tissue had left the skin empty as a pocket. The touch made him queasy, as though he had

152

caught some of his father's illness. "What's it like for you to be here?"

Lon swayed a little and came up straight again. "The first twenty years are the hardest." He gave a dry chuckle. "But when you get it that this is your life and there's nobody to impress or move, you make a place for yourself, and it's not too bad. I learned what the good jobs were and got some of them; I worked to get a good cell placement; I learned what classes and extras to sign up for, and what advantages to get from letting people study me. Study, not treat. Before I got sick I had a fair setup, and even now I'm as good as free within the system." He had begun to breathe a little harder as he spoke.

Steven said, "There's a wheelchair—over there. I'll get it."

"No," Lon said. "If I take it slow, we can walk. There's an elevator. God, I remember this prison before we got air conditioning. Wait—I'll be all right in a minute." They stood, Steven holding his father, wishing it could be without disgust. They began a shuttling walk. "It's okay," Lon said. "Don't sweat it."

Chapter Twenty

Because of all the traveling he did, Steven tried to keep his car in top shape, but driving back to Denver, the afternoon heat was so severe that he kept a watch on the temperature square for the trouble light. There was no leisure for the scenic trip this time; it was hot highway there and back.

Connie lay stretched out in the backyard hammock, which she had moved to the cramped but cooler north side of the house. "This is nice," he said, "and the garbage cans add just the right down-home touch, don't you think?"

"I made a salad," she said dreamily. "The air conditioner is on the blink again and it's too hot to cook."

Here it was, and Steven felt relief. "Connie, let's eat our salad and bring the coffee out here. It's been a long hard day and I have something important to tell you."

"What is it?"

"I can't do it all at once. It's got too many parts."

She got out of the hammock, looking intently at him, and he all but saw her mind beginning to pick over the possibilities: medical—that he was ill, very ill; business—that bad trouble had happened in the practice. Was he being sued for something serious? A friend's husband had told her suddenly that he wanted a divorce; another that he was seeing a lover, a man. Which was this to be? "No—don't worry, please. It's—it's all right," he said.

She brought out the salad, rolls, and coffee, and he helped, putting the food out on the wooden porch table in silence, relieved at the comparative coolness of the yard. There was enough space there so that the sounds from the neighbors were muted by shrubbery and trees.

They ate hesitantly. He saw she was still anxious. "This needs to be said, Con; I've been carrying it long enough."

He introduced his subject in the lawyerlike way to which she had become reconciled years ago. It was the way he had proposed marriage, the way he had introduced his going off on his own when he had been doing well with Blakely and Milan.

He began with Annina's death, reminding her how they had searched the old valise and not found a death certificate for his father. He saw her face ease. This wasn't to be basic or essential to their lives. He said that he had mentioned the absence of a certificate to Terry, that Terry had casually, almost absentmindedly, played with the skip-trace program on his computer. He told her of Terry's learning that Alonzo Howe—Lon Howe—had not died after all, but was in prison, had been in prison since 1957.

He felt her listening intently, but she offered nothing, waiting, perhaps, for all of what he had to tell her. He forced himself along. He told her about his visits. "I know it sounds as though I've been keeping this from you—and in a way, I guess I have. I wanted to be sure, to know what he was like, before I told you." He couldn't discern in the shadowless afterglow if she were pale or if her stillness was disbelief or simply patience, an intensely focused waiting to hear the whole story.

"First I thought the sentence might be for murder. I had the idea of a bar fight and thought that maybe he had been fighting in prison also, or been in other trouble that would explain his long sentence. But it wasn't murder."

"What was it?"

He couldn't say the words immediately. He began moving their plates. "It was child molesting."

"Oh my God." Her hand rose quickly. "That can't be."

He spoke on. "No, listen, Con. The little girl who died was run over by accident, by another person. I've looked up the records. It wasn't felony murder, murder as we imagine it, it was accidental, really, and he's been paying for it—is still paying. . . ."

He stopped. Connie sat absolutely still, saying nothing. The afterglow had given way to dusk. He had purposely moved to stand facing away so as to spare Connie his courtroom technique of the level gaze. Now he turned and looked at her. Her hands were gripping the edges of the redwood table as though a wind or a wave might sweep her away.

"Connie?"

"Let me catch my breath." Some moments passed. "I should be used to hearing about men who do that, all those priests who were predators. Are you telling me that your father is one of those?"

"Yes, one of those."

"With boys?"

"Boys or girls."

"That's not supposed to be, either. It's supposed to be one or the other."

"Sometimes it's both."

"And it was so bad that they sent him to prison for life?"

"A death happened—a girl was killed running away from him."

156

"He raped them?"

"He says no. He says he fondled them. I can't be sure. The papers and the charges don't tell what he did. They dump it all into one big designation."

"It makes me sick."

Steven remembered how ill he had been when he had seen the headline in the *Ute River Voice*, the first delighted recognition of the picture and then the overwhelming sickness and horror.

"Listen, Connie—I'm still me; we're still us. My father's compulsion has nothing to do with me or with us."

"And you saw him? You talked to him?"

"Yes. He molested children, but he says he was never violent with them, never."

"Never mind. . . ."

"He's also a sick old man and what he suffers from isn't contagious."

"I think it is. I feel sick. It's awful. I can't talk about this yet. Don't ask me to think about it any more tonight."

"Connie—only this. You know me; you know Annina—knew Annina. Lon Howe is not a monster. We can go down to visit him, and you'll see. Ask the guards, the people who know him. . . . Think of the suffering Annina must have gone through, the terror, the shame."

"It's not Annina we're talking about. It's your father who abuses children."

"He's still only a man. Connie, Lon never murdered anyone, and I'm not defending what he did, but . . ."

He stopped speaking. He saw her trembling. They stood facing each other.

Connie said, "What have you given us?"

"If the man had been *your* father?"

"He couldn't have been. That's what's awful, that some people are predators and they look like anybody else, and act normal, but they're not. My father could never be like that. How can you say such a thing?"

She turned abruptly and went into the house. And as he came close, he heard through the open door not her usual purposive movements, the competence of familiar action bringing order out of chaos, but her stop-and-go steps. A piece of silverware clattered to the floor. Something scraped against a pot.

He brought in the plates and the half-eaten salad and went back outside, where he sat down to wait in what was now darkness. At last, the few stars the city's glare allowed for appeared. Steven realized he had to go in. He pulled himself up from the bench and went through the kitchen to the living room. She was watching TV, but when he glanced at the set, he saw that it was a program to which she would never have given a minute of her time.

They went to bed with only the necessary words. The bed was king-size and so perfect in design that one partner might never know if the other were sharing it.

Chapter Twenty-one

Connie was up early, dressed and ready to go out, when Steven got downstairs to have his breakfast. "I didn't want to go before I saw you," she said. "I was in shock, I guess, and I said things I shouldn't have said."

"So how is it now?"

"I feel like somebody with altitude sickness."

"I'm still me, Connie; we're still who we were before. My father's compulsion has nothing to do with me or with us. The man, though—I've seen him, and I want to see him again."

"My worry isn't about what he can do to me, but his compulsion, as you call it, does affect us. People are learning that genetics is the"—she shaped the words with her hands—"the base, the bottom of what we are. We have diseases; we pass them on. I've been up all night—maybe you were, too—seeing the pictures of what your father did to those children, and how that evil might go on down the generations."

Steven had slept relatively well. His relief at finally opening up to Connie had overwhelmed his tension and unhappiness at her response. "I want to tell you to look at me carefully, and at the kids. Have they changed in your mind between yesterday evening and now?"

"I see those pictures in my head, what child abusers do, and then I see that picture of your father. . . ."

159

"What pictures are you seeing, Con? I think I know. Rape, murder. He never did those things."

"I'm not ready to hear about him. Give me some time."

"I will, all the time you need, and I need to apologize for keeping what I knew from you after I had found out. It would have been better if we had both learned all this together."

She gave him a wan look. "Who else knows?"

He took a deep breath. "Terry found out, which I told you, and I told the rest of the committee."

"Your lunch friends?"

"Lunch friends" made the group sound too casual for what his relationship with Terry, Paul, and Jack was and had been for years. "Connie, I'm sorry. I wanted to find a way, some way to tell you so that you wouldn't take this so hard. Lon Howe isn't a monster. I'm not saying that anyone can forget what he did, but he's spent almost fifty years in prison. He's in prison now. I needed to go there and see him. I'll need to keep going, because I lost a past when I lost him, and I need to clear up who he is and what really happened."

"Don't you know how they hide, those people, how they look and act normal and seem normal? Ted Bundy had friends. Jeffrey Dahmer looked like the boy next door."

"I don't want to talk about people who have nothing to do with who Lon is or what he did."

"All right," she said, "all right."

They went to work.

A run of clients appeared, as they sometimes did, for which he used all his persuasive skill to advise each to carry his case no further. Kindle had been drinking at the lodge in sufficient amounts to cause the staff to take notice. Frailey had been skiing in the trees and had not been in control. The Oslers claimed that Arlette, five, was a good-enough skier to be negotiating heavy powder alone.

The good news came in a final settlement to the Todd Harmon case. There would be no appeal of the generous judgment, and money would come for Todd's rehabilitation and all the care he needed if he couldn't work. Steven called the Harmons and Mrs. Harmon expressed their gratitude. "Todd works hard, and if he's able to be proud of the progress he's making, I think he'll be happy. He still mentions your visit."

The spring and early-summer wedding season was over, and in August, Steven and Connie usually took two weeks and did a little traveling. "I was supposed to plan," Connie said, "but Annina died, and Jennifer's trouble came, and then . . . well, I just don't feel like going anywhere."

"Let's not, then. I can use two weeks off. I want to go through the house and see what needs doing. Remember, we should find a way to catch the rain that's running down the side of the garage."

Connie opened her mouth for the words she had used throughout their marriage—"Okay, pioneer." She stopped before she had drawn the breath.

Steven had always done just minimal repairs on his house or car, but when Connie had first learned that the Howes had homesteaded in the Ute Valley, she had seen them and, by extension, him as having gifts of handiness and a knowledge of nature she assigned to the early settlers. He'd laughed and fallen in with the idea, looking up at a bell-clear sky and predicting the rain he'd heard about on the weather report he listened to while shaving. Now the joke, the fun of the fantasy, had been shattered and replaced by pained silence.

"What if we took a day or two and went out to see Jennifer?" Steven said. "We can check out one of her plays, if there's one on."

"Maybe," Connie said. "I'll talk to her about it."

Three days later, Steven said, "When are we going to tell the kids?"

"Are you crazy? Why?"

"Because if we don't, they may find out on their own. You're the one who investigates this lineage business. Don't you think it'll occur to Mike that my side of the equation is missing? He's already moving toward it, thinking you'll be pleased by what he produces. Terry got the information; why shouldn't Mike? Isn't it better that we tell everyone and not be haunted by their finding it out? Con, part of your anger is that we didn't learn all this together. You feel betrayed."

"Don't tell me what I feel."

"I haven't done well by keeping this from you. I don't plan to make the same mistake again. The kids'll have to be told, and so will your family, I think, and soon."

"Don't you see? Telling the kids will ruin the picture they have of who they are. I grew up proud of my family and it gave me a good childhood and a boost through the tougher years, a boost I very much needed. You'll be hurting them, ruining some good image in them."

"I hope their understanding of who they are has been pretty well set by now, and I think the Scotts are a little too pleased with themselves anyway. This is reality. Lon Howe's existence isn't anything we can finesse or control. It's here."

"Why? You didn't know about it last year. What's to stop us from simply forgetting it?"

They had endured angry moments before, mostly as a consequence of their personality quirks. Steven's

162

past poverty and the caution it bred seemed to Connie like stinginess; her overconcern for her appearance and her impulse buying worried him. He disapproved of the exaggerated demands of the children, which she overlooked. She sometimes thought him inconsiderate. They fought about vacations. Their disagreements, however, had never overshadowed the good times or the positive parts of their marriage and had seldom interfered with their satisfying sex life. Connie was a joyous, eager bed partner, even though her pleasure reflected her general mood more directly than his did. His needs were less determined by his daily ups and downs.

He began to imagine himself telling Jennifer, Jeremy, and Mike, sometimes separately, sometimes together. Each of them would take the news differently, he thought. Their personalities were very different. Each would react differently. He imagined Jennifer being intrigued by the drama of the story. The plays she costumed were set in superheated moments. Jeremy might turn away and not wish to go deeper. He was more judgmental than Jennifer, more self-protective. Mike would wonder about his own responses; he would place himself in the molester's role for a few moments, sympathizing, wanting, more than Steven had ever wanted, to know what Lon's life was like, what his thoughts were.

"Are you doing this on purpose?" He had been held up at the office again.

"I call, Con. I always call."

"You call when dinner's already up and it's too late to matter, when I've already canceled my evening."

"I call as soon as I know."

"And the towels."

"What towels?"

"The towels you leave on the floor after your shower. I feel like a servant, picking up after you."

"That hasn't happened in years."

"It happened this morning."

"I was late and it was a court day."

"Annina always picked up after you."

"Connie, I'm going to Cañon City again, so get used to the idea. Look—there are books about this we can read together and learn."

"No."

"There's even an article in the *Law Journal.*"

"Not interested."

"Why, because he's my family and not yours? You and your mom were Johnny-on-the-spot when Grandma Scott started to go downhill. You and Suzanne stayed with her, spelling each other at the job, keeping her alive. If Annina had been ill, I know you would have done the same. Why not stretch it a little further?"

"Not for a monster," she said.

Interrogatories were in process for *Peppiat v. Catania.* The respondent had, for a prank, removed danger flags from a rocky area and replaced them downhill of the obstruction. Criminal charges had been filed; civil damages would be high. The insurance lawyers were friendly and took Steven to lunch at an upscale restaurant, where he never would have gone himself. Opposing counsel all skied, and during the meal they regaled him with stories of trips they had taken, trips combining legal work with ski vacations in foreign countries. Their status play and self-promotion were expressed in talking about such travel and in name-dropping, mentioning the colleges their children attended and the trips they'd made. "Kendra's in India now, on a Yale study expedition. She'll be gone a year." "Justin is in Siam, doing photography." Steven fought a desire to say, "Jeremy is on the moon, collecting for our rock garden. Mike is in Cañon City, visiting his grandfather."

When he thought objectively of this new form of status inflation, he was proud that if his kids wanted a year abroad, he could afford it. Perhaps they were cutting their dreams to his more modest pattern and would in time come to feel cramped in what he had tailored. Connie had accepted his need for a careful, debt-free existence, but she disliked his anxiety, his worry that the prosperity they now enjoyed could melt away overnight into nothing. The life she had with Steven was narrower than the lives of her sister and brothers. It sometimes made her feel imprisoned, but he reminded her that it was liberating to spend less than you earned.

Chapter Twenty-two

Jeremy came in occasionally from his summer work at the conference center in Estes Park. He radiated a new sense of contentment. The people at the center were pleased with the job he was doing, he told his parents. "This year, I'm not a mere Indian—I'm one of three chiefs, and that means I do it all, from helping unload cars to assigning conference rooms and setting up any equipment that's needed. We handle meetings of every size, from conventions to family reunions. I even take group pictures."

"I can tell you're enjoying it," Steven said, "but what makes the work so interesting?"

"Challenges of all kinds—there's always something coming up, always something new."

They could see he was steadier, less manic than he had been studying chemistry in the winter at school. "There are all the conferences," he told them, "religious-study groups, business-management seminars, writers' workshops, Aikido conventions—I can dip into any one of those I'm interested in and leave when I'm called away."

Late in August he came home again, and stayed the night. At breakfast, he announced, "They've offered me a full-time job—assistant manager. The pay is good, I'll set my own hours, and there's the possibility of advancement to manager, which can be very well paid. There's a medical and retirement package. If I stay for a year, I'll get a house on the grounds. If I get

married, a wife and I could make a career in it together."

"What about college?" Steven asked.

"If I go into the position, I'll have a contract. The
job doesn't require a business degree, but if I want
one, I'll be able to pick it up at CU."

"Have you decided?"

"I think so."

Later, Steven and Connie talked. "Are you happy
about Jeremy?"

"What can I do about it? He's there and that's that.
Like certain other things, I have no say." She was
sitting on the bed, putting moisturizer on her face.

"I think that after awhile he'll decide to go to
college, probably part-time, the way I did."

"And that's okay with you?"

"No—I wanted college life for all the kids, but the
decision is theirs."

She got into bed and turned away.

A week later, Jeremy called from Estes Park. "We
have a packed campground and the center's full for
Labor Day, or it was until one of the reunions canceled. Why don't you get Gram and Grandpa to move
their Labor Day bash up here? I want to give you a
tour of the place, and I've initiated some things I'd
like to show you. Why not bring the party up here on
Sunday and go home on Monday. Hot tubs, buggy
rides—what do you think?"

The Scotts' Labor Day picnic was a tradition going
back to Connie's childhood, but her mother and father
surprised Steven with their immediate agreement. "I'll
call Jeremy myself," Barbara Scott said, "and set
things up." Neither of the elder Scotts had mentioned
their genetic testing, which had cleared them and their
family of being the cause of Jennifer's condition. They
were cautious about discussing it in front of Steven,
and were so tactful as to seem uninterested. In

Connie's sister and brother, the silence rang like an accusation.

Steven called Jennifer, who sounded eager to come.

"I want to see everybody. It's been a hectic time and it'll be good to get away, even if it's only for the weekend."

"How are things going, Jen?"

"Fine. Did you get the pictures I sent?"

"Yes. I think we'll start a scrapbook."

"I'll see if I can get in on Friday."

Connie was beaming when she hung up the phone. "I'm so glad she's coming."

"How did she sound?"

"Fine. She always sounds fine. She would sound fine if she was wandering in a jungle at midnight."

"The kids will miss Annina at the party. She would have liked it up there. She so seldom got out of the city."

"I was good to your mother. I won't see your father."

"Connie, give it a rest, will you? While we're there, I want to take the opportunity to get the kids together and tell them about Lon."

"No—you can't."

"Connie. . ."

"You can't. Not yet. Promise me you won't."

"They'll have to know sooner or later. I won't wait until they find out by accident. Their grandfather is alive and they need to know that."

"Sometime, not now. Promise me you'll wait a while, until . . ."

"Until when?"

"Until they're old enough."

"Forty or fifty?"

"Not yet, *please*. Promise me."

"All right. I'll wait, but we can't put this off too long."

She softened. "I know you appreciate what I did for Annina."

"Her dying took all the answers away. I miss her. And I miss what she took with her. What did she feel about him? About what he had done? Did she really know?"

"I don't want to talk about him, not a word."

"This has been some year," he said, "and it's still not over."

"I feel like a punch-drunk fighter. The wrong person died," she said. "If only that other one had died."

Jennifer came in on Saturday and Jeremy picked her up at the airport. By the time they reached the house, they were arguing.

"About what?" Steven asked.

"About gas prices in Peru," Connie declared, "about the number of stars in the sky. Those two never needed a specific topic."

While she spoke, Steven saw Connie evaluating Jennifer out of the corner of her eye, and he was glad for Jeremy's argument, which reestablished the normality of the day.

Sunday's weather cooperated. It was mild and warm in Denver, although they all knew it might be another climate entirely in the mountains where they were headed. The four of them filled Steven's Explorer with talk and laughter. They had coffee, pop, and fruit for the hour-and-a-half ride to the campground and conference center. The trunk of the car held Connie's bean casserole, as well as their big insulated box of meats, punch, and picnic supplies.

The first wrangle of the day was whether to drive the highway or to take the longer route, traveling on scenic roads now all but deserted. Connie and Jennifer wanted the remembered route they had used before beltways moved in, malling and blurring the dozen small towns between Denver and the mountains. "We have lots of time," Connie reasoned. The men gave in with token complaint.

The ride was pleasant at slower speed, with the intimacy to the landscape the narrower roads afforded. Mike talked about losing a girlfriend and finding another; Jennifer told about technical advances in the work she was doing. "The whole process of buying and fitting has changed because of the computer. You have the measurements of the entire cast, cost of labor and material for each one."

"You kids are so at ease with the computer," Connie said, "I'm still a novice."

Steven thought, Thank God Mike hasn't decided to play genetics on his.

"It's going to save me," Jennifer said. "That little screen—as long as I can see at all, I can focus on that little screen."

She hadn't been so direct before. At the time young people rise into selfhood and independence, she'd been shot down by her condition and had to be careful not to say anything that would bring them galloping to her aid. Connie was unable to stop herself. "Wouldn't it be better if you lived here, where everything is familiar?"

"Ma, don't plan it. Don't work on it, please."

So Steven listened, his jaw tight. He, too, wanted Jennifer home. Connie kept urging him to apply the force of his logic to reason her home.

"You could get somebody to work with you for all the hands-on stuff," Mike was saying, "while you just designed. You could get projects from all over the country."

"Put a stopper in it, will you?" Jennifer could say to Mike what she couldn't say to Connie. "I'm not a dress designer; I'm a costume designer. I need to be in the same world as the directors, actors, set designers.

'Great cape, Jen, but it's cumbersome onstage and hides the actor's face.' 'Great long scarf, Jen, but it might strangle the leading lady if it got caught in the furniture.' I don't want to sit at a computer; I want to be in the mix, in *life*."

She had become intense. Protect and defend, his fatherhood commanded, but how is it done to help and not harm? He caught himself going over the yellow line and a driver coming the other way hit the horn.

Chapter Twenty-three

Connie had been right to press for the scenic route, because it lifted their mood, and by the time they got to the conference center, Jen and Mike were wrangling about nonsense and enjoying themselves. Connie and Steven were enjoying the landscape.

Jeremy put them into the hands of an assistant, then disappeared. The assistant was a pert young girl. "His folks! Did you have a good trip? We got you a suite in the Aspen pod." Steven smiled and caught Connie's eye. They had a family joke about the Aspen Room in every hotel and of Aspen Street, Drive, and Way in every development all over the state. Behind him, Mike subdued a guffaw.

The Scotts were in full cry in the suites next to theirs. "Jeremy must have worked like a maniac to do all this. The staff will cater what we bring." Steven was grateful for the noise, the family jokes, and all the traditional fussing, into which Connie disappeared as daughter, sister, and aunt. When he visited the prison again, he wouldn't tell her and she wouldn't ask. Now they were unpacking the big cake—Connie's blueberry, strawberry, whipped cream specialty. The picnic would be held in a grove within easy walking distance. Mike, Jennifer, and the cousins began to take the baskets to the grove, where there was a fireplace ready with charcoal.

Steven saw Tony Scott, who waved him over for a drink—his very good scotch—and they sauntered over to the tables that were being readied. "Women like all the fuss, but I could eat lunch meat on a bun," Tony said.

Steven nodded. "The liquor would have to be as good as this."

"Oh, I saw one of your cases in the paper a few days ago. Big win."

"Not that big. The decision was so far overboard that the defendants will appeal, and it'll get scaled back."

Steven liked Connie's father, a tolerant, easygoing man. They watched the setting up.

Jeremy appeared, checked things, disappeared, then reappeared. Steven began to understand the attraction the job held for him. The work was active, physically engaging, and detailed. There were fifteen other parties going on at the same time, of which Jeremy was indirectly the host. He seemed on top of his game: his family members were his guests, and he was in and out of the other suites and pods, checking on the other parties, pleasant, helpful, and in command.

Soon the family gathered, babies and toddlers there to provide the uproar. The techniques of classical grill cookery were argued over; there were the familiar bathroom runs, falls and scrapes, howlings, wet washcloths, sticky fingers, mustard in hair, Frisbees in trees, an argument over how to cut the watermelon. Jeremy was everywhere. Steven also noticed that he and Mike were unobtrusively looking out for Jennifer, who had several times been on the verge of stumbling or dropping what she carried or bumping into things she hadn't seen. Babies and small children were outside her visual field, and now and then Mike would lure one of them out of her way.

Steven found himself swinging between awe and annoyance. Jennifer wanted to play her part to the fullest, carrying picnic things, helping children, eating, laughing, unaware of near misses with knives, pitchers of juice, and babies' heads. Only once did he catch her in a clouded moment, and that was when all the older cousins went to where there was a volleyball court and began to play. She had begun to follow them as they went, all of them making up a parody of a rap song Steven didn't know. He saw her stop and sweep the group, like the slow pan of a video or movie camera, taking in the scene. Then she turned away and walked slowly back to the picnic tables, studying the ground.

Later, the women decided on a hike through the woods, and Steven saw Jennifer weighing the proposition and deciding against it. The moment might have been sad, but Tony called her to help him. The men, being left alone with the children, organized a relay race, in which anyone who could walk participated. The final section was run by two toddlers who didn't know what a race was and kept wandering off the course. Everyone got hoarse cheering. Jeremy returned. "I'm free for a while. Later, I'll be running a film."

In the evening, he gave Connie and Steven a tour and they met the other two managers of the area, an older man in charge of the campground and a woman who ran the cafeteria and did the catering. Jeremy managed the conference center. He had a staff of nine. "And he's only twenty-one," Connie whispered to Steven as they watched him with staff in the open reception area. His style seemed friendly but authoritative. They knew he had taken them on this tour so that they might see him to advantage. Three women came up to him, dressed in the light green uniforms of the center. Steven and Connie watched him explaining something as he received their nods of understanding. "Wow," Connie said, "I wonder if he staged all this."

Steven murmured to her, "It would be tempting."

On Monday, they didn't gather until after lunch, when Tony and Barbara and many of the cousins would be leaving for Denver and taking Jennifer to the airport. It was another warm, windless day. After lunch, Jennifer said good-bye and left with them. She had argued over their taking her to the gate. "I'm not an invalid—you can just drop me off."

"Silly creature, it gives us time together," Barbara said.

Tony took her arm and said, "Honey, learn to accept loving help gracefully. It's going to be a part of your life."

Steven shook his head, marveling at how she accepted the words and the help from her grandparents that she would never allow from Connie or from him.

Connie went off with her sister. Steven found a lawn chair in the sun and shadow of a pine tree, then turned the chair away from the center building so no one would see him and feel a need to come over for a talk. He lay limp in the canvas seat and let the afternoon bless him with soft sunshine. He dozed, letting his mind go.

When he woke, a little boy had come to a sandbox that lay at the other end of the small strip of ground. The child wasn't one of theirs, so Steven felt free to do no more than enjoy his presence. He began to watch the boy, who, he guessed, was about four, dipping water out of a bucket into the sand and making mounds in the sun, patting them with care and a certain aesthetic judgment. The child was talking to himself animatedly. His contentment, his absorption in his work, was complete, but after making five mounds, he seemed to tire. Abruptly, he stood up, turned, and realized he was alone. His face creased with worry and he began to cry.

Steven saw Jeremy coming out of the campground's woods. He stopped when he saw the little boy, came close, and squatted before him so that their faces were level. Steven heard the sound of their voices, Jeremy's friendly and engaging. Jeremy rose and took the little boy's hand. They began to walk away together, the boy looking up at Jeremy, squinting in the late sun.

Steven was struck with a horror so overwhelming that he was momentarily unable to move. The boy and the man. Lon Howe had sought work where there were children. What better cover could a molester find than a campground, where everyone felt relaxed and safe enough to let kids play by themselves? Who would question an employee seen with a little child? What if that compulsion were genetic also, murmuring its coded message down the generations? His rational mind was no match for the picture that had been summoned up.

The pair was walking toward the center and then past it, around to its side. Steven's heart was beating in his throat. If he ran and caught up to them, what could he say? He began to frame reasons and excuses he could offer if he showed up breathless and red-faced. He would be forced to explain, and what could he explain? You look like the Howes. Your body—its compactness—and your coloring are like my father's. Steven had argued the obvious, that he had none of Lon's propensities and that his sons were clear of them. He and Connie had conceived their children under another set of truths from what was now emerging, all this gene thing to explain everything from shyness to obesity. They had worked all through the growing years of those beloved children in the belief that how they were raised was what they would become, predictably, as sparks fly upward.

So he stood in the late sunlight, unmoving and unable to extricate himself from the tangle of pictures and conflicting ideas. Jeremy's obvious gifts for organization, his love of novelty and challenge, his ease with people, particularly children, all were part of his personality, a successful, charming part, and suited him uniquely for his job here.

All that wit and skill might be used at the service of darker things.

Connie found him standing, stunned, in the twilight. The afternoon was cooling and it was time to leave.

Chapter Twenty-four

Steven would never tell Connie what he had seen at the campground and what his imagination had made of it. With all the anger she had already, she would turn his fears back on him. The gap between them was widening. Everyone had praised the weekend and been delighted with Jeremy. His confidence and competent management offset the family's disappointment at his not finishing college.

Connie had a run of late-summer garden weddings. Steven had a short lull. "We're out of sync again," he said, and they both realized that even if they had been free, they wouldn't have wanted to go away together.

"Con, I kept my promise at the party, and now I want to tell the kids. The secret isn't going away; it's getting worse."

"No, not yet. Wait."

"They'll find out."

"They haven't until now."

"The fact is hanging in the air like a vapor we can't force back into the bottle."

"What do you do with poisonous vapor? You get rid of it. You don't call the family in to smell it and get sick."

"When they find out, they'll also find out that we knew and kept it from them."

"Just the way you keep poison from the people you love."

"He's not poison. He's not a monster. He's a man, a person who is in prison for having committed terrible crimes, but he's the grandfather of your children."

"Why don't you stop reminding me? You get rid of poison, and speaking of getting rid of things, why don't you go downstairs and get rid of all that beer you have in the utility room."

"I got it for the guys, for the Fourth of July, and forgot to get it to them."

"It's been sitting there going flat."

"Connie, stick to the point."

"Going flat. . ."

Later in September, a day when the light cut everything it touched with perfect clarity, Steven headed south again to Cañon City. Lon had had his dialysis the day before and said he felt washed-out, but he looked better than at the previous visit. They sat outside in a small cleared space in back of the building. Now and then, Lon dozed, mouth slackly open, face relinquishing its frozen stoicism for something like trust. Waking, he would murmur a comment or two and then be still. Steven had never been able to appreciate the silence in which companionship flowed unimpeded. He was bruised by his disagreement with Connie and tired by the extra effort of the drive to the prison and the tensions of the check-in. A guard had told him that they all knew he was Lon's son. "How long did you think that lawyer story would last?"

"I *am* a lawyer."

"Not in here you're not."

At last, Lon seemed to wake more fully. Steven said, "Things aren't good at home. I want to tell the kids about you, that you're alive and that you're here. Connie says no. We argue about that."

"Why kick a hornet's nest? Last year I was dead and you had a fine family. Why fix that?"

"Because you're not dead and because I'm still coming down here and because in spite of what I know about you and the pictures I see in my head, I like you. The guard I first met said you were a good man, the woman at the desk likes you, and I believe them, and that means I have to wonder what a good man is. Part of me can't believe I'm saying this. Part of me is just scared that one of the kids will find out and blame me for my cowardice. Something bad happened a few weeks ago. I saw my son, the older one, with a kid, a little kid, and I panicked. It wasn't suspicion or any hint of something he might have done. It was a moment of blind fear."

"That what I have is catching?"

"What do you have that made you do that to children, that got you this?"

"A dozen theories. Take your pick."

Again, silence. From far away, the sounds of voices rose and fell. A summer indolence hung over the place, even as the summer was drawing to a close. "I haven't been a husband or a father in a long time," Lon said, "and I don't know what family life is like anymore."

"This isn't about family life; it's about people talking to one another. Something I need is here and I don't want to be ashamed of it."

"What is it? I don't have anything to offer you."

"I have very little of my childhood. There are a few disconnected memories of places I can't identify, and people who weren't related to me. Where did we go? What did you do. Your jobs, I mean."

"I can tell you some of those things. . . ."

Silence again. Then Steven asked, "Why did they give you life with no parole?"

"I came at the beginning of a scare, which we get every forty years or so. I'd been up before the same judge four or five times and then I took those

180

children, and that's kidnapping. I took them and I used them to masturbate. That's a sex crime. I felt it getting worse. I kept remembering Italy, when it was being offered to me, anything I wanted, for food. Then that little girl was run over. The scare blew us up. I was part of a job lot coming down here that year. Ten years later, only the killers and rapists were getting life sentences."

"Were you attracted to me like you were to the other children? Did you want to use me?"

"I think I was afraid I might as you got older. I was narrowing in my habit, but it was getting more intense."

"What should I tell your grandchildren?"

"Are they too swell for their own good? Do you think they need some humbling, and you'll use me to do it?"

"That's not the way I would put it."

"How *would* you put it?"

"Let's say there's a need—"

"I'm not someone's punishment."

"It came out that way. I'm sorry."

"I used the kids," Lon said. "I got into a terrible hunger and I needed to feed it; it was more powerful than I could stand. I was ashamed—I am ashamed—but I see now that I let you and Nina down, and I shouldn't have done that. I thought disappearing was protecting you, but it wasn't." Steven opened his mouth to say something, but Lon spoke first. "Don't talk about love, either, or faith. They're syrup words, like TV medicine, that are poured over everything from juvenile delinquency to war. Ask a drunk if he loves his wife and kids, and then ask him if so, why doesn't he stop drinking? Ask a believer on his knees why he can't stop the ideas he has even while he's praying. Some people can give up smoking; others

181

would rather die coughing. Where does love fit in, or faith?"

"There was a ranch you worked at. . . ."

"The Speyer place—that was up in Wyoming. I wouldn't think you could remember that."

"What happened?"

"It was the best job I ever had, but summers they'd have city kids up to visit. It was there I found out what would happen to me if I didn't use the kids. I was like a blind dog in a slaughterhouse, all but raving. I didn't touch one of them, but I had to quit. I lost hope after that."

"If I brought Jennifer, Jeremy, and Mike here, would you see them, talk to them?"

"Sure, if I'm not hooked up that day. I wouldn't want them to see me like that."

Lon's vanity surprised Steven, who raised an eyebrow.

"Look, I'm not a symbol, not only a prisoner, a child molester, or even a grandfather. I'm a man; I come with all the fittings."

"I'm aware of that," Steven said, and Lon surprised him with a chuckle.

"God, you didn't get that mouth from Annina's people; that mouth's pure Kendrick."

"Your mother's folks?"

"Those Kendricks raised more sand than the Howes ever did, though neither of those families was what you'd call chatty. The Howes were quiet; the Kendricks—you'd be home half an hour before you realized you'd been cut off at the knees."

"Why didn't you try harder? Why did you let the compulsion win?"

Steven's voice had risen.

Lon's stayed level. "I guess the biggest disappointment I ever had was when I prayed. I called on God and I gave myself up, believing in every way. I found that God couldn't help me. God was there, but my hunger was there, too, and when it came, it blotted out everything else, like the hand you put in front of your eyes blots out the sun."

Steven sighed. "I never had the talent of believing."

Lon said, "I did—I still do. Shame on you." And they laughed.

Lon pulled his chair out of the sun and sat down again, closer to Steven now. "All the interviews I've given, the studies, the probing, years of it. . . I did them partly as some payback, something to help science, to make myself feel less worthless. I never thought all those years were getting me ready to talk to you."

"I've been seeing you all this time, versions of you on your motorcycle. Now I think I see Mama driving a car, which she never could do."

"I tried to teach her, lots of times. Do you remember that?"

"No, I remember you on the motorcycle, riding it or fixing it. I kept seeing you on it, all these years. You never aged."

The sun had moved again and Lon got up to reposition the chair, but Steven rose quickly and took it from him, moving both chairs into the shade.

"I suppose I should answer your question," Lon said, "the first one you came here to ask. After I do, it'll probably be the end of these visits. The answer is no; none of us was blind anytime before old age. We run to skin things, rashes, impetigo, psoriasis. The Howes were heavy drinkers, but only one or two of them ended up drunks. They bred like rabbits but none of them was blind. The Kendricks—I remember many of them, but their history is wispy in my mind. Heart, I think, is what they died from. They got deaf in their old age, maybe because they were tired of the meanness they heard from one another. None of them was blind."

"I need to start back now. Is there anything you want me to bring next time?"

"No, but thanks."

"Is there anything you want to tell me?"

"This thing I did—that some of us do—this compulsion—if people wanted to, they could help us overcome it. They could put science on the problem. There are people who treat this, and they have successes. I'm not a monster."

Chapter Twenty-five

To leave, Steven had to check out at the front desk. He was turning from the guard's station when a woman came quickly toward him.

"Mr. Howe. . ." She looked harried and her clothes were wrong for her figure. The plastic ID card showed her smiling. Rare, he thought. Her skin was so perfect that she seemed healthier than the other prison personnel he had seen. "I wanted to talk to you before you left. I'm Janet Winters, a social worker here." She extended a hand and shook his manfully.

He stood without speaking, wondering why he felt caught out, compromised, as though he had lied. The response was an old one, due to years of welfare employees and caseworkers questioning him about his part-time jobs and any money he might have kept out of the monthly reckoning.

"I wanted to speak to you about your father," she said.

He felt a flippant reply beginning, but instead, he said, "Is there some problem?"

"If you can just stop for a moment at my office, just for a moment. . ."

He let out a breath in resignation.

She led him past a line of offices with names and positions; he had the feeling he was in that old Chaplin movie, *Modern Times*, watching Chaplin being caught in one of the great gears of the factory. The thought amused him and by then he was ready to hear what the woman had to say.

Her office was small and bare. He took the chair she indicated. She was saying, "Violent crime is a young man's game, and sentences for it have been getting heavier. For some sex crimes, juries give life sentences, meaning parole in twenty years. For others, the board doesn't want to let the offender go, especially if he hasn't had therapy or special counseling inside. The system fills with sick old men." She looked at Steven, expecting a murmur, a sign that he understood her. He didn't give her any help. "Then there are the drug convictions. We still have the drug offenders of the sixties, people that juries gave life sentences to, all getting old. Mr. Howe, we are by far the biggest geriatric facility in Colorado." She waited. He gave no word, just a little nod, and she went on. "Your father was one of those statute-mandated cases, life without parole. It was a travesty, of course—he never murdered anyone."

Steven thought: Three cheers.

She had seen that he knew what was coming and was arming himself against it. "Mr. Howe has never made an effort on his own behalf. He participated in a number of prison programs that might have persuaded the board to look favorably on his release, but he never put in for parole or mitigation of his sentence."

Steven gave no word. He was making her work.

"He's an old man now, a dying man, who'll be dying in prison."

"You're cutting slices off the octopus to make it look better on the plate," Steven said, "but it's still an octopus." He thought she might laugh, smile, loosen up, but he saw then that she was well-meaning, earnest, and utterly without humor. "Okay," he said, "tell me."

186

"With a court order, you might have him removed from here, placed in your custody. He might die with dignity, out of prison."

"Don't you think I know that a move like that would make me financially responsible for him, including his dialysis, all his medical costs?"

"He's your father. You look pretty prosperous to me, a lawyer. Why shouldn't you carry your part of the load?"

"Because the state took over my father's life and made what it wanted out of him. He had lots of people testing and evaluating him, students getting degrees, papers getting written, theories getting made, but no meaningful therapy. The work was all for the students and the doctors, not for him."

"By the time the sex offenders come to us, therapy is less successful. At his age, we think these people can be safely returned to the community."

"What's a community? Who's 'we'?"

"We think—"

"I think you want to stop paying for my father's incarceration because he's sick and old and expensive, and no longer a danger. You never really treated him or prepared him for life outside. Now this is where he lives; this is his community."

"The community we mean—"

"Come on, what community is that? A nursing home? Our house? My wife can barely hear his name mentioned, and she's a woman I never would have called bigoted. Our sons and daughter are unaware of his existence. Do you know what reception he'll get from the schools and churches in our nice neighborhood, from our neighbors?"

"Are you that concerned about what your upscale neighbors think?"

"You're damn right I am. I don't want any drive-by mudslinging. I don't want my neighbors hating me because having a registered sex offender in the house lowers home values all over the neighborhood."

"I know that the so-called Megan's Law has had a chilling effect. . . ." Her gaze lowered, but he bored his own into her the moment she looked up.

"That law provides that when a sex offender comes into your fabled *community*, said community must be made aware of his presence there. What possible chance would my father have for a normal life? That old man would signal open season for every macho bully and wanna-be vigilante in a ten-mile area. He'd be on the Internet and so would we—name, address, phone, fax, and E-mail."

"You could put him in a nursing home."

"What do you bet the good ones wouldn't accept a sex offender and the bad ones would be worse than here?"

"They're overcrowding the facility."

"Not my problem."

Even to his own ears he sounded cold, as though he had said, Let him die in jail. Don't bother me.

"He'll have Medicaid anyway, so what are you worried about?"

"I'm a lawyer, as you reminded me, and I'm aware that if I contract to underwrite any part of my father's care, I will be legally responsible for all of it. He's a sick old man, but he's also a stranger, someone I thought was dead. If I followed your plan, I'd be wiped out financially. What you're asking is impossible."

Outside the barred window, a tree had begun to make the transition from summer green to a drier olive color. The leaves had gone papery, making a scraping sound in the developing breeze, which, in the evening, would work itself into a wind.

Ms. Winters reinstituted eye contact with a baleful stare. "You have a responsibility," she said. "Wealth and social position shouldn't be protecting you."

"Hire a hall. Go on TV," he said, and left.

He used the long trip home to shout in the car, and he was still shouting as he pulled up to a traffic light on the outskirts of Denver. The driver in the next car, a young man, flipped his thumb up in approval.

Connie was at a meeting, Mike at a late class. Steven turned off the electric crock-pot, where his dinner was warming, and sat in the dusk, watching the day fade. He went to his CD cabinet and chose a Scarlatti disc, which he played louder than he would ordinarily have. Years ago, Connie had introduced him to classical music, concerts, theater. His deepest everyday pleasures had come from her, but now he felt a bitter, thwarted annoyance at her. He wished he could make her more sympathetic. She had conceded to him before in her bright, kind way. She'd understood his drawing back before the cheerful inundation of her family, his caution about food, money, change. This challenge, of course, was different. Her fear and love were bound up in protection, her loathing in what she saw Lon Howe doing in her imagination. He sat in the dark and let the music cleanse his mind with its intricate rational mathematics, the restrained order that had often stunned him with its beauty.

Chapter Twenty-six

Although the spring wedding season was so much a part of her family life that Connie was attuned to it subliminally, the autumn wedding had become almost as popular, forming a bump in the gradual incline in the year's long silhouette.

Her work piled up and Connie began looking harried. The weddings Ring and Wreath organized were becoming larger and more detailed. There were now two every Saturday and one every Sunday in October and November, the maximum Connie could handle. It had become fashionable to marry in the mountains and she had begun to travel some distance to rural churches. Mike, who helped, and was employed by the business on weekends, described the process for Steven. "Two mule trains leave Denver, twenty mules in each, starting at daybreak. Each pulls four loaded Conestoga wagons up into the mountains. Scouts and outriders guard the lead wagon, which carries the cake and champagne."

"It sounds like it takes all your mom's organizing skills."

"It's more than that. I've been to lots of Ring and Wreath's weddings by now, and I think the hardest part of any of them is dealing with the personalities of the participants. Grooms show up drunk or spaced on drugs; brides go wild, throw up, break down; in-laws get into the act. High-heels collapse, dresses tear, and maids of honor remember old grudges. Sisters tussle;

190

mothers have vapors, fathers heart attacks. Last week, they had to move the ceremony off a mountain at the last minute because of an avalanche warning, and the bride's language would have made a biker blush. Mom sails through it all, not being cute or too sweet, just kind of serene. People look at her and their blood pressure goes down."

Steven had often been awed by Connie's descriptions of wedding crises. He couldn't help wondering how she could mastermind all the problems Mike described and be at such a loss when it came to sitting with her own sons and daughter while he told them about Lon Howe. He had kept his fears about Jeremy from her, too, saying, "He looks like a Howe, but he's a Scott in his tact and organization skills."

Steven had told her that he would meet with the kids at Thanksgiving and give them the facts about their grandfather. He hadn't wanted to set a deadline, and especially not when three huge weddings were coming up for Connie. When he compared her elaborate weddings to his complex trials, he felt a stab of sympathy for her.

"We're having a gay wedding soon," Mike told him, "or half a gay wedding. The groom told Mom he didn't want to be gay, so he's marrying a straight woman. He's saying good-bye to gay life by having the flashiest wedding since one of Liz Taylor's."

To Steven's surprise and annoyance, Jennifer called on the first of November and told them that she wouldn't be coming for Thanksgiving. "Too much work, Dad—isn't that great? I will be in for Christmas, though, and I won't look like a refugee, either. Something's happened."

"What, something bad?"

"Not bad, good. Tell you when I see you."

191

The wedding was Castello-Milani, and as Mike and Connie described the struggle, Steven had no trouble seeing the couple as though they were litigants and it was Castello v. Milani. The groom was striving for Louis the XIV, the bride for Ralph Nader.

"Who's paying for this catastrophe?" Steven asked.

"He is."

"Maybe she should tell him that her parents would be insulted and hurt if he took over their responsibility. They have their pride, too."

"What a great idea. I think I can let her suggest that. It will cut our profits, but unless she does something, I'm afraid she'll self-destruct. A week after Thanksgiving, I'll be going to the fights. I hope a wedding will break out."

Thanksgiving came and with it the anniversary of Annina's death. Steven had been warned that he might feel grief or depression, but he found himself surprised at the intensity of his emotions. Sorrow was like a predatory cat, belly-creeping to spring out at him from hiding. He found himself weeping at traffic stops and before his shaving mirror. Connie's sympathy was present but diffused by work. She was being besieged by calls morning and evening from the Milani-Castello combatants.

As it grew—Connie's word was *metastasized*—the home calls grew more frequent. Only Thanksgiving Day gave her some reprieve. The family met at Connie's sister Suzanne's and comforted her with two generations of wedding war stories. "What about the time the automatic sprinkler system at the park went on in the middle of that reception?" "What about the freak May snow that drifted over a lovely outdoor mountain wedding miles from shelter?" "Tell about the power outage that darkened Tisdel-Roma, and the fight at Henderson-Harlow that brought the police and ten arrests."

"Milani will soon be over," Suzanne told Connie, "and will join the roll of its illustrious predecessors, holding its own title. We've had dangerous weddings, black-eye weddings, black-out weddings, whiteout weddings, and now the winner in the tasteless category."

After Thanksgiving, Steven's mood slowly lifted, leaving him feeling drained and weakened, as after an illness. His friend Paul was impersonating Lincoln in the Lincoln-Douglas debates, and he and Connie went and enjoyed the break in routine.

On December 3, the overwrought Milani-Castello wedding was loosed on stunned guests at the Denver Cathedral. The reception made the papers.

Connie had carefully monitored the bride's ingestion of tranquilizers, as she told Steven later, but before she could intervene, the bride had downed two glasses of champagne, which interacted with the previous chemical smorgasbord and rendered her almost catatonic. The groom seemed unaware that his bride was not, strictly speaking, in attendance.

The ceremony had been a long one, and to serve champagne without serving food at the same time was courting disaster. By the time the toasting was over, many of the guests were past interest in food. The shower of confetti landed in the hors d'oeuvres and drinks, to be picked off or fished out by only the fastidious few. By that time, most of those in attendance lacked the dexterity to perform the act anyway. Belligerent guests had to be dealt with, and the groom's plans had not included pouring fifty drink-sodden revelers into taxis that would take them home. The bride maintained a dignity that was aided by a glassy-stared incomprehension.

Connie told Steven all this at 1:00 A.M., as he sat in bed. He'd been reading and waiting for her. "I was really frightened about some of it," she said.

"Can you sleep in tomorrow, at least?"

"I'll take the time. I'm just tired enough to declare a dictum."

He put down his book. "Declare away."

"I think the worst weddings are those where the dream overwhelms the reality of what's best for the couple and for the guests, and even of what makes sense. Then there are the weddings where form and spirit separate, and people go with the form and forget the spirit. I will not visit him down there, or take him a fruitcake, or call him Dad."

Steven began to laugh. "For one thing, they won't let you take a fruitcake in there at all, except a factory-wrapped one."

"I'll be there when you tell the kids. I'll try to listen to you when you tell me that people like him, that you like him. He's your father, and I'll try to remember that and that you loved him and missed him when you were growing up. I'll try not to see him as a—"

"Monster?"

"Monster," she said.

Chapter Twenty-seven

Jennifer called with plans for the Christmas trip. "If costume design has a season, it's now," she said. "Three kids' shows, costumes to be on the hangers by December fifteenth.

"Jen—"

"I'll be home for a week and I'll tell you my news. Meanwhile, I'm building a reputation here."

"How are you doing with that young man you mentioned, the one you met at the audition?" Connie was on the other line.

"We're going to be good friends. He's gay and I don't drive anymore."

"And that director?"

"Just a friend."

The tone was quick and light, but Steven heard a pause, which he was sure Connie heard, as well. She told him later that had the communication been by E-mail, she would have glided by what the words really meant.

Jennifer's voice didn't fail at the job of keeping light. "We see each other, but he's very ambitious and he isn't ready for the big stuff."

"When did it happen?" Connie sobbed to Steven later. They were about to go to bed; years of being together had choreographed their nighttime preparation moves into a graceful, satisfying dance, but she had broken the rhythm to sit on the bed in forlorn bewilderment, half-undressed, holding a hairbrush she wasn't using. "She's so wonderful, and I think she sent him away."

"You don't know that it was Jen. He might have—"

"I heard it; it was in her voice. What's this need to be so strong, to turn away someone who might have been right for her?"

"You think she'll never have another chance?"

"Who wants a blind wife?"

"I don't know, but someone might love Jennifer enough to want her, blind or not, and to be as strong as she is."

"Steven, was it only last Thanksgiving when we were all so happy and I was worrying about nothing and you were worrying about Jeremy's vocation hopping and getting Annina out of her apartment? The whole year seems like an elephant falling on us in slow motion, part by part—here comes the front, now the back."

"Come on," he said. "Let me take you to a place that's warm and soft and not always perfectly quiet." He took the brush from her. "Let's do what we're good at."

When they lay side by side, she said, "Would you be disappointed if I cried again?"

"No. Go ahead. It's been a hard year."

"It seems unfair for our work to be frustrating also."

Steven reached for her hand. "Even with my best friends, even with you, I don't like my pain to show, to let people know that the elephant has just rolled over. Connie . . . At Christmas, I'll tell the kids. I've waited long enough."

"You said you would. What about my family? Do you want all of them to know?"

"No, but they'll have to be told," Steven said. "Things happen. Terry found out, and he was only half-looking. Somebody will see something on the

196

Internet or on a list somewhere. This is the age of information, not the age of wisdom. We can't hide the elephant."

"It hurts me how little their generation has to hang on to these days. Community is gone, neighborhoods are gone, nothing is shared anymore, and families are fragmented. At least we can give them a sense of pride in their backgrounds, a reason to feel blessed. . . ."

"My father's alive. That's a fact. We should acknowledge that and live with it."

"Why? We don't discuss our sex lives with them or detail our financial situation. When I had that cancer scare, I didn't tell them."

"When it was over, you did, and if it had been cancer, you would have told them. Lon has begun to see us as family. What if he leaves them something in his will? Won't they know then, and from strangers?"

"What could he leave them?"

"I can't keep wondering, looking both ways and waiting for something awful to happen. We don't have to bury them with details; we don't have to give line and verse, case citations. I'll tell them together. You said you'd be there, but if you can't, that'll be all right, too. I'll do it alone."

"Let me see what Christmas does for my charitable spirit."

Steven remembered having looked forward to Christmas as an adolescent because he could earn money he kept from Annina and from the welfare department, money he spent on food and movies. She liked Christmas for the sentimental holiday stories on TV, tales in which people were reunited and God answered an embarrassing profusion of children's prayers.

Family-loving Connie had been careful of Annina, helping at the apartment, stocking the pantry, seeing to her needs. Only a tremendous revulsion would

197

keep her from her natural wish to include, care for, and find a place for a family member. Steven had never thought of his father and mother as an adult would think of them, as individuals apart from the roles they played as his parents—not until now, that is.

What an unlikely match they must have been, the Colorado job-jumping ranch hand and biker and the Neopolitan war survivor, both hiding enormous weaknesses and desperate strengths. How much had they known about each other, really? Steven would find himself pondering these things when driving to a deposition, when his mind should have been working on the questions that would reveal a hole or an inconsistency in a deponent's testimony.

The Christmas weather was raw and cold, with possible snow to come. When Steven met Jennifer at Denver International, he drummed his fingers and tapped his foot for two hours in expectation of her late plane, and by the time they were sitting in the car, she was too tired for all but the most desultory talk. Once home, she turned down Connie's offer of a late supper and went to bed.

The next day, Steven took Jennifer to lunch at Le Central. He found himself trying to watch her without making her conscious of it, tracking for any little changes of behavior that might signal a narrowing in her vision. He thought he found a few, but he wasn't sure. The differences were subtle and might even be her tiredness or his concentration on her movements, the turning of her hand, her response to sound.

"Mom wants me to get a man, to get married, to be safe. There are guys I've dated who are kind and gentle, who are bright and creative and have a good sense of humor, but I haven't found one with all those things, someone who has the kind of staying power I need and will need even more later on."

"Your mother's scared, and I can see that now. She hides it well; she's energetic and full of ideas. She's so competent at work that you'd never think of her as fearful."

"What about you, Dad?"

"You'll hear more about me after the Christmas party."

"You're okay—your health—"

"I'm fine."

"Is it about me?"

"No; that much I can tell you now."

"Could you do me a favor?"

"I'll try; what is it?"

"Could you get Mom off my case?"

"I don't know if I can help you there, sweetheart. I'm disappointing you in the first big thing you've asked of me, but I can't make your mother unafraid, and I can't stop her from doing what she sees as her duty. Meanwhile, you said you had some news."

"I've been approached by a pattern company to make a line of costume patterns for school plays. I'll be starting with the standard stuff—the tomato, the mushroom, et cetera, but if things go well, it will be nice income and steadier work than what I do now."

"Jen, that's great!"

"I'll tell Mom tonight. Act surprised."

The Scotts' Christmas party was quieter than usual. Some of the children had grown past the tantrum stage and others into preadolescent sweetness. One cousin brought a girlfriend, one a fiancée. Suddenly, Tony and Barbara Scott looked older to him. Steven thought Connie or Suzanne would soon begin to take on the party burden. Jeremy missed some of the day but came in the afternoon. Steven had told him that his presence was important.

"What's up?"

"Wait till we get home."

"It's not something awful, is it? Somebody sick?"

"No, nothing like that."

"Why isn't Mom coming?"

"Aunt Suzanne will drive her home later. They're doing the cleanup."

"Shouldn't we wait for her?"

"No, not this time. She said she wanted me to start. She'll be home for the latter part of it."

They were all sitting in the family room, waiting for Steven to begin. Jennifer said, "Something was wrong with the party this year. Nobody told us they were sorry Nonna wasn't with us. It was as if she'd never been part of the family at all."

Mike nodded. Jeremy asked, "Is what you have to tell us something about Nonna? Is it something about her will or something you want to donate in her name?"

"No, although she plays a part in what I have to say."

They waited, watching him.

Steven's plan had been based on his courtroom summation approach. This was a slow accrual of facts to form a structure. The picture he strove to make was reasonable, rational, and balanced. He had planned to use this structure to show Lon Howe to them. He had planned to begin with Lon and Annina in Callan, then go on to the genetic base of Jennifer's condition and his casual mention to Terry of Lon's missing death certificate, and then on until the whole picture was there before them. But their faces defeated him. He dropped the pieces around him. "I've found out that your grandfather, my father, Lon—Alonzo Howe—is still alive. Alonzo Carl Howe is in Cañon City, in the penitentiary."

Silence. They stared at him blankly. Then, Jennifer said, "Wow." Of course, *wow*, Steven thought. These young people had no memories of Lon himself, no sense of him as a grandfather. Steven thought he might have been speaking of a great-great-uncle, hanged as a horse thief on the frontier in 1886. Distance lends enchantment.

Then, Mike said quietly, "You must have had a hell of a time with this, Dad." Steven nodded. There it was again, that compassion. Where had Mike come to it—in what gene?

"How did you find out?" the other two said at once, as though it had been rehearsed, and they all echoed a nervous laughter.

"The computer," Steven said. "Terry Shannon did the work, I guess the way a musician would doodle around with a theme on a piano, half-engaged until something began to form itself. Then he followed the little idea here and there—you know how you fool around with a skill you have. He did, until, bang, there it was."

"So he knows," Jeremy said.

"Yes, he knows."

"And Mom—what about Mom?"

"She's had a very tough time with it."

They were silent again. The distance was shrinking, the enchantment fading. "Who else knows?" Jennifer asked.

"Terry found out, so I had to tell the others, the Witty Committee."

"Not Grandma or Grandpa?"

"No, not yet."

"And you want us to keep it that way, a Howe secret?"

"Yes, I think so, for a while at least." Steven thought they might protest. They were close to their Scott cousins.

Jennifer said, "It'll be nice to have a Howe thing for once, just for us."

Nice? A Howe thing for once? Of all the predicted responses, this was one Steven hadn't begun to guess at.

Mike asked, "What happened? What did he do?"

Again, Steven wanted to begin with all his own defenses, taking them away one by one; again, he couldn't. "Child molestation. He molested children. One of them ran away from him and was killed by a car. He was charged with felony murder."   Dead silence. The romance died out of their eyes.

Jennifer said, "Have you seen him?"

"A few times."

"What's he like?"

"Old, sick."

She leaned forward. "Is he still—is he still like your dad, the one you remembered?"

"I can't tell anymore. When I pull away the parts of what I created as a six- and then a seven- and eight-year-old—the biker, the exciting hero, the homecoming dad—there isn't much left. I'm just now meeting the real Lon Howe."

Near midnight, Connie returned.

"Con, what happened? Something's happened."

"Not yet . . .just let me be. I'll be ready for you soon. Did you tell them?"

"I said I would."

"How did they take it?"

"They romanced it until I told them what he'd done."

"You told them *that?*"

"Connie, they're not six-year-olds."

She began to cry. "It's so awful. A grandfather like that . . . " And then she said, "Oh, Steve, that bitch *stiffed* us!"

"What is this? What happened?"

"Castello, the wedding I worked so hard over, listening to her, trying to get the ceremony and reception toned down, bunny-mothering her, explaining to him . . ." She was sobbing and all Steven could do was to sit beside her and wait for her to pass through its stages.

He offered her a handkerchief. "It's okay—it's clean."

"Don't help me," she said, but she took the handkerchief and blew her nose. "He was supposed to pay for the wedding, but she ended up sending us a check, which bounced. Bry told me at the party."

"You're sure it wasn't an honest mistake?"

"It was a check on a closed account."

"The kids want Lon Howe to be a Howe secret. Connie, Lon Howe won't ruin us. The happy couple haven't skipped town, have they?"

"I don't think so, and I won't let it slide. I'm going after them. I'm going to nail them for every petal, every sequin."

"I know you've been worrying about genetic propensities. Maybe I have, too. I think I worried about Jeremy, because he resembles Lon. I watched him when I told them about Lon. Had Jeremy recognized any of those needs in himself, there would have been a glimmer. There wasn't. Whatever urges Lon has—"

"How can you tell by an expression what was in his mind?"

"Connie, this is our son, a boy we know."

"Isn't that what every mother says? Watch them all on TV, all those mothers protesting how good, how innocent their sons are. Watch their neighbors, who all say it was impossible, such a nice man, such a good neighbor. Your father has brought all that here."

"Talk to a psychiatrist about this. Talk to Mike. He's solid and sensible, and he isn't hysterical. Experts are recommending—"

"Experts don't know how frightening it is to see all those mothers, all those neighbors, to be reminded that our streets and homes aren't safe, that our careful plans are never careful enough. He's your father, yes, and his last crime was—"

"In the mid-fifties."

"But don't you understand? I just couldn't listen to you defend him to our children. God, what a long day this has been."

Chapter Twenty-eight

The trip was pleasant, the traffic light. They made good time. All of them had been subdued at the beginning, thinking of the solemnity of a prison visit, but solemnity wasn't natural to them and they soon responded to the day, the snow-heaped fields and radiant mountains. Steven stopped at Penrose for breakfast, having left too early to eat. They told war stories. Jeremy's were about strange or comical incidents at the convention center, people who stole things and offered bizarre excuses when caught. A family had driven off with their baby, in its basket, on the roof of their car, waving back at all the waved hands of those trying to alert them. "I called the police. They stopped the car in downtown Estes Park, with the baby still cooing in its basket." Jennifer told about the two bolts of special fabric she had ordered, found impossible to work with, and had to replace one day before a performance of eighteen fairy dancers. "I still have nightmares about that one."

"My war story is from back in the summer," Mike said, "when I was working at the camp. About half the kids there were in wheelchairs and protective of their chairs, because they represent their freedom and mobility. We had kids who wouldn't let *anybody* touch their chairs, and the chairs had to be right next to their beds. One kid, Freddy, was so unhappy, at camp he decided to escape. He had cerebral palsy, and though he started out at four A.M., it must have taken him over an hour to get himself into his clothes. Then it must have taken another hour for the bathroom, crawling there and then back to his wheelchair, another hour to get into it and roll it down the halls to the back doors. God knows how he got them both open and the wheelchair outside. Then there was the hill. Out back was a stiff drop-off, which he misjudged. I don't think he could have made it even with the brakes set, but he got launched down that hill and the chair turned over and over, he and it down the hill, and he ended up under it. We found him at eight o'clock, still struggling to untangle himself from the chair without damaging it. I had all kinds of trouble lifting it off him. He was crying, his face was cut, his right ankle was swollen, and he was filthy. He looked up at me and said, 'I can't even run away like other kids.' His mother raised so much sand about the whole thing, I thought we'd never hear the end of it."

"It's a sad story," Jeremy said, "but I can't help thinking that the kid at least had the excitement of a getaway and four hours of full freedom, hip-deep in something all his own."

Jennifer began to whistle and stamp. "Yes!" she said. "Yes and yes. Freedom, autonomy, like other people."

"You will admit, though," Mike said, "that we care-givers have a different agenda, and who can blame us? What do we want for those kids? Safety. Safety first, second, and third, and that means little freedom and no risk."

"Why should we be less free than anybody else? Why should we be safer than anybody else?" Jennifer's voice snapped with indignation.

"Because if I let there be freedom and risk, parents and supervisors would call it dereliction of duty," Mike insisted.

206

"Freedom is worth sacrificing a lot for," Jennifer said, "and I'm willing to give a pass on some of the superstringent safety for more of it."

"Hold on there," Steven said. "Now you're playing with some of my rules. Those rules undergird American civil law. In any case, I don't know how much freedom any of us have. Aren't we controlled by lots of conditions, external and internal—reputation, needs of others, money considerations, health, age? It's a matter of degree, isn't it, freedom and risk?"

"A glass of water is water, and so's the Gulf of Mexico, but you wouldn't compare them," Mike said.

They argued down the highway with increasing spirit.

At the prison, they were almost an hour checking in. Steven thought that because of the young people, the search was more punctilious than for Steven on former visits. They passed through two sets of doors and then were led by a guard to another part of the building, where Lon waited in a small meeting room. Steven saw them noticing the still-present Christmas decorations on desks and walls and the set expressions of guards as they rang their keys and clanged the doors open and shut.

Lon had obviously spent time on his appearance. He looked like a teenager ready for a date. The combination of eagerness and fear, the adolescent's hallmark, was on him, and his stiff body language and measuring glance underscored the effect. His clothes were new issue, and he must have practiced the ploy of putting his shirt and pants under his mattress to press them and preserve a crease in the pants. He had a fresh haircut and his shave was only an hour old.

Everyone measured. Everyone stared. The young people were looking for hints to the prisoner's personality, the gestures, facial expression, landmark nose or jaw that marked him as a criminal. They took

207

in the scar with fascinated awe. Steven hoped they didn't notice the features of the Howe family reappearing in Jeremy. He watched each of them for reactions. Only Jeremy could easily be seen as son or grandson. Would Lon see himself in Jeremy?

They uttered hesitant words. How was he? Fine. How were they? Fine. Jennifer said: "We all got searched, and you can't have any homemade food. Is that—does everybody go through that?"

Lon relaxed a little. "It's a feature of the place. We're like the outside, only more. Some guys arrange for dope deals or make knives. If the stuff gets found, a new reg comes down about tighter security and everybody pays."

"They told us that nothing could leave the room— we have to eat it here. It seems so . . . rigid," Jennifer said.

Lon's expression didn't change. "Rigid is what prison is, rigid but undependable. Things change at a whim, the warden's or someone else's. Privileges are there, then not there, sometimes on the same day. It's why prisoners get superstitious."

They were slowly beginning to relax. Steven opened the paper plates (a factory-wrapped set) and the plastic forks and knives (also factory-wrapped), poured the juice into the Styrofoam cups, and, unable to cut the plastic on the lunch meat, bit the edge to open it. Jennifer apologized. "Our mother's a great cook and so am I and so is Mike. We wanted to get you a ham or turkey with corn-bread stuffing, and Mom's *great* pecan pie, but they wouldn't let us bring that."

"I was used to the issue stuff, food, clothes, all the rest. Guys who were rich, used to better, they suffer more. I never had much better than prison chow, so I didn't miss it."

Mike told a joke about food and Jeremy kidded him about how his tastes would make him a happy prisoner. At that, Lon began to laugh, a low chuckle deep in his throat.

Steven found himself gaping. He was close to tears. The sound of his father's laughter had been rare in his childhood, and the laughter he had heard at their first meeting, and since, had been a prisoner's laughter, carrying no hint of fun or simple pleasure. This laugh was Lon's open delight, an old memory, older than words or judgment. It was the sound of that laugh. All is well, it said, sleep will come with no unease, and tomorrow, at least, no packing boxes scratching a gritty floor with their signal sound, the move again, the uprooting, the dislocation, the silent, patient pain of his mother.

"Maybe that was why I never liked travel," Steven murmured. No one heard him. They were telling jokes and Jennifer was trying to convince Lon that what his generation thought too risqué for mixed company was now freely shared around. He saw they were taking turns gleefully, trying to shock Lon, and for a moment he thought of stopping them. The jokes made them brave at Lon's expense, but after he swallowed the last forkful of store pound cake, Lon said quietly, "It's fun, joking with you, but I think you came here for something else. Is it answers? If it is, I guess I'm ready. What I did was a long time ago."

"You kidnapped kids. . . ." Jeremy said.

"I got them to come to me."

"And you—"

"I fondled them."

"Their bodies. . ." Mike's mouth must have been dry. His voice was thick.

"Through their clothes."

"Did they know what you were doing?"

"Some did, some didn't." There was a silence.

209

Jennifer was shaking her head. "Hey, this is three against one."

Lon's scarred side was turned to her. "You're the one with the eye trouble," he said. She was caught off guard.

"Yes."

"Can you see me?"

"Not now. You're too far over to the side. I can see perfectly what's in front of me."

"You think my people gave that to you?" It was a question but spoken flatly.

"I don't know," Jennifer said. "My mom is busy with that genetic stuff, I don't have time for it."

"The Howes . . . well, I wouldn't put it past 'em, but I never heard of any problem that way. I don't call 'em long-living, because too many of 'em died young from accidents they had when they were drunk. That was the men and some of the women. I don't know what they could or couldn't see."

Mike asked, "Nonna—Grandma—did she know what you did?"

The fine day had changed. The wind, channeled and sifted through the endless canyons and watercourses of the Rockies and hell-bent for liberation, had poured itself over and through the last barrier and spilled down on to the plains and a thousand miles of freedom. It brought heavy clouds with it and the day had darkened in the space of fifteen minutes.

"She didn't know at first—I mean when we moved or I got arrested or spotted talking to kids and had to leave. The thing that got me in here, kidnapping, the felony murder charge, yes, she knew about that."

"Did she help you? Did she get a lawyer?"

"No; she faded away. It made my folks angry that she didn't stand by me, not after she knew. I was bitter then, but not now. She barely spoke English or knew how things were done here."

Steven thought Jennifer must be blind in this darkness. Lon was saying: "I didn't marry to trick people. I married to make things all right. I had it good with Annina, and I thanked God. I thought I would be healed and was being healed by being with her—a fool's paradise for almost a year."

"Did you feel bad afterward?"

"Sure. It's not easy talking to a son and grandkids about what I did. I thought about being a picture for you. Dad, Grandpa. Then I realized I might never see any of you again, and there's the urge to leave something, like they do on the outside, keepsakes, words of wisdom." He looked around at all of them, a natural look, one not prison-issued. "And what would that be but the best I had to give? So now I need to be as straight as I tried to be with any of those shrinks and students and people who came here to get college credit or prove their theories on me."

"Why didn't you let us know you were here?"

"Fear, pride, laziness, cowardice—everybody's big bouquet of weaknesses."

The talk stilled, but the room was noisy with the buzzing of a bad fluorescent lighting and there were parts of conversations passing by outside, creating sound that was meaningless but intrusive. "How did I seem to you when I was little?" Steven asked.

Lon shrugged. "I remember things you said and did, little-kid ways you had. You would pick up things we said and give them back just the way we said them. Once—you must have been around three—you sat down on the floor one afternoon and put your arms out in front of you and said, 'Tough day all around.' I never realized I put my arms out until I saw you doing it. 'Tough day all around.' Nina laughed, and she had about quit doing that by then."

Steven was looking away from Lon. "You left us alone a lot of the time."

"I couldn't stay too long in any one place. It's not easy to find places where there are no kids."

"Or where there are." Steven could hear Mike exhale beside him.

Lon said, "I had to go where they didn't know me, and that got harder all the time."

"And your arrest made all that moot."

"Spoken like a lawyer. Yes, it did."

"Do you think about that little girl, the one in the park?"

"The law said 'kidnap' and 'manslaughter,' but doesn't that show how strong my urge was, how much further than my safety it went, how it was running against all good sense, all my experience?"

"If the urge is greater than you are, why shouldn't you be jailed?" Steven asked. Rage had come without his realizing.

Lon suddenly stood as if pulled. He made a grunting sound.

A guard opened the door and poked his head in. "Everything all right?"

"Yes," Steven said. "We were just being emphatic."

The guard scowled. "Well, move it along. You ain't got much more time."

Lon was breathing heavily, as though at the top of a long flight of stairs. "I didn't mean to scare you. There's treatment, and no one trusts it but those who've been through it. The citizens are too scared to trust it. We're all kinds, like you're all kinds. Some of us use kids and don't care, rape and don't care, and murder them after and don't care. Others—there are better men." The words were emphatic, but a life in prison had taught Lon the dead-level expression. This time the knife scar was pallid, not red. His pain gave him away. Steven wondered if Mike noticed that. Lon sat again.

Mike said, "There must be lots of other men here with the problem. Do you talk about it?"

"Not among ourselves, no. It's the professors and the penologists who do that. Some of the prisoners are getting therapy now, and there's therapy on the outside. I wouldn't trust therapy in here without more when a guy got out. Therapy's easy where there's no temptation. I wouldn't be in any of those programs anyway—too old."

"What about the families of the. . .offenders?"

"Don't be delicate. What are you getting at?"

Mike was the student now; there was a clinical tone in his voice. "Is there a genetic thing, some kind of markers in the DNA that would go on down the line? We don't have it, but our kids?"

"I don't know, and I'll be dead before science finds out." He contemplated them for a while in silence and then said, "Your mom, what's she like?"

It was softly, deftly hostile, but Jennifer, to Steven's surprise, turned the stiletto off with a natural tact—learned where, he wondered? "She's had some bad shocks. She's a bridal consultant. They design and coordinate weddings. That's all about making people and things look good. How things and people look gets to be very important. Sometimes how a thing looks is more important to her than what it is. Mom wants to fix what happened to me. She has a huge need to fix, and there's no way to fix this thing. When Dad found you, it was too much for Mom and she closed down. The way she's been acting now is nothing like her usual self."

The guard looked in again. "Time's up," he said.

They began to gather the paper plates, plastic utensils, and plastic wrap.

"Listen," Lon said. "We have our cells and we call them our houses. We're very private with our beds and the walls by our beds, where we put up pictures or mementos—things that mean something to us." He waited for them to follow his thought, and when he saw they were unsure, he cleared his throat. "Some guys have pictures of their family. I have a picture of a ranch I worked on." Again he waited. "I want a picture of you, one you take to send to me, not one you happen to have, and with all of you in it—Stevie—Steve—you, too—and all of you dressed nice." He thought he might have gone too far, so he said, "If that would be something you could do."

Another guard came in. "Hello, Lon, how're you doin'?"

Lon's face showed no expression. "Hi, Charlie. How's life in minimum?"

"Okay. I got some extra duty in, so I'll be able to take the grandkids to Disneyland for the anniversary coming up. Marlys is all excited."

"Three days with that bunch," Lon said from his unchanging face. "You sure you're up for it?"

"Well, it's one of those things I figure is better having done it than doing it." He turned to the four visitors. "This your family here?"

"Part of it," Lon said, and carefully introduced them. He gave a short sketch of what each one of them did. Steven listened in surprise; Lon had remembered everything that had been told to him, kept it, refined it.

Charlie shook hands gravely with them. He had spoken naturally and easily of his own grandchildren, as though Lon Howe were not a child molester and the words about children had no special resonance to him. "Lon," Charlie was saying, "it was good to see you. I'll take these folks back through." He turned to Steven. "You going to Denver?"

"Yes."

"Time to get started, then, if you want to beat the snow."

Chapter Twenty-nine

Everyone stayed for supper, pleasing Connie, whose silence on the subject of where they had been was as pointed as her paring knife. She had made dinner a festival of their preferences: guacamole and tomato salad (Jeremy), marinated duck (Jennifer); stir-fried mushrooms (Mike), and her special dessert, pecan and coconut bars. The kids dug in. Steven saw her working with all her skill to restate the attractions of home—warmth, good food, comfort—in the face of an exciting trip to prison with its rules and ugliness and factory-wrapped food.

Now and then, the three returned to their experiences of the day. Jeremy mentioned the friendly guard, Charlie. "He came over to see Grandpa Howe, Mom." Steven saw Connie wince at the "Grandpa." Mike told about their joking; Jennifer described his scar, his lack of facial expression. "It was like showing feelings had been trained out of him, and it was weird, his saying things with a kind of dead face."

Connie took these comments with her own lack of expression, changing the subject whenever she could. "I heard there was snow down there. Did you get any on the trip? Oh, and have I got a wedding for you. Marcie Timson and Hector Thompson. Yes, Timson-Thompson, and it's on the slopes at Beaver Creek, ceremony at the top of the lift where they met. Then the whole wedding party skis down to a reception at the base."

"Might I advise against that?" Jeremy asked.

Connie said, "I've tried myself. She wants to ski in gown and veil."

"Dangerous, if not deadly," Steven said.

"I know what she's seeing in her mind," Jennifer said. "Perfect weather, sun and blue sky and the white bird she wants to be, flying with her mate. The photographer will catch them darting past in glorious youth and graceful motion." She was silent for a moment and then said, "Dad, *we* have to make plans to take a picture."

"What picture?" Connie was puzzled.

"That's right; I would have forgotten it," Mike said. "Grandpa Howe wants a picture of all of us to put on his wall. Dressed up, he said, posed by a photographer. We'll get the guy you use, Mom, Mel."

"I can't be part of this," Connie said. "I can't. You've been down there and seen him, and that was something I didn't want, but you did it, and it worked out, but I can't go there with you. I see pictures in my head and I don't want to be on somebody's prison wall."

"Mom . . ."

Connie was busy clearing the table. She carried a tray of dishes into the kitchen and then, coming back, said, "I told Marcie Timson that the grandparents would get altitude sickness. She told me we should supply oxygen canisters."

"Back to the wedding," Jeremy said. "Okay, then, what does a wedding like that cost?" he asked.

"It's going to be in blue and white," Connie said. "With all the extras, I put it at just thirty thousand eight hundred eighty-three."

"Whew," Steven shook his head.

"That bride—she was taught to see herself like that," Jennifer said. "Open any catalog of high-fashion winter clothes and see the models posed in luscious light, with open slopes, untracked trails through the trees. Some girls were raised on those catalog and the ski-magazine pictures. They forget the hours and endless primping it takes to get that light, that look, and how no one skis holding hands."

Jennifer started helping clear the table. The kids' normal volubility turned to joking as they worked. "Mike, you talked more than all of us put together. Your greatest triumph among the handicapped will be with the deaf," Jeremy declared, "although you'll find a way to yatter even more in sign language."

"*You* did us proud," Jennifer said, pinning Jeremy with her centered vision. "I see the day you introduce a line of gourmet foods for prison visits: factory-sealed pâté, inspected by retired wardens, Brie, caviar, mousse, Ball and Chain brand. Why not an ethnic line: Chinese, and two kinds of soul food."

"Listen, sweetheart," Jeremy answered in Humphrey Bogart mode, "you'll be busy designing jumpsuits for the svelte look in maximum security."

Connie walked past them as they were kidding and began scraping and stacking the dishes they had cleared from the table. "How can you joke about that man, about visiting someone in prison?"

"He's an ordinary guy," Jeremy said, "that's all."

"He's a child molester. Don't you understand? He wounds little children."

"He's not only that," Mike said, "and he did something I don't know if I could have done—he took himself away from the kids and from freedom, too, from normal life."

"How did he do that?" She was scraping loudly, and loading the dishwasher with short, hard motions.

"He did it by not putting in for parole," Mike said. "He could have been paroled years ago, Ma. I don't think I would have had the strength to do that to protect other people."

"How noble," Connie said, scraping hard, "no need to work, no worries, no daily hassle."

"Ma, he was cut in prison. He has a scar all down his face. He's been beaten."

"Too bad."

"I don't get it. You're understanding. You understand the wacky brides and grooms and the crazy families. You're sympathetic to homeless people, to alcoholics and unwed mothers. What's different now?"

"I draw the line at men like him. Maybe you think he's picturesque, quaint in some way, and he's old and soft and pitiable."

Steven said, "He's none of those things, and he's not asking for anything, not our sympathy or our time. Everything came from our side."

"That's what I can't understand." Connie's movement made them stand back. "Why you would want to see him, go down there, all the way down there to visit him, to hear him, to take him food? It's inconceivable to me."

Steven sighed, a sound she bridled at. His voice was patient. "You've never had poverty, Connie. You've always had health and beauty. You've always had family, friends. I don't think you can feel the same kind of hopelessness Lon lives with, or the loneliness I lived with. Do you remember Mama and me at our wedding? The bride's side seated a hundred people in the church, and, of course, they flowed over to the groom's side, where there were my six friends and one family member, a tiny nervous woman who didn't even fill her own place."

Connie shook her head violently. "There was enough family for both of us on my side. Didn't I treat Annina as family?"

"Of course you did, but would you now, knowing that she had married someone you consider beneath contempt?"

218

"He's not some poor old man. He kidnapped children and made them into sex objects."

"It's over. It was over in 1957."

"That was because he couldn't get to them."

"We don't know that. We don't know what treatment might have done, had he been given any. He was desperate not to be what he was. He tried. . . ."

They suddenly realized that the three children had been trapped in the flash flood of their wrangle. Everyone stopped breathing and looked around and then the boys rose, murmuring something, and left. Jennifer got up and moved into the kitchen with the butter dish, giving a small intake of breath as the kitchen doorway's molding reached out and bit her hip. Connie gasped and put out a hand; Steven thought quickly, She isn't paying attention. She needs to pay attention.

With the young people gone, the wrangle crept back, hushed this time. Steven had involved all of them in the visit, exposed them to the ugliness of a prison. It had been their choice from the beginning. Why was she, who had always been so eager to volunteer for the mentally ill, the homeless, all the less fortunate, stopped before this man? Why couldn't she listen to what experts who had studied the issue said of his illness and his need?

"Connie, we aren't talking about anything we'll have to do. The country is still in witch-hunt mode. Don't you remember the recovered memory craze? The multiple personality craze? The Satanic cult craze? Now we have child abusers lurking behind every tree. We're still living in terror of one another. Lon wasn't a rapist, nor a murderer; he wasn't violent. Some people are amenable to treatment; some are not. Some are violent psychopaths; most are not. I don't understand why we can't separate violent psychopaths from

219

others who can be treated, maybe from people like my father."

She stared at him. "Now you're calling him 'my father.'"

Connie was moving as she had moved thousands of times, sink to dishwasher, dishwasher to cabinets, sponging, wiping, putting away, making ordinary order out of ordinary chaos, cleanliness out of mess, all with efficient reasonableness.

"Remember," he said, putting the glasses away. They were glasses she had just bought to replace the normal attrition of a Christmas set he had given her eight years ago. "It was you who started all this, set it in motion. You got everyone busy looking up family, trying to nail down what genes were responsible for Jennifer's handicap. I still think that had we found Lon together, your reaction wouldn't have been so strong."

"I have pictures in my head," Connie said. "I can't help that."

"Get a picture of me," Steven said. "a picture of an orphan, a man who had to create a father. Help that man. I found my father, and because I found him, I've stopped having to look for him at traffic lights, or on the highway, or in dreams. Be glad for us, Connie; I'm whole in a way I never imagined I would be."

She turned away.

Chapter Thirty

The Witty Committee had voted itself a ski day in the middle of the month. The weather was bell-clear, the sky a ringing blue, the cold just enough to keep the snow light.

Steven had once been too competitive on skis, trying to outperform Paul, who'd been a medalist in college, and Jack, whose form was showy and whose daring sometimes horrified the others. More recently, Steven had stopped working so hard and, being less tense, found his skiing had improved.

When they rode up on quad lifts, they spoke of general things—the fluctuations in the stock market, party politics and its media blare—but riding the two-person lifts, the talk was more intimate.

"You've been seeing your father," Terry said. "What's he like?"

"He's honest, a little prickly. He's a man I don't remember except at special times, when he laughs or uses some small gesture that lets me see him as he was when I was six or seven. The kids have been down, too."

"Really? How did that go?"

"Better than I thought it would. Connie's still holding back."

"It must be hard for her; she likes to be part of things."

"Very hard, but at least I've stopped having to look for him or run after him in dreams. The kids have heard the names of my family from him—the Howes, the Kendricks, the aunts and uncles, people whose names I haven't heard in years. Not all of my family are genetically damaged child molesters or terrified immigrants. My father did well under fire. He said that his buddies respected him. Some of the guards like him. He received a bronze star. I looked it up. He's a veteran of the landing at Salerno. Howes homesteaded in the Ute Valley, and the Kendricks had mines on Prospector Mountain and the Hungry Mother. The kids are seeing all that now, maybe in a more realistic light, and—"

"Maybe they like him. That would get Connie blazing."

"Yeah, they do like him. He's an entirely different version of a grandfather, and maybe that adds something. They seem to take him as he is. I hope they see more in him than a rebel or a romantic figure."

"It's been a hell of a year for you," Terry said, and they looked out into the wind-played snow.

"I don't think I've examined any of it, and some of it I haven't even felt yet, because I was so busy fielding what was thrown at us."

"I did too much after Suzy died," Terry said. "I wanted my ordinary life back so much that I tried to force it on all of us. If I hadn't tried so hard, I'd probably still be married and life would be a lot closer to what I wanted it to be. Do the prison people want you to take him?"

"Yes, dialysis and all. I think Connie imagines Lon being paroled in my custody and me asking her to take care of him. If I'd found Lon in a VA hospital somewhere, she would have swung into action, the way she did with Annina." The wind dropped a little and the cloud passed. "She can't break out of her fantasy that what he did was somehow worse than murder."

"Do you know, actually know, what he did?"

"No, that's the strangest part of all this. I have his statement and I think it's honest, but he may be lying to protect me and himself. The papers and even the court records covered the crime with a single blanket word: *molestation*. What was it? Fondling, touching, kissing, holding, raping, sodomizing, brutalizing— what? There's no degree here, no way to know exactly what was done or how much pain he inflicted, or even if there was physical pain suffered at all. Shouldn't there be a question about that?"

Terry shook snow from his hood. "Are you sorry I found him?"

"No, I'm not. I found out that I wasn't abandoned. I'm not part of a mystery. There are reasons for what happened to Annina and me, for what she did and what happened to us, and I'm learning more every time I visit him. But we don't have lots of time." Steven looked out into the muffling snow. "Lon might die any day now, or decide to die and quit taking his dialysis."

"Connie's not asking that you stay away, is she?"

"No."

"Or punishing you afterward?"

"No, not really."

They came in sight of the dismount and moved their poles, checking the positions of their skis. "We're wrestling over the kids," Steven said.

Terry leaned forward. "That's what happened to us," he said, "and it was the worst part of what happened."

Steven shifted and got ready to dismount. When they stood at the top of the hill, waiting for Paul and Jack, Steven said, "Mike likes Lon. Lon fits his idea of what his life's work will be. He's fallen in love with rehabilitation, with changing the world in some concrete way. He sees his grandfather as part of that. I don't know about Jen."

"Do you like Lon?"

"Yes, I think I do. He wouldn't be a friend, and prison has pulled him into himself in a way that's disturbing, but yes, I do."

"You've changed," Terry said.

"How?"

"I don't know, eased up maybe."

"Jack thinks I was too respectable before all this happened. Connie's afraid that my heritage is flawed and that a genetic shadow will continue in the blood after we're both gone."

"We're romancing DNA right now," Terry said. "Tell her that in five years, scientists will pull the molestation gene out and zap it into churchgoing respectability."

Paul and Jack skied over to them. "Let's try Not for Grandma this time. The weather's perfect for it!"

"I'm going to be downtown near your office." It was early the next morning, and Tony Scott was calling. "Any chance for lunch?"

"What about the Athletic Club, Sixteenth and Sherman?"

"Fine."

Steven's first appointment that day was with Melissa Carney's parents, who sat close together his office. Melissa loved to ski, they told him. She reveled in its freedom and the doctors said it was excellent activity for her because she was severely arthritic. It was the only sport she practiced for fun. Steven wondered yet again at the world's confluences: a daughter's handicap made the world bloom with handicapped people. Melissa wore leg braces, Delia Carney told him. She was a dark, vivacious, attractive woman. That would help. In spite of the law's insistence on blind justice, the nice-looking and the well-spoken got better compensation. "We are careful to protect her with layers, never without great care." She was foreign, judging by her use of words. Spanish, Steven thought.

"We were skiing at Aureole, on beginner slopes," Mr. Carney said, "the run called Cady's Cruise."

"I know the run."

"There are markings there that tell the expert skiers to slow down. A woman coming from behind was speeding and ran into Melissa. The fall triggered an arthritic crisis. The woman's insurance company says it was an accident, with no blame attached. There were three witnesses."

Steven thought he would enjoy the case. Over the years, the secondary research he did had begun to interest him as much as the legal ideas involved. He had become knowledgeable in some areas of physics, was conversant with the properties of wood, metal, and the modern polymers, and was now well versed in alcohol absorption rates, blood chemistry, the physiology of hypothermia, and much more. He was pleasantly aware of an excitement he had been missing.

His client, Melissa Carney, was twelve. He hoped she was bright and articulate. Dullness evoked pity, brightness evoked sympathy, and sympathy got better awards from juries.

"Will she be ready for vigorous questioning?" He saw the two glance at one another and slight smiles pull at their lips.

Chapter Thirty-one

The Athletic Club had been a good choice. Tony was already seated when Steven got to the table. He soon realized that the lunch wasn't meant to provide a pleasant social break in the day. Tony's look was tense and drawn; his fingers played with the tableware. They ordered and then chatted for a while, Tony becoming more uncomfortable with the passing minutes. The food arrived and Steven ate, watching his father-in-law for the moment when he would open up.

"Steve, you know Peter's been having problems."

"Peter? Oh, Pete, yes."

Steven hadn't known much detail about his nephew's problems, undoubtedly because Connie hadn't told him. He covered by saying, "What's going on now?"

"It's more serious this time. After the shoplifting incident, Suzanne and Bob got him into therapy. They thought things were going well; his attitude seemed better and his grades were improving. Wednesday afternoon, he didn't come home from school, but they weren't worried—he's almost seventeen, and they figured he might be out with friends. At eight, the police called. He and Zach were DUI and had outrun a police car. They'd turned the wrong way into a one-way street and I guess they realized it and tried to back up, so when they crashed the car, they were going fairly slowly."

"Zach? Zach's only fourteen."

"They were both drunk. The officer told Suzanne and Bob he wondered how the boys could see or walk, they were so bombed."

"And they need lawyers."

"Yeah."

"I'll give you two names. Both are excellent men, but I should tell you that there's not much a lawyer can do—if you're thinking of getting them off, I mean."

"Zach was the one driving."

"Whew."

Steven got out his PDA and retrieved the numbers. "Call this man first, for Pete. It would be best to separate the boys' cases. Two lawyers. It will cost." He wrote the information on the slip of paper that Tony offered, aware of the look of bafflement and misery on his father-in-law's face but knowing he couldn't put a hand on Tony's shoulder or arm or offer any but the most casual sign of sympathy. "You'll have counsel. Follow the advice you're given," he said.

Tony nodded. "It's Peter I'm worried about. Zach is just a kid, a follower, always wowed by his older brother's daring and glamour. Zach'll learn, I think, but Pete . . . Will they have to go to jail?"

"They both might, but to a juvenile facility."

"If only the authorities would accept this as just the youthful prank it was—no one was hurt, after all."

"I don't think they'll see it that way," Steven said. "People's lives were risked and the boys tried to evade arrest."

"My God, Steve, they're *boys*. They can't be jailed."

"They might be. And for Pete, it might be a rendezvous with reality: bad choices have results."

"You don't understand."

"What don't I understand?" Steven hoped that Tony, who was a kind and gracious father-in-law, wouldn't try to tell him that Suzanne's two boys were different, better than the common run of teenage offenders, deserving of special treatment.

Tony gave a long sigh. "I'm scared, Steve. I'm scared about what Pete might do. I had a brother, Ed—Edmund, who died when he was eighteen. It was 1942, and I let people think he was killed in the war— even Barb thinks so. Ed was in the army, but he had a furlough in Denver. He and a buddy got drunk and ran over a kid. He was in jail, waiting transfer to Fort Carson and a military trial, and he took his own life."

"That's bad, Tony, I'm sorry."

"The family thinks he died overseas. I never corrected the impression because, damn it, he was a good kid and a great brother and I didn't want the last two acts of his life to overshadow all the rest. I tell the Ed stories and reminisce about the fun we had as kids. That way, I can show my sorrow that he died without letting the kids and grandkids be ashamed of him."

"Are you afraid there's some kind of family weakness, something Pete has inherited?"

"No, I'm not saying that."

"Are you feeling that?"

"Maybe a little, like the superstitious twinge you get at a coincidence. You must have been through the same thing with Jennifer, thinking that one bad gene might spoil your children's and grandchildren's lives."

"Your side of the family is free of RP anyway. Didn't you all get tested?"

Tony had been drawing a line in the tablecloth with his thumbnail. He stopped but didn't look up from the table. "I didn't. I told them I had. Connie was all hipped on it, and she got Barb steamed up to make sure that *we* were free of the gene. I can't see what good it would do to find out just whose DNA has the secret message."

"I haven't been tested, either."

"I thought you wouldn't be. The kids, when they marry, fine, when they want to start a family. I'm happy enough knowing what I know right now." His brow furrowed. "Pete worries me, though. There's a gratitude for being alive that some people have and that keeps them from demanding things the world can't supply. Barb has it; Connie doesn't. Your Jennifer and Mike have it, but Pete never did. If a person doesn't have it, there'd better be something powerful to keep him on track: love, or fear, or the disapproval of his neighbors, or his religion."

"Maybe that's why the system ought to take its course with Pete. Can Suzanne and Bob think about not bailing him out?"

"I don't think so. They're not strong enough."

"I don't know if I would be, either," Steven said.

Tony rose. "The lunch is on my tab here, Steve. Thanks for the names. I have no doubt that Suzanne is on the phone with Connie about this right now. She'll tell you all about it when you get home, but I imagine that in her version, the police will have been overzealous and the DUI someone else's fault."

Steven wondered whether or not Connie would tell him about Peter and Zach. Suzanne's sons were among their favorite nephews, although lately adolescence had carried them into sullenness and secrecy. Steven had seen their moods lighten when they were alone with him. Pete's engaging curiosity and inventiveness emerged then. He had occasionally invited them singly to lunch or to boys' night out shows or ball games and found them open and considerate. Would Connie tell him because she knew the boys needed legal help?

On the way home, he'd been ready for disappointment—a recital of her ordinary day—but he was gratified by her all but meeting him at the door with the news. "They spent the night in jail. Can you imagine? Suzanne says they had to appear yesterday in those prison suits and wearing handcuffs."

"That must have been hell for their folks to see."

"Thank God we never had to go through it."

"Thank God there weren't people in the way of their car."

"Suzanne said the police had records of them running more than a dozen red lights and going over sixty through town."

"Did you know that Zach was driving?"

"No. How did you know?"

"Tony told me. The boys each need a lawyer. You probably have more of the details of what happened than I do. Go ahead; Tony didn't give me any more than the basics."

"What will happen to them?"

"I don't know. A harsh judge or a judge who's just had a bad experience will dole out a stiffer sentence. A lenient judge will see it as Pete's drinking problem and a joyride for Zach and give them the lightest mandatory time, drug rehab, and community service."

"Pete's drinking problem?"

"Maybe. Maybe it's only that he's starting and needs to learn when to stop."

"What was Zach doing drunk—a kid?"

"I have no doubt that Zach was a follower, aping an older brother. He needs good counsel to make that argument."

"If only they'll see it as a medical thing, an illness, and send him for therapy."

"That could have happened for Lon."

Her face went rigid. "How can you compare them?"

"How not? Back then—"

"Getting drunk and joyriding—you can't compare an adolescent misstep—"

"I wonder what would have happened if Lon had been caught early enough to break his habit, not by beatings in back of the jail, but with therapy. Of course, there was no medication for sexual obsession back then."

"Habit? You call that a habit?"

"All right, a compulsion. But what if before the habit becomes a compulsion, it can be stopped? Wouldn't that be worth trying?"

"Weren't those people born that way?"

"I don't think so. I don't think Pete was, either, or Zach."

"You're still drawing lines between them. I don't want to talk about this any more."

"Talk about something less painful."

"I can't. To top off this awful day, Mike told me he's moving out—he's found a place close to school. The news hit me like a falling rock. We'll be alone together, you and I."

"Is that wow or yikes?" As soon as he said it, Steven knew he was afraid of the answer. Two years ago, he would have laughed at such a thought. "I'll miss Mike, too, despite the relief of not having to live in the blare of what goes for his music."

"Oh, yes, and Timson-Thompson, the ski wedding, has been called off, not only the wedding but the marriage, too. They won't want to pay us for the work we've done, and I said things to Bry I shouldn't have about the billing. I have a headache and I just want to sit here and cry."

Steven fought a desire to take her in his arms and pat her head. "The Thursday from hell," he said. "What is it Jennifer says—'You stand there and get pissed on.' Everything falls jelly side down."

231

"And I'm supposed to be glad about Mike, to pretend I'm not feeling old and sad at his leaving."

"Have you started dinner yet?"

"No, I've been too upset. I'll go now."

"No, Anderson's Cafeteria. Listen to this: fried chicken and mashed potatoes with plenty of butter. No salad. No steamed vegetables. For dessert, chocolate pudding with whipped cream."

"With sprinkles."

"Of course. Would I take you to a place with no sprinkles? After that, we come home and get the dumbest tape in my collection and watch it while we drink Irish cream. Then we go to bed and make love to the sound of our arteries hardening. Sound good?"

"Then I cry?"

"Sure."

Chapter Thirty-two

The hospital sunroom was at the end of the hall and gave a healing view of the mountains, their summits radiant, the white shawl extending almost to the foothills, blessed with the recent snows. The girl, Melissa, a tiny, pale child, sat facing away from the scene that formed a backdrop to her.

"You're the lawyer." It was a declaration. "On TV, lawyers are handsomer than you, and younger."

"Older means I have more experience," Steven said. "It's worth the sacrifice of some good looks."

"That bitch took me out," the little girl said. Steven had thought her pinched expression might be pain, but he saw now that it was chronic rage. "I want you to make her poor forever."

"I can't guarantee that." Steven looked to the far end of the hall, where Melissa's parents sat. "Our case shouldn't be about vengeance, but about getting you a fair restitution for your injuries. Her homeowner's policy—"

There was a shriek shaking Melissa's twisted body, and the parents looked up quickly. Down the hall, people's heads came up and some turned to look over at them. "I don't want any fucking insurance company to pay. I want *her* to pay."

"I know you've suffered a lot of pain."

"Easy for *you* to say."

Steven thought, Here sits the world's worst plaintiff with a valid claim. "Tell me what happened," he said.

Melissa told her version of the accident, how she had been skiing ahead of her parents, feeling free of their eternal worry. Steven took note of this as his tape recorder wound her anger. He would need to account for that legitimate wish, and it would have to be carefully explained to a jury. Where the beginners' hill led down to the lift, there was a feed-in from an advanced hill, marked with a SLOW sign. The woman saw her, Melissa said, and purposely steered in front of her, upsetting her and causing the torqued fall. She had risen and skied again, but the next day the remission, in which she had been for almost a year, ended and heat, swelling, and pain retuned with cruel force. Steven began a series of questions and explained that the opposing counsel would be asking those same questions and that preparation was the best defense. But the little tyrant screamed at him, "You're supposed to be on my side, damn you!"

At the end of the two-hour interview, he told her he needed statements from her parents. She greeted this information with a scream of outrage. Her energy amazed him. After two hours of close examination, most deponents were dazed and vague. She was ready for more.

Now and then he looked down the hall, catching quick glances from the parents. He saw sympathy in their looks. At the end of the interviews, the father saw him to the elevators.

"All these swollen, inflamed joints," he said, "and the 'procedures' they do—the tests and more tests, the injections into her bones. You have to make allowances because of the awful pain."

"I know that," Steven said, "but if we can't get a settlement and there's a trial, she'll need to be told that juries are more sympathetic to less abrasive people." The elevator came and the doors closed on the man's helpless look.

Celia Havemeyer, the respondent, was deposed at home. She was a pleasant woman who told them she had slowed to a staid pace as she merged from the expert run. There were three or four skiers on whom she was keeping tabs, including one who was bombing her on the left. Steven hadn't known of other skiers nearby. Celia said that the little girl was crossing the entire line of skiers. "I kept waiting for her to turn. She seemed to have begun a turn, but then she didn't. I found out that she has some sort of bone condition. That's such a shame. We barely touched, because I veered hard away when I saw, too late, that we were ready to collide. Was it her fall that did the damage? I'm so sorry if it was."

Steven imagined the scene as Celia was describing it and thought the two skiers might truly have been parallel with each other, Melissa demanding the right-of-way, and Celia surprised and unable to act quickly enough simply because she had, in fact, sharply reduced her speed. The slower the ski, the slower the turn.

"My easy case is evaporating like a mirage," he told Connie that night. "I would have liked it better if Ms. Havemeyer had been a reckless, careless, gum-chewing teenager, not a quietly responsible industrial designer with a library card."

She looked at him and sighed. "'When the bride is foulmouthed and the mother whines, when the guests mistake the reception for a hockey game, the job one has done may be the only joy at the end of the day—that and the fee.'—Constance Scott Howe."

"Something was learned, as we say. I'll need to give Jen's speech about risk versus safety. Has Mike left yet?"

"End of the week."

"He's not in Siberia. I hear they have excellent phone and E-mail service between here and downtown."

"It's a minideath," Connie said, but then she waved her hand at him. "You didn't hear me say that."

"Say what?"

"As for your client, maybe you can put the little imp on Prozac before the trial and she'll turn sweet."

"I can comfort myself by thinking of what a sweet kid Todd Harmon is, and how much I like Marie Doolittle, my seventy-year-old museum piece, and some of the others. It strikes me that most of the people you and I deal with are young, or if old, are in very good health. We don't notice much blindness or illness or weakness in age, because those things aren't in our ordinary day's work."

"We will, in the not too distant future," Connie said, "begin to see them in each other."

"Good," Steven said.

Jennifer's weekly call wasn't the usual recitation of triumphs and action. "I've started back to a support group," she said, "but not the RP one."

"What others are there?"

"There are groups for every condition you can name, but the one I found has people of all ages with chronic problems—all kinds."

Connie was on the kitchen phone, Steven on the cordless.

Jennifer's voice had suddenly risen on a swell of near weeping. "Oh Ma, the world is closing down on me, getting tighter and tighter, and I know now what I didn't know before, even though everyone told me—"

"Sweetheart—"

"That it won't ever stop, reverse, open up again, never. I don't want the world to pinch closed, Ma. I can't tell the RP support group because those people know it already, and most of them have gotten themselves past it, and they want to tell me that I'll get past it, too. Of course I will, but not *now*. They are so damn *positive*, so relentlessly cheery. No one gets up and says, 'Because some idiot great-great married another great-great, I wake up squeezing the light out of my eyes.' We can work, they tell me, be self-sufficient and even self-supporting. We can have independence and self-respect, but all that seems like gabble, cut from a bolt of gabble. I want to do costume design, turtle suits, a gown for the queen of Egypt." She paused for breath.

His cordless phone didn't have good tonal quality, but through it Steven could hear her struggling with tears. "You have a lot to go through," he said, "and some of it's awful. Cry, sweetheart, and be glad you're not on E-mail."

"My complaining sounds so weak, so drag-ass."

"If you don't cry to us, then to whom? Here's the good news. You can cry and your mom and I won't drop everything and fly out there and rescue you."

"Did you hear about the lady who was so nasty that her support group told her to go to hell?" It was Connie, barely keeping her voice steady. Jennifer began to laugh.

"I have to go," she said. "I have a play to do."

"With turtles?"

"A Chinese play. Dad, I didn't tell you about how good it was, the trip to Cañon City to see Granddad." He heard Connie take in her breath. Granddad.

"I'm glad you feel that way."

"I can't say why yet, only that it was good for all of us to go. And Ma—"

"I know," Connie said.

"I only wanted to tell you how awful I feel about what Pete and Zach did. What's happening?"

"It's not good," Steven said. "The whole equation's changed since the Columbine shootings and all the other teenage stuff. There's a lot less give in the system now. Judges who might once have been lenient and seen what the boys did as adolescent idiocy are now reading heavy messages into that recklessness and handing out stiff sentences."

"Aunt Suzanne must be frantic, but the boys will only be in juvenile detention, not in prison or anything like that."

"You're talking as though it's not a big thing," Connie said, "but it is—out in public, our family in a criminal case. It's awful."

Jennifer paused a moment and Steven heard her embarrassed. "I guess so." Then she said, "Dad, how about that awful little girl, the one you told me about last time?"

"She's still awful, but I want a good judge for her case, too. Like it or not, a judge can tilt a case. My garbage-mouth client won't appear, so I'll be fighting uphill in the rain, and a nod from the bench would help."

"You once told me that a case taken to trial is a kind of failure."

"Certainly the attorneys are less in control then. But if we took no cases to trial, with no potential of doing harm, no one would settle."

"Do you still wear your lucky clothes and eat your special breakfast?"

"I do."

"Keep doing that," Jennifer said. "It's a relief to know. When does it start?

"Monday."

"Good luck."

She stayed on the line with Connie, chatting, and Steven wondered again what women could talk about for so long.

He told Connie the paradox of the case the next evening. He faced a potential jury missing its share of skiers, many of whom would have fled jury service for the slopes. These were the last weeks of ski season; the areas were closing and white slips excusing people from jury service now fell whispering on the desk of the court clerk. These days, many people called for jury service simply failed to show up.

He would set the scene with photographs of the hill and of the spot where the event occurred. He would be careful not to use the word *accident*. Jones would say *accident* as often as he could. He would describe the conditions, wet snow at the edges of the run, making turning more difficult.

On Monday, the trial started. The jury was, as he predicted, made up of non-skiers. Steven led witnesses one by one through the experience and encouraged them to stress his points: Melissa's careful swathing, how slowly she was skiing, how careful her parents were with her. Melissa herself was not at the trial. She would remain, for the jury, frail and sad, her little tumble triggering a massive medical crisis. The jury saw the small girl traversing the beginner's hill. There was the other skier moving from the expert run on the left. There was Melissa, still traversing. Steven elicited the growing anxiety as the skiers neared each other and then colliding.

Havemeyer's lawyer underscored the fragility idea at cross-examination. Why had the parents let so fragile a child out on the slopes? Had Melissa seen the other skiers, and with the entire hill to turn on, had she continued her traverse to encounter Havemeyer, who was skiing far over on the left and out of the way? The mother, well prepared by Steven, answered the questions with quiet control, never raising her voice, never dropping her eyes. The fingers that were shredding Kleenex were safely out of view.

Havemeyer's testimony was simple, quiet, and full of sorrow for what had happened. She saw the little figure traversing lower on the hill. "I had no other place to go," she said. "If I'd turned to the right, there were other skiers I would have been forced to avoid." The collision was a bump only. "I reached out to her when she was falling and she said something and turned away quickly and then had a twisting fall."

Steven's cross-examination was quiet, lighting on inconsistencies between Havemeyer's testimony at the deposition, as well as at the scene of the event, and now, months later. Once, she seemed surprised at what she had said. His closing was simple and not dramatic. Havemeyer knew the little girl was inexpert and not quite under control. There were a few seconds available when she saw the girl approaching and could have made a better choice than collision. In essence, she had let the collision happen.

The jury was out for four hours and back with a good judgment in Melissa's favor. It was a nice win, a very nice win, because if the sum had been much greater, the insurance company would have appealed. Steven suspected that the words Melissa had uttered, and which Havemeyer claimed not to remember, had been coruscating.

The courtroom cleared. Steven was standing, stretching surreptitiously, as he replaced some papers in his briefcase. A breeze of contentment flowed about him in his relaxation. He would have an interesting story to tell Connie that night. He would describe the win and the turns the case had taken. As he moved to leave the courtroom, he thought of telling the story to Lon, of explaining some of the fine points of tactic and strategy. He imagined the questions Lon might ask about the details that turned the case, and there would be his slow, rare grin.

Chapter Thirty-three

"They thought I was blind, the little bastards! They thought that until I decked one of them with my tote bag, the one with a flashlight the size of Peru."

"Are you all right?"

"Oh, sure, I didn't fall or anything. They made me so mad."

"It happened because they thought you were blind." Connie was on the other phone.

"I've been using a cane for curbs and stuff, and for things that are on the ground that tend to trip me up, garbage bags, dogs, all that. It means I don't have to walk looking straight down, anymore."

"And . . ."

"And that means that for a certain segment of the population, I'm fair game."

"Oh darling . . ."

They knew she had sculpted the event in the telling, made the outcome her triumph, and no harm done. They also knew they had to listen to her manicured version as though it were objective reality, to listen without protest and accept the words with only a shadow of the incredulity they felt. Jen and Connie chatted for a while and then Jen asked to talk to Steven. "Lawyer stuff," she said, and Connie made her good-byes.

"Dad, I had one of them down and someone kept him there until the cops came. They took us both to

241

the station house—the other kid had run away. This one was maybe fifteen, big for his age, and a real rotten apple. Apparently, he was so well known to the police that they had his mother's number on automatic dialer. I'm okay, though, really."

"You will press charges."

"I sure will. Once they understood, the police were very cooperative and I did identify the other kid."

"But they wondered about you at first?"

"I thought they did. I puzzle people—blind, not blind, faking? Tunnel vision? Legally blind with twenty-twenty vision? Yessir, that's me."

"Jennifer . . . "

"I have to learn how to do this, how to be this person without losing who I am. I need to make a life, an everyday life, out of what's here."

"That's why the support group."

"I don't want to hear about RP as a singular thing all the time. Don't old people lose their sight? Don't Ménière's sufferers stumble around and aren't they taken for drunks? I'm still designing costumes and I want to do that until the curtain falls, but I need to see all the others who ride the hope on down. I need to learn how it's done."

"You're doing this awfully well, Jen. I'm proud of you."

"Thanks. Dad, and I want to go back to Cañon City and see Granddad."

He hung in silence until she said, "Dad, are you there?"

"Oh, sorry, yes, I'm listening. I'm only trying to figure out what your problems have to do with him."

"I think he would understand me." Suddenly, she was hearing how her words sounded. "Oh, no—it's not that *you* wouldn't, but you're tied up in feeling and what you want for me and how three years ago I was still a kid and falling into and out of love and being clumsy and getting hysterical when assignments I wanted went to someone else. It's too hard for you and much too hard for Mom to deal with that. Grandma and Grandpa Scott are sweet, but the family—they're all too *happy*, somehow. My difference is too difficult to talk about with them. Couldn't we call down there and ask if he'll see me, and could you take me down, because"—her voice broke—"I can't drive anymore."

"You'd make the trip in just to see him?"

"Yes. Mom has to know, but I don't have the energy right now to argue it with her. Will you help me out?"

Lon sounded defensive. "Last year, none of you knew I was alive. Now you want me to be Granddad."

"And a year and a half ago, we thought our daughter was clumsy. Now she needs your help, or thinks she does, and I'm willing to ferry her down there to see you. She'll be making a special trip if you say yes."

"What am I supposed to tell her, to do for her? I can't even hold all my own piss anymore."

"I don't know. It's between the two of you."

"And that's tying you up, isn't it?"

"A little, yes."

"And your missus is still scared I'll get out and move next door."

"Yes."

"And you'd take all the static she would give, and your kid's going around you, and your own mind working on you just to do what the girl wants."

"Yes."

There was a long pause, and then he said, "A man forgets, when he's inside, how it's supposed to work, families and that. Okay. Bring her on down."

"Thanks."

"Maybe."

243

Steven met Jennifer at the Colorado Springs airport instead of at Denver. He was shocked at the swelling at the side of her face and the large band-aid near her eye. He watched her careful stepping, her checking side to side, ahead and down, now tentative, now confident. He saw her use the wandlike cane, which telescoped up and disappeared when she saw him.

"This airport is a better place for RP," she said. "It's smaller, simpler. A slow sweep takes it all in. Does Mom know we're doing this?"

"I won't lie to her. And I've betrayed her enough already. Some people think that affairs are the only infidelity in marriage, but I think there are others as harmful."

"She's hurt. I know that."

"No doubt she is, but she knows where we are and what we're doing. I think that before Lon dies, she'll get a little more comfortable with his existence. After he dies, she'll be able to pave him over. We'll never agree that the pictures she sees in her head may be more about her own fear than about what he is and how he should be treated."

"You're different lately," Jennifer said. ""Mike noticed it, too."

"I'm tougher."

"No, you seem to be easier to talk to now. Something got untied and made you less . . . formal."

"I've never thought of myself as formal."

"You had a plan for the way things were supposed to be."

"I still do."

"It's a bigger plan now. There's more room in it."

They left the airport, appreciative of its closeness to the parking lot and its modest proportions. "No hiking," Steven said, "but I've never driven down from here before. Get the map and take us on to I-Twenty-five south."

Jennifer guided him capably and soon they were on the interstate. He realized he hadn't done anything special with her for years, not since high school and the father-daughter dinner dance. Were they still giving those, or were changing tastes and the incest blight now great enough to sweep the old rituals away?

"I know this is killing Mom," Jennifer said.

Steven shook his head. "She'll die a little less every day, but you need to be sure you're not romanticizing your grandfather. Don't build him into some kind of lone hero. His dealings with two generations of psych students and mental-health people have given him a sensitivity to bullshit and faking."

"You forget that I've been to see him before."

"That was a social call, and this isn't. Lon's life isn't based on family or love. Don't make him your guru because he's suffered."

"All right, but did you know that Mom is on a committee to stop released sex offenders from moving into neighborhoods where there are children?"

"I've heard."

"And now we have a pedophile in our family and some genetic mess."

"I've heard about that, too," Steven said, eyes on the road.

"It's not a Scott picture," she said.

He looked quickly at her and grinned. "In the Scott picture, even pregnant brides wear white." Jennifer began to laugh so hard, he found himself laughing in sympathy.

245

Chapter Thirty-four

They were driving opposite to most of the traffic, Steven catching glimpses of the brown April and the bare foothills to the west, below the still-white high peaks. The right-of-way was dry-looking and patched with decaying, discolored snow. Even the majesty of the sky overhead was lost in gray overcast. Its Creator, having heaped some places and leveled others in preparation for a great work, had lost interest in the project and left it bare and dull for another time.

"You didn't fly into the Springs for the convenience, did you?" Steven asked her.

Jennifer shook her head. "Mom would have thought she had to come out to the airport, and if she had seen me, she would have gone ballistic."

"Did they hurt you badly? I noticed the swelling."

"Not really, and it didn't hurt till the next day. I got it all checked out at the hospital. And yes, I have pressed charges."

"It's very scary, having you out there alone."

"I may not be out there for long."

"Oh, Jen, thank God! You've decided to come home."

"No, Dad. The San Francisco job has come through, and I'll be going out in the summer. Three of us have been asked to work with a big theater out there, a rep company that does a fantastic amount of work in a

246

huge variety of styles—Brecht and Shakespeare, Shepard, Stoppard, and Baitz."

"Those last three sound like a law firm. I'm supposed to be happy about it, but you may have to wait for that."

"Love isn't always the easiest thing, is it?"

"No. Well, what's to be the drill here, for the visit? I wait for you in the car or what?"

"We both go in, we both see him, and then you leave and I see him alone. How does that sound?"

"I hope it's not too complex for the system to allow."

It was Lon's day after dialysis and he looked pale and fragile. For some reason, the usual informality wasn't allowed this time and Lon was brought out into a visiting area by a guard who sat too close.

Lon looked at Jennifer. "Someone's been at you," he said, with no other greeting.

She nodded. "Yes, it's why I'm here. Suddenly, it's open season on me. If I use a cane, the other hand had better be cradling a semiautomatic." Lon said nothing, but Steven saw him watching her intently. "As a matter of fact," she said, "I've signed up for a self-defense class. I'll be going with a friend, so I can take the class at night. My friends have made all the difference. I couldn't function as well as I do without them."

"Yeah, the friend thing. Your dad told me that his friends know about me."

"I shouldn't have told them first, but I did. I guess that contributed to Connie's feeling separated."

"I had friends in the war," Lon said, "and that was what made the war the best time I had. Afterwards, I was friendly, but no one knew me. How could they? In here, the friendships you have are even more about power and safety than they were in the worst of the war. I guess I never had friends the way normal people have them."

All at once, Jennifer was weeping, and Lon turned his gaze on the guard, who had been staring and who then looked away. Lon's hand went out and for a moment hung over Jennifer's bent head. Then he slowly lowered it to caress the dark hair that was like Annina's. The hand was so tentative that Steven didn't know if she felt it there, until it began to move, a long stroking, as though petting a cat. Steven wondered for a moment if that was how he stroked the little children at first, before he began to work on himself. Then he thought, Maybe it's only what anyone does in a gesture of love and comforting. When was the last time Lon was able to give anyone comfort?

After awhile, Jennifer sniffed and blew her nose. "I don't want to lose my life," she said, "to go into a zoo because I'm too scared of the jungle."

"The zoo isn't always safe, either," Lon said. "I was fair game in here because of what I did, especially back when I was new. The attitudes inside the zoo may be harder than they are in the jungle, and in the zoo, there's no place to hide."

Again, Steven was surprised at how self-centered the old man was, but thought again how few Lon's chances were to complain or be heard in his world of silence and stoicism. He looked for any change in his father's frozen expression, some easing of the set lines, the hard mouth. He saw none, but Lon's hand still moved down Jennifer's hair, patiently, lightly.

There was the sound of a key unlocking the big door and the guard who had come in during Steven's third visit stood in the doorway. "Hey, Lon, I thought your visitors might like some coffee." Steven all but cried out in annoyance. He had almost seen Lon begin to open something deeper in himself, to speak as he had only rarely spoken on past visits. Even a friendly act here could be a violation of rare privacy and rarer personal will. The guard backed through the door with a tray on which were three Styrofoam cups and packets of sugar and creamer. "Come on, Ken, give us a hand." The first guard rose and the two exchanged whispers. The first guard shrugged and went out. "I got you a little more time, but I'll have to see you off before shift changes. If Lon here gets too tired or needs the toilet or something, don't go out there; you can knock on the door and I'll come and escort you."

"Thanks, Charlie," Lon said.

"Don't mention it."

Steven looked at Lon quizzically. "The security wasn't this heavy on the other visits. What's up?"

"Who knows? Maybe someone's escape plan was discovered; maybe the warden and his wife had a tiff. A rule's here and it's gone." He turned to Jennifer. "You had your purse at the desk. Maybe they searched it and maybe they didn't. Maybe you'll be patted down when you come again, maybe not. They do it to keep things interesting."

"But you don't complain," Steven said.

Lon gave his matter-of-fact nod. "No, you don't do that."

The coffee was everything Steven expected: cold, bitter, and sour simultaneously. He saw Jennifer wrestling with her features as she tasted it, and they both made heavy use of the creamer packets.

To his surprise, Steven found that he was telling Lon about the Malin case, about the five boys, his airtight presentation, all the work that had gone into making it perfect, only to be lost in an elevator and a parking lot. Then he told about *Carney v. Havemeyer*. He didn't shade Melissa Carney's meanness for Jennifer, who might be defensive for a handicapped child. He found himself watching Lon's face for the slow nods of understanding. Jennifer began to talk about

249

theater and why she loved designing. She spoke with urgency against the closing hands of the clock. She talked about men she had dated who had been interested in her until they saw the degree of her handicap. She described feelings that Steven hadn't known or had heard and had not understood as deeply as he did now, in Lon's presence. Suddenly, she was talking about the narrowing of vision itself, about its frustrations and the life it imposed, and about her fears for the future. Steven had risen to leave in order to give her the time she wanted with Lon, but she took his hand, so he sat again and listened as the two of them talked. He saw Lon's tiredness, resisted for their sake. He noticed his father's age and frailty, and the dry pallor of a bad day. They might be overwhelming him, but they saw he didn't want them to stop. Jennifer truly believed that Lon shared her isolation. Steven ached to fill years of imagined conversations with the father he'd thought had died.

Then Lon told them about the scar, and other hatreds visited on him over the years, about the few guards and fellow cons who looked beyond the designation of child molester to the man he was. They were all speaking almost in whispers, urgently, sitting close together, aware of minutes passing and of wanting to cross vast distances in those minutes to reach one another while there was time.

Steven asked Lon if there were a cure for compulsions like his.

Lon said, "I hear there's a treatment being done, and it works with some but not with all of us. They tell me it works best if they start it young." He looked appraisingly at Steven. "I can see why you went into the law. Guys here are hooked on it, some of 'em. I had a cell mate who knew more law than the Supreme Court, but the con's need isn't the same as yours."

Steven felt called to defend his work. "It's true that my kind of law seems to be about money, but it's really more than that; it's about justice, too, freedom of choice and quality of life, the same things everyone wants." He saw Lon's quizzical look. "Think of a paralyzed boy getting the therapy he needs to make him healthier in spite of the paralysis."

Lon said, "You take a lot of care of those folks of yours, don't you? If someone came into court with a three-day beard, you'd tell him to shave, wouldn't you?"

Steven laughed. "I might shave him myself, if it came to that."

"I didn't have a lawyer at all," Lon said. He waited the storyteller's three beats and then added, "I didn't have a barber, either."

Steven remembered that Lon's pleadings and trial had come years before *Gideon v. Wainwright,* when the Supreme Court mandated counsel in criminal cases. No lawyer, no therapy, either, no help at all. Then, before he could stop himself, he murmured, "What a waste that was! What a terrible waste."

To his surprise, Lon's hand came up before his face, hiding the telltale scar. When he lowered it, he said, "Thanks, Stevie, that means a lot to me."

"Why? Where's the compliment?"

"You wouldn't say it was a waste unless you thought I had value."

The door opened. "Say your good-byes, folks," Charlie said. "It's time." He looked around. "Let me get rid of that coffee stuff—it's not supposed to be in here."

"Thanks, Charlie."

They were silent, working to help Lon to stand and get his balance. "Will you be back this way?" he asked.

"I will—*we* will, and I think Mike will, too."

There was a high moment as they held together supporting Lon. Steven hadn't been sad enough, he knew, and not angry enough, not yet. Next time, maybe.

As they left the prison, Jennifer took her telescoping cane from her capacious purse. "It was a good visit, Dad."

"Try to convey that to your mother."

"I don't think I can. She's adamant."

They drove away into the late-afternoon glow. Behind them, Steven heard a sound, and as they turned on to the highway north, a lone biker, black-clad and powerful in helmet and gauntlets, coiled sound in the air around them, lassoing the traffic with it, and then was off, moving among the home-going commuters.

Acknowledgements

My thanks go to Jim Chalat, an eminent personal injury attorney specializing in ski law. He gave freely of time and wisdom. To read his cases is to enjoy an esthetic encounter with his careful building of a structure of logic with and skill. Any weaknesses in my legal understanding are mine, not his.

Harry Ledyard's training in ski lore and some of his ski patrol experiences have been used here. His years on the slopes have given him a special kind of wisdom.

The impetus of this book is the result of my many conversations with Dr. McCay Vernon, whose comprehension and compassion are as wide as that of any person I have ever known.

Dr. Fred Berlin opened his clinic to me and allowed me to meet with many sex offenders in treatment. On a wall near his office is a picture of a little boy of two or three playing with his toys. The boy is Adolf Hitler, and the message—in the clinic of a Jewish doctor who lost relatives in the adult Hitler's camps—was stunning to me. I asked him how he felt about one of the violent sex offenders we had heard about in the news. He said, "First, I want to take someone like that out and shoot him. Then, I think." His therapy is successful in enough cases that it challenges those who say that the condition of all sex offenders is hopeless.

I also want to thank those sex offenders in therapy who let me in on their sessions. It's one thing to read what experts say. It's quite another to learn what the range of behaviors is from those suffering from them, who are working hard to overcome what is in essence an obsessive-compulsive disorder. As horrible as some of these offenses are, I believe that if treated properly and consistently at an early age, the behaviors might be changed.

In any case, we don't know enough to put the label "hopeless" on anyone.

LaVergne, TN USA
20 December 2009
167683LV00001B/147/A